the
hospital ship

the
hospital ship

MARTIN BAX

A NEW DIRECTIONS BOOK

ACKNOWLEDGMENTS

Certain sections of this novel have appeared in the magazine *Ambit* (London) and in *New Directions in Prose and Poetry,* to whose editors the author is grateful for permission to reprint.

Lines from "Spain 1937" by W. H. Auden (Copyright © 1940, renewed 1968 by W. H. Auden) are reprinted by permission of Random House, Inc.

"Overt Transference," by James L. McCartney, M.D., originally appeared in *The Journal of Sex Research* (Vol. 2, No. 3). Excerpts are here reprinted by permission.

Manufactured in the United States of America
First published clothbound and as New Directions Paperbook 402 in 1976
Published simultaneously in Canada by McClelland & Stewart, Ltd.

Library of Congress Cataloging in Publication Data

Bax, Martin.
    The hospital ship.

    (A New Directions Book)
    I. Title.
PZ4.B3545HO   [PR6052.A845]   823'.9'14   76–16033
ISBN 0–8112–0584–3
ISBN 0–8112–0585–1 pbk.

New Directions Books are published for James Laughlin
by New Directions Publishing Corporation,
333 Sixth Avenue, New York 10014

To p.p.'s et al.

Contents

Acknowledgments

The author gratefully acknowledges the following for permission to quote from works in which they hold the copyright: A. & C. Black Ltd., for A TEXTBOOK OF MIDWIFERY by R. W. Johnstone and R. J. Kellar; Churchill Livingstone, for MANUAL OF OBSTETRICS by Holland and Brews and QUEEN CHARLOTTE TEXTBOOK OF OBSTETRICS by J. S. Tomkinson and A SHORT TEXTBOOK OF MIDWIFERY by G. F. Gibberd; Philippe de Pirey, for OPERATION WASTE; Hamish Hamilton Ltd., for NEW WORLD ARISING by Harry Hopkins; Harcourt Brace Jovanovich Inc., for THE ROBBER BARONS by Matthew Josephson; Harvill Press Ltd., for SOMETHING TO DECLARE by Iovleff Bornet; William Heinemann Medical Books Ltd., for A TEXTBOOK OF OBSTETRICS by John F. Cunningham; Hutchinson & Co., for THE ANATOMY OF JUDGMENT by Jane Abercrombie; *Journal of Pediatrics*, for 'Early Infantile Autism' by L. Kanner; H. K. Lewis & Co., for 'Behaviour Patterns of Groups' by F. Kräupl Taylor from THE PATHOGENESIS OF WAR edited by Margaret Penrose; Liveright Publishing Corp., for THE STORY OF AMERICA by Hendrik van Loon; Macmillan & Co., for A HERO IN REVOLT by Claude Barrès translated by Humphrey Hare; Christopher Ounsted, for *The Psychopathology of Everyman*; Passages magazine, for the article by Col. Willard Rockwell, © 1971 Caldwell Communications Inc.; *Paediatrics*, for 'Human Maternal Behaviour at the First Contact with her Young' by M. Klaus, J. Kennell, N. Plumb and S. Zuehlke; Sir Isaac Pitman & Sons Ltd., for MANAGEMENT SURVEY by Frederic Hooper, © 1948 Sir Isaac Pitman & Sons Ltd., reprinted by

ACKNOWLEDGMENTS

permission of the publishers; G. P. Putnam's Sons and Souvenir Press Ltd., for CHARIOTS OF THE GODS by Erich von Däniken, © G. P. Putnam's Sons, New York; Grace Thompson Seton, for POISON ARROWS; Spastics International Medical Publications in association with William Heinemann Medical Books Ltd., for THE INFANT CRY by Wasz-Höckert, Lind et al.; *The Times*, for an article by Michael Leapman in the Business Diary, reproduced by permission.

The author has made every effort to trace all copyright material which has been used here, but apologizes to any author or publisher whom he has been unable to contact.

Tomorrow the rediscovery of romantic love;
'*Spain 1937*', W. H. AUDEN

1   Night Round

Unless he chose to ride with the emergency ambulances, Euan rarely set foot on land. Then it was not in any well-known harbour that his feet touched soil but at some peripheral point — an island in an archipelago or an abandoned fishing harbour far from a centre of population. Such a landfall had been made by the hospital ship some three nights ago and the scene was fresh in his memory. Just after dusk they had slid slowly into a deserted coaling station and Euan, like Conrad before him, had had his first view of the East.

As the ship had touched the quayside, men had leapt down with heavy ropes to moor her to the old bollards. The captain had brought her in so skilfully that Euan and the other medics standing with him had been concentrating on his miracle of seamanship, unconscious of what waited for them on shore. But suddenly they were safely tied up and the captain ordered the ship's searchlights to be turned on to the quayside. There had been silence, stillness while they all stared down at the rusted railway line below them. The line seemed somehow deformed, with sleepers above and not below the rails, and then they had realized that they were not sleepers, but stretchers which were lain across the rails. Long lines of waiting stretchers.

No one had moved on shore. No one had come forward to greet them. Then the watchers became aware of small movements from the stretchers — a hand moving to pull a blanket, an arm thrown out in a disjointed fashion as an unconscious patient turned restlessly over. There were small noises too. A faint moaning of someone in pain, the slight rustle of the trees where they ended some fifty yards away from the quayside, and Euan was sure he had heard someone call out in a clipped Boston accent, 'Bring me some iced water, Orderly, please.' Afterwards it had seemed to Euan that the scene had stayed like that — the relative quiet, the small movement, the stage-like picture — for almost five minutes before someone on the ship stirred and started giving instructions. Gangplanks had shot down. Mobile electric trolleys had been off loaded. The emergency medical teams had rushed ashore. Euan had hurried down to his own receiving room and the cases had begun to reach his unit within minutes.

The patients, as usual, were of all ages, all nationalities, all races. Some seemed to have been involved in a violent affray, others had recently sustained a coronary or had prostatic enlargement with urinary retention. Many, indeed, were the run-of-the-mill cases of any busy city hospital admitting room. They had already had some sort of cursory medical examination and labels had been tied to them with their names and a few brief clinical notes. 'Brenda Unwin, 33. Multiple pelvic fractures. ? ruptured spleen. Urethra intact, bladder functioning normal as of this time' — time and date were indecipherable. Sometimes a brief note of some therapeutic intervention — 'Morphia stat' — and again an indecipherable dosage but a clear date, '3.25 p.m. May 27th,' no year given.

The patients they picked up this way were unable to give a coherent account of the way things were in the world. They were concerned to tell you the details of their own particular misfortunes but it was impossible to obtain any idea of what was happening in general.

'Betty Emery and I had just slipped out to do a little shopping, looking at silk scarves for my daughter, when I suddenly has this breathlessness, you know, Doctor.'

'Sah. I am walking along the street and boom, the building, he had collapsed.'

'But was it a bomb?'

'I don't know, sah.'

Many of their patients of course spoke no language the

doctors could understand and their team of interpreters were involved full-time asking essential medical questions. They often found that the patients were simple people — peasants from villages, cleaners from office blocks, long-distance truck-drivers — people who don't read papers except for the sporting ones and who were hazy in the extreme about what actually was happening.

Had the holocaust occurred? It was maddening, Euan thought, that although most of the personnel on board were highly skilled at their particular jobs, the radio and com-munications section was under the control of a schizophrenic middle-aged Welsh lady who might have been able to run the postal service of a small village shop but seemed incapable of keeping the ship in regular contact with any major news source. Aware that the crew were hungry for information, Tafteria had her clerks type out anything they could pick up. The results were pinned up on a board outside the radio station for all to read. There seemed, however, to be a chronic shortage of pins to fix up the reports, so that in consequence they blew away and anyone in the stern of the ship could reach out a hand and collect bulletins from the air as they drifted by in an endless paper-chase over the stern of the boat and on into the sea.

Sometimes the information that was thus collected seemed to suggest that business was much as usual all over the world, while at other times the suggestion was that total collapse had already occurred. But whether there had been a war, a new plague or what, Euan was unable to assess. His own collection of bulletins he kept clipped in a book in his cabin, and he had become quite unable to decide whether he was reading an advertisement for pharmaceuticals, a travel agent's blurb for a brighter holiday or a piece of essential information which, when fitted into a complex jigsaw, would reveal to him just how and when the human race took its final downward dive into extinction.

The patients from that landfall were still with them. Time

for his night round. Euan threw his stub away, walked over to the elevator bank and stabbed the button for C deck.

YOUR HOLIDAY IN VIETNAM

Vietnam is situated in the south-eastern corner of Asia, with Cambodia and Laos on the west, and the China Sea on the east. According to the agreement signed at the Geneva Conference on July 20th, 1954, the national territory was divided at a line of demarcation along the seventeenth parallel.

South of this parallel, the Republic of Vietnam covers a 65,000-square-mile area with an estimated population of fifteen million. The coastline is about 625 miles long, with numerous off-shore islands. With its sophisticated temperate-climate resorts in the Highland country, its white beaches, its ancient Imperial City, its vast hunting reserves and its numerous other attractions, Vietnam is becoming a 'must see' for thousands of foreign tourists.

THE PEOPLE

The Vietnamese people of former times probably came from the Yangtzekiang River and had clearly defined ethnic traits: divergent big toe (Giao-Chi), short hair and body tattooing. They called their nation Van-Lang, the nation of 'cultured people'.

During their long southward march, they mixed and amalgamated with the aboriginal elements of the Indo-Chinese peninsula. This ethnic mixing through long centuries of common life gave birth to a relatively homogeneous race. Being of a peace-loving nature, the Vietnamese nevertheless know how to react vigorously against adversities to defend their freedom and right of living, for they were constantly threatened during their long history by their powerful neighbours to the north and attacked several times by their neighbours to the south.

'TET', LUNAR NEW YEAR

The most important of the traditional festivals is 'Tet', i.e. the Vietnamese Lunar New Year. This celebration usually falls in February with the coming of spring. Although 'Tet' has primarily a religious and family character, the general atmosphere of festivity is most exciting. Preparations begin many days in advance. During about thirty days before Tet, nearly all shops and streets become as busy as ever. People rush out in the streets to do their shopping all day long until late in the evening when most places, especially the markets, are illuminated with paper lanterns.

In Saigon, the festival is particularly brilliant. The pavements are flooded with flower shops, and boulevards are adorned with long luminous garlands. Houses are especially decorated for the occasion with flowering branches, and for at least three days running, from the eve of the Tet, fire-crackers are let off everywhere. 'After dark, no strangers enter here,' I was told. We walked past several checkpoints where young women under the age of twenty, dressed in the black-pyjama PSDF uniform, some of them carrying carbines or other weapons, were on guard. 'Yes, we have more than 600 women and girls among the total of 2,400 PSDF volunteers in this district,' Mr Cong said. 'Some of them have volunteered for combat, if need be, although most of them are trained in such fields as first aid and public health.'

OUT OF TOWN EXCURSION TRIP

A sign on the neat, arched gateway out front proclaims 'Tan Phat Ngan Pig Farm'.

Miss Hanh's farm, a short distance on the opposite side of Bien Hoa city, already features two modern sheds for her two hundred pigs. In July construction will begin on a third, larger shed. Miss Hanh plans eventual expansion of the farm to one thousand pigs.

She is a member of the Dong Nai Co-operative Association's Board of Trustees and is its technical adviser. She says she joined the co-operative to obtain help in improving her swine stock and as a means of providing better feed at reasonable cost.

Like the fourteen other pig farmers in the co-operative, she is looking forward to the sorghum crops their new plot will produce.

Euan decided to do the men's ward first. Elaine, the senior nurse on the women's side, was more to his fancy than Sister Windsor whose office was on the men's side. She rarely took much notice of the female patients of whom she was nominally in charge. She didn't seem to like women much. Unfortunately, men didn't like her too much, and although she'd press him to drink coffee Euan would hurry away as soon as he could.

He pushed open the double doors and held them so that they made no noise as they closed. Sister was not in her office — she was probably manically checking drugs — so he was able to go into the main part of the ward unaccompanied by a nurse. This was how he liked to do his night round. Alone. He nodded to the girl on the duty desk in the centre of the ward and she smiled back. Then he began his slow stalk from bed to bed, pausing by each one, peering in the dimness at his patients.

He had to admit that his nightly visit to the patients in this way had no very rational basis. It would be more logical to go over to the duty desk and look through the patients' charts, where he could obtain all the information he needed to check that the patients were doing what was expected of them. The nurses would tell him of any significant change since he'd last been on the ward. Yet he relished the opportunity to take this somehow private look at each of his patients: he stood by their beds and watched their gentle respirations — sometimes if a hand was exposed he'd feel a pulse — but mostly he just stood there and watched.

Some of the patients would be awake and he'd have a word with them and ask them if they wanted a sleeping draught or not. Others would be dozing and would open their eyes and start slightly when they saw him standing there. And he'd smile reassuringly and say 'All right, Mr Williams' and they'd smile back and close their eyes again. It made them feel cared for. Sometimes he'd overhear conversations in the morning. 'Dr Gregory — saw him on the ward after midnight last night,' and that made him feel good. He liked to imagine they saw him as the really devoted doctor — the man of infinite compassion — and this night round seemed the best way of building up the image. It was also in his contract. Junior house staff were required to make two personal rounds each day.

The drip on Mr Williams had not stopped. Before tea, when he'd opened up the valve a little, the drip rate had hardly gone up at all and he'd thought the vein was blocking off. But it had probably been some temporary effect due to movement of the arm. Now when he opened the valve the five per cent dextrose fairly poured through. Williams had been transferred back from the surgeons two days after surgery because he was thought to be about to go into cardiac failure. The problem was to get enough fluid in but not too much. Euan got out his pencil torch and looked at the neck veins. They were O.K. Williams was asleep and didn't stir while Euan padded round the bed checking that his arm was secured so that the drip would not be jerked out by a sudden movement.

Two or three of them were awake of course and he noted their names to order them drugs, but no major disasters occurred. The chronic bronchitic from Fulham looked terrible, puffing and blowing, cyanosed as hell, uncomplaining, cheerfully asking to be allowed a cigarette to loosen up his phlegm. Every day Euan told him that the cigarettes made the phlegm and damaged his respiratory mucosa into the bargain, but Mr Stevens just looked away while he talked and then said, 'That morning cigarette, you know, loosens it up lovely.' At night Euan omitted the lecture, saying, 'No, sorry, no smoking in the ward at night. You get to sleep.'

So finally he was down at the bottom of the ward and into the side cubicles. 'The Terminal Cancer', 'The Organic

Psychosis' and, in the end cubicle, his most bizarre patient, 'The Man from the West'. He was called this because he lacked any other name. When brought in he had been curled up in a foetal position, his head tucked well down and covered by his hands. This flexed posture he had maintained rigidly so that Euan had had difficulty in bending his head back to shine a flash-light in his eyes. He wouldn't talk or respond to sound. Occasionally he had let forth a series of noises which had reminded Euan of a cat. Sometimes he rocked in the bed. After a preliminary examination Euan, at a loss for a diagnosis, had reached with relief for the label that the unknown doctor had attached to the patient's wrist. But the scrawled handwriting offered no real diagnosis, just the words 'Man from the West'.

It was Bob, in fact, who'd come up with what seemed like a practical suggestion. The mewing, he said, sounded like a baby's cry. Why not get the paediatricians to look at him? Maybe they'd be able to interpret the cry and tell Bob and Euan what the patient meant by his mewing. Let them get going with their sound spectographs, Bob had suggested. This the paediatric team had been pleased to do. A relief from their own problems was welcome. But they'd not really come up with anything. They unplugged their recorders, looked at their tracings, shrugged their shoulders and wandered off, saying 'He's in some sort of pain — it's a pain cry.'

'Random', 'non-expressive' and 'diffuse' and similar terms have been used to describe the utterance of babies (Gesell 1940, Osgood 1953, Spitz 1965). Other writers such as Miller (1951), Sherman (1927) and van Riper (1954) suggest that the cry of a baby has little intent or meaning and that the nature of the discomfort that causes it cannot be identified by the type of vocalization. Developmentally orientated representatives of the behavioural sciences (such as Allport 1960) have approached the subject of the baby's cry from the standpoint of the well-known theory of response differentiation. They also maintain that the infant's vocalization at birth, and for some time thereafter, is random and undifferentiated and that it gradually becomes differentiated as a function of age.

We believe that infants' cries are meaningful, and if correctly interpreted could convey information to the adult. This view accorded with that of Bühler (1930), Hurlock (1950) and the more phonetically orientated Trojan (1957) and Berry and Eisenson (1956), who all argue strongly for the expressive function of pre-verbal vocalization.

The problem was to select cry signals for study which might be expected to be specific signals. It is clearly not possible for an adult to know what a particular baby 'feels' at a given time, and we decided to use easily definable situations as constants in order to facilitate the collection of a sampling of cries, which we shall call situational cries.

In describing the situations one is faced with the problem of deciding what language one should use to describe the baby's state. Is it permissible to speak of the baby being 'happy' or 'angry'? In our opinion the baby's total situation can only be explained from the adult's point of view and therefore we have not been afraid to use adult terms to describe the baby's behavioural state. The four situations in which we have made recordings are as follows.

1. BIRTH CRY

The recorder attended the delivery standing beside the midwife with his microphone. This he held to the baby's mouth as soon as the head had been delivered. Sometimes a cry was recorded before the rest of the body had been delivered. Death cries have not so far been studied.*

2. PAIN CRY

Cries were recorded when the baby was having the BCG or PDT (triple) vaccination or simply after pinching the skin

---

*Yates (1935) records the case of a fellow who, as he died, mewed like a cat. 'A very shocking noise on the lips of a man,' Yates comments.

over the infant's biceps. In future studies we plan to use a more standardized stimulus (a prick from a modified Heaf gun) but we do not believe this will alter our results. These recordings were made 5–30 minutes after the meal when the infants were dry, calm and comfortable but fully awake in their cots or in the arms of the nurse. The babies were in the state described by Prechtl (1964) as State 3. It would clearly have been wrong to use painful stimuli when the baby was in State 1 as the cry might then be interpreted as one of irritation at being woken up.

3. HUNGER CRY

Cry has been recorded at 4 hours 20 minutes after the previous meal when the infant is crying steadily and all the motives for his discomfort, other than hunger, have been excluded as far as possible. The intake of food at the previous feed must have been average and the behaviour in the intervening period not remarkable.

Even so, it is not, of course, possible to be certain that the cry is given entirely because of hunger. It may be that the baby wanted handling. However, the eagerness with which the baby accepted the bottle or the breast after the recording made us feel certain that our explanation of the cause of the cry was the right one.

4. PLEASURE CRY

Signals have been recorded in a situation where the infant, having been fed and changed, was lying comfortable on the bed or in the arms of the mother or the nurse. This is the first sound the baby makes that can be readily identified and associated with a specific pleasure situation.

The average pain signal is rather long. However, the variation in length is considerable, the standard deviation being 1.5 between 0 and 1 months, and 1.1 between 1 and 7 months.

The melody form is usually falling (very rarely rising-falling). The maximum pitch tends to be high and shift is quite often present in about one-third of the cries. Sub-harmonic breaks occur in about half the cries and vocal fry in rather more than this. The signals are usually tense. There are no very sharp changes between the first month and the next six months. The length of the cry tends to increase and the maximum pitch to get a little higher. Glottal plosives are less common after the first month, when half the cries have them. Sub-harmonic breaks become more common.

The possible influence of the sex on the character of the cry in our study has so far given negative results. We have done some work on infant cries both in South America and Japan and believe that babies' cry signals are culturally free and represent a truly international language, although further work is needed to confirm this hypothesis.

There is a mythology surrounding this subject. It was believed that intra-uterine crying foretold the birth of great men. Napoleon and Mahomet are among those reported to have let forth these prenatal sounds. However, although man appears to have believed in the importance of crying from the earliest times, the incomprehensibility of the signal (and possibly the vanity of great men) has meant that little attention has been paid to them in the past. Now, however, that we begin to understand their nature we believe that the study of the infant cry will achieve the significance it deserves.

'Nothing fancy to his problem,' said Sheila Braun, smiling encouragingly at Euan. She had been left behind by the paediatrics firm to pack up the sound spectrograph. 'The guy's in pain.'

'I knew that already,' said Euan feebly, irritated too because he liked Sheila but somehow she'd always managed to keep her distance. He could ask John Walters whom she did sleep with.

'I don't know what to do next, we've run bloods on him and got nothing.'

'You're going to have to call in Psychiatry, aren't you, boy — that should make you both happy.'

'Yeah.' Euan stood swinging his stethoscope. 'I wish I was doing paediatrics; kids who are sick get better and are grateful for it. I doubt this guy wants to live.'

'Yeah,' Sheila mimicked him, 'five of the last lot we picked up were autists and it's supposed to be a rare disease. Come over and see them some time.'

'I might at that,' said Euan. Sheila smiled at him, patted him gently on the arm.

'Try a little Maximov therapy, it might do us all good.' She was gone, up the ward, tugging the contraption behind her.

On the round next morning his chief, Van Thofen, listened to the absent history sympathetically. He even cursorily examined the patient.

'Have you been over his C.N.S., Bob?' he asked.

'Not yet, Jan.'

'I think you should,' said Van Thofen. 'What does he do to pin-prick, Euan?'

'I couldn't get him to respond at all.'

'He's about fifty, I suppose.' Van Thofen ran his hand over greying short-cut hair. 'Do you notice he has no chest or pubic hair, although the genitalia are normal enough.'

'Alopecia, did you think?'

'Hardly adds up with the rest of the clinical picture, in so far as there is a picture. Ask Nanda Verkun — do you know her, endocrinologist — to have a look at him and do his hormone levels. Is he always curled up like this?'

'I tried to uncurl him last night when I thought he might be asleep but he went straight back into this foetal position. Of course I don't know if he was asleep.'

'We ran EEG on him for an hour yesterday afternoon and he wasn't asleep at all then, according to record.'

'Anything in it?'

'Nothing.'

'Well,' said Van Thofen, 'let's give him a good dose of

chlorpromazine and see if that will straighten him out — some sort of psychic shock I'd think.'

'I was wondering ... ' Euan paused; Van Thofen was not exactly a young physician.

'Yes?'

' ... I was wondering if we should try Maximov therapy on him?'

Van Thofen laughed. 'The girls would have a hard time if he was all curled up like this, but if he relaxes you might give it a shot. Sir Maximov himself is coming — visiting lecturer — indefinite stay.'

'What!'

'I thought he'd never leave Aberdeen these days.'

Euan and Bob were amazed.

'Well, maybe things are more broken up than we know — any rate he's coming. Yes, we'll get Sir Maximov himself to consult on this case.' Laughing, Van Thofen hurried from the ward.

'He knows him well, I believe, they were at the Royal Free together.'

'I thought Maximov Flint was trained in Vienna.'

'Postgraduate course when he first went to England, I think. Before he went to the U.S. and before he went to Scotland.'

'How much chlorpromazine shall I give him?'

'Oh, I should pump a fairly heavy starter I.M.* and see what he does with it.'

'50 milligrammes?'

'Why not 100 and then you can go on to oral if he seems to like it.'

'Supposing he won't take oral?'

'Try suppositories — he's a rum enough character, he doesn't budge an inch when you ram a pin into him. Reflexes are sluggish but I suppose you'd have to say he was hypertonic. That doesn't fit either. He's a case for the trick cyclists. I'd love to see one of them analytical bastards at work on him. I suppose

*intramuscular

he'd lay him on a couch and go to sleep himself for an hour and call it negative transference. I see the nurses are getting him to swallow water so I'm going to assume his palate moves O.K.'

Euan had been watching Bob examine the patient, occasionally lending a hand to turn him or to hold a limb so that Bob could use his reflex hammer to effect, but he'd not really been listening to what the first assistant was saying. He'd been trying to figure out how their patient — a man from the West — had got to the East. Perhaps he'd come there on some sort of mission.

'Do you think maybe he's studying Buddhism — Zen, don't they call it? — and he got stuck into one of those abstract trances? I mean everybody was going in for that sort of thing when we left.'

'Buddhism — no, this guy is a straightforward nut from the West. Put him in a grey suit and you'd lose him in the crowd at Atlanta airport. No, he's just a Yank who couldn't take it. All the Yanks are pepped up to the eyes with tranquillizers by the time they're fifty. This guy — he was probably a stock-broker.'

DIFFICULT DAYS ON WALL STREET

Things are not like 1929, the experts constantly and ever more frantically assure us. In spite of the remorseless slide on the Wall Street stock market, we are not about to see brokers and businessmen plunging in despair from skyscraper windows.

In the past few weeks, any Wall Street broker doing that would have stood a fair chance of landing on the massed hard hats of flag-waving construction workers, or even on the backs of the numerous police horses which have been crowding into the financial district almost daily. For while Wall Street is suffering one of the blackest patches in its recent history, it has simultaneously been picked as the scene of a sustained series of demonstrations, some of them quite violent.

At first it all looks like the fulfilment of Marx's most gloomy prophecies — or his most optimistic ones, depending on your point of view. Inside the halls of capitalism, men's fortunes are whittled away in minutes while outside the disgruntled populace are on the march, squaring up to armed and helmeted law enforcers.

Where that image collapses, though, is over the identity of the marchers. The most vociferous and plentiful of them have been construction workers, parading not to show their disillusion with the order of things but their entire and complete satisfaction.

'U.S.A. all the way' they chant, carrying flags and banners proclaiming support for President Nixon and Vice-President Agnew, specifically over the war in Indo-China. One banner read: 'God bless the establishment.' There have, too, been anti-war and anti-establishment marches but these have been smaller and less noticeable.

By some canons, there is a link between the market fall and the war protest. One man the other day was standing on the corner of Wall Street and Broadway, carrying a sign which read: 'The stock market will not rise until there is peace.' It is true that the Dow Jones index fell dramatically the day that the Cambodia adventure was announced — although when I was younger it was the conventional wisdom, at least among my radical friends, that wars were good for business.

The bars remain awash with urgent conversation and the occasional wry joke, all being assiduously scribbled down by a flock of reporters doing their 'how Wall Street faces up to the crisis' stories. Some brokers slip away from the depressing hurly-burly to the gardening shops, where they browse through the seed packets to stock up their Westchester gardens, or to the outfitters, where the shirts they buy get more dazzling as the index sags lower.

The New York Stock Exchange, overcome by it all, has temporarily closed its public gallery — overtly because of the demonstrations, but I suspect it is because the proceedings there are considered too gloomy for public inspection.

Its brash younger sister, the American Exchange, where the stocks of smaller companies are traded, is still open to visitors, who watch white-jacketed dealers dash round the floor at a racing walk occasionally yelling in apparent agony and making passionate tic-tac signs to anyone who is watching. It is an eerie way for fortunes to evaporate.

One of those most worried by the market decline must be the owner of a chain of city restaurants who is offering 'Get well, Dow Jones' dinners. Customers can choose what they like and are charged in proportion to that day's closing index. Thus, if the closing mark is 650, the price of the meal is $6.50 — almost giving it away by some New York standards.

The offer is set to last until the end of June, by which time, the advertisement says, Dow Jones should have recovered. Either that or the restaurant, like most of its customers, will be on hard times.

At any rate the largactil straightened him out. An hour later when Euan went back to look at him he was lying flat on his back. Looking at his patient Euan felt Bob was right, the patient could be an American businessman. He didn't respond to any remarks Euan made and he was still apparently unresponsive to pin-prick or super-palpebral pressure. It was only when he was out of the ward, having ordered Maximov therapy to commence at once, that Euan became conscious of what he had unconsciously observed while he was in the ward: reacting to pain or not, the patient had been quietly smoking, chain-smoking, those long American filter tips, Winstons probably. How on earth had he got hold of his filter tips?

Now, at this mid-point on his night round, Euan halted for a moment, he had just recalled this enigma and meant to ask the duty-nurse who had supplied the patient with his cigarettes. There was no smoking on any wards in the ship without special licence. Indeed Euan himself had to smoke at odd moments and on deck as the habit was frowned on by most of his colleagues. As he turned back towards the duty desk, however, he saw Sister hastening down the ward to meet him. He hurriedly swung round again but she caught him up with whispered complaints that he should let her know when he was on the ward. Why? he wondered. Well, he'd fix her, he thought, and began telling her about the cigarettes.

'Cigarettes,' she said, ' in *my* ward!' Blessedly she didn't ask for more but hurried back to the duty desk to see if there was any nursing note on the patient's smoking habit.

Euan pushed through the doors to see how the Maximov therapy was proceeding. He quickly saw that it was not proceeding at all; both nurses were asleep and the patient lay between them in the middle of the big double bed smoking placidly. 'Your nurses are both asleep, Doctor.' Euan ripped back the covers and smacked them both hard on their bare bottoms. They both spun round with a start and looked up at him with dismay. He knew what was going on. They knew Sister disapproved of Maximov therapy so they guessed she wouldn't bother to come in.

'I said four hours,' Euan grunted. 'Come on, what's the response?' To his embarrassment he recognized the dark-haired girl, Sally. He could even smell the body powder she used, could even see a greyness in the lustrous black of her pubic hair where she had accidentally shaken too much powder. He knew why she was tired on night duty — she had spent an hour or more with him during his off period that afternoon. She must have had a rush to wash and get ready for duty.

'It's not a bit of use, love,' she said, 'we kept it up for an hour or two but he hasn't even turned over.'

'Come on,' said Euan, 'give it another try for half an hour. He may relax as it gets later.' Dutifully they started off on the prescribed exercises, pressing their naked bodies against his body, murmuring endearments in his ears, stroking his shoulders and chest and very occasionally allowing a hand to drift to his belly and down over his penis to his thigh, but flicking back again quickly as they felt the lack of response in their patient. Euan watched them for a moment and then pulled the covers up over them. 'I'll tell Sister to see you stop at twelve o'clock.'

He hurried out into the ward and met Sister still breathing fire about the smoking.

'It must have been a patient who gave them to him.'

'We'll find out in the morning.' Euan brushed her apologies aside with an 'O.K., O.K., let him smoke. At least it's a sign he's alive,' and rushed out of the ward. As the doors swung to behind him he suddenly leaned back against the lintel and took a deep gasping breath. The man from the West had spoken to him, after three days! 'Your nurses are both asleep, Doctor.' Not a great line, but something. In English too.

Euan smiled and turned his mind to the female side. The diabetic coma. The terminal uraemia. And his most enigmatic female case — V. The girl from Saigon.

2   *The Female Side*

As usual we went in at dusk — this time in a heavy rain squall. We moved only a nominal distance, perhaps three hundred metres, through the thick tangled growth and stopped. Without moonlight we were making too much noise. It rained all night so we had to wait until first light to move without crashing around. After moving very cautiously for about an hour we discovered a deserted company headquarters position, complete with crude table, stool and sleeping racks. Reporting this by radio, we continued on our way. The area was criss-crossed with well travelled trails under the canopy. A few hours later we came out of the undergrowth on a small hillock and looked down at a few huts that made up the village of M.N. We reported our position by radio.

All day we lay up above the village. Through our glasses we could see almost into the huts. People were moving about their daily lives peaceably. 'There's a whole battalion of V.C.s in the area,' they told us over the radio. 'It's in the village.'

'Well, we can't see them.'

'You must go and look. It is imperative. The whole success of the mission depends on your report ... over.'

'Are you screwy or something? There's no battalion strength V.C.s in that village. My answer is: will not comply.'

'You must go. That is an order from way up.'

'I say again, will not comply.'

'Why will you not comply?'

'If they're about they are not in the village. They're in the jungle around us. If they are, one step out of this jungle and it's all over. I'm not going to have this whole team wiped out for nothing.'

The mission had been planned on information that V.C. was there in at least battalion strength. There's no such thing as a typical mission. Each one is different. This one seemed at first less screwy than some: to confirm V.C. presence, then mark out landing zones round the area. Further troops were ready to be called in to make simultaneous landings. Then when the bombers came in, the Viet Cong would leave the housing area for the jungle. Between the bombs and the jungle they would be caught. But it was another screw-up. There was no sign of the Viet Cong. We never saw any real ones that whole mission.

All day we lay up above the village. There was the problem of keeping the men alert and active. They tend to get edgy on this sort of mission. They divide into those who turn on and those who don't. Towards evening half the men were turned on. They were a bit hazy and uninterested. The other group were officious hyper-military, keeping the villagers we could see in their sights all the time. There were two or three men or women — you can't tell which from their dress — who worked all day in the fields not far from the village. Finally TOC (Tactical Operations Center) came through again: 'Abort mission. No Viet Cong in your area.' Later we learned they had the name of the village wrong. We should have been looking at another miles away.

They told us to return to our LZ and prepare to leave the area. We did not believe that there were no Viet Cong in the area and we moved out cautiously. Most of the men were just depressed, bored, and went quietly off. Some of the men were swearing and cursing. Just as the last were about to leave one swung round and shouted, 'I'm going to get me some V.C.s.' Taking up his weapon, he opened fire suddenly at the peasants in the fields. Everyone jumped at him and began to hustle him away. They were scared stiff the shooting could attract real Viet Cong. I was the last to leave and I looked back for a last time at the village below me. The workers in the fields were no longer visible. They were on the ground, either dead or taking cover. But a small figure, a child, ran from a nearby hut and

flung herself to the ground, beside a black shape which I took
for a body. I could almost hear her weeping even at that distance. We went on our way to the landing zone.

On the female side no one attempted or rather bothered to
escort Euan on his night round so he carried the whole operation forward a great deal more smoothly. He actually went to
the nurse's desk and asked the duty nurse if she had anything
new to tell him.

'Mrs Violet complaining again, that's all.'

'What's it about this time?'

'About being in the ward opposite Mrs James. Mrs Violet
says she doesn't like the way Mrs James snores or the way
she looks and she wants to talk to you about it, and she wants
to have something stronger to make her sleep. The pills you
gave her aren't strong enough because of the snores. I couldn't
fob her off with Night Sister, she said she must see you. She
knows you do a round because she's always awake.'

Euan wandered over to that part of the ward. The problem
was that for once Mrs Violet probably had cause for com-
plaint, but it was difficult to know what to do about it. He went
first to look at Mrs James. She was sitting propped up with
pillows in the special cardiac bed but this did nothing to ease
her snoring and you could hear her from right across the ward.
Closer to, even in the dim light, one could see how ill she
looked. One huge, swollen foot had somehow got through the
sheets and dangled obscenely away from her bed. Euan felt the
oedema and pushed the foot back. He felt her irregular pulse.
She was fibrillating, among other things. He glanced more
closely at her face. Her upper lip appeared long like a horse's
with protruding teeth. Euan realized this was because her top
set of false teeth had slipped out of position and indeed looked
as if they might fall from her mouth at any moment. He decided
the best thing to do was to remove them, but, as he reached
towards them and tried to grab them with a swab he'd picked
up from her bedside table, Mrs James half woke up. She jolted

herself back, shot her teeth firmly back on to the gums, murmured something and dropped back into her comatose sleep.
The teeth stayed in. Euan made a note to talk to Sister about
them in the morning, although the chances of her inhaling
them in this position were, Euan realized, remote.

He switched on his pocket torch and looked more carefully
at her face. Every day she managed to rouge her cheeks with
an almost crimson rouge. This colour clashed with the horrible
blue or even violet tinge of her cyanosed face. Her hair, he
supposed, was meant to be blonde but it was a rather nasty
yellow, the result of nicotine, although it was many days since
Mrs James had smoked.

Mrs James had been picked up by a helicopter team which
had spotted her sitting on a beach all by herself in a wheelchair.
The cruise people, she had said, had just dumped her there.
As far as Euan remembered their ship had been somewhere off
South-West India and she was the only person they saw or
found near that particular landfall. It was difficult to gather
whether the cruise people had dumped her ashore and sailed
on, or whether they had left their ship for some reason and
headed inland. Mrs James was too sick to supply all these
details but she could not have been sitting there long or she
would have been dead. A valiant effort was made by Tafteria
to raise the cruise ship via the wireless.

Needless to say that attempt was a failure, as doomed as
the attempt to treat their new patient. Mrs James would die
soon. Mrs Violet was another matter. She would not die. It
was true she sometimes had genuine attacks of acute ventricular
failure. Euan had thought she induced these and had tried the
trick of giving her saline instead of aminophylline. But it
hadn't worked. The attacks might be self-induced but they
were genuine enough. Nevertheless Euan felt she'd be with
them always. He had once tried to discharge her and had sent
her off with a shore party, but shortly after the ship sailed
emergency room had called him up to say one patient didn't
make it. She's back waiting for you. And there she was, sitting

puffing in the emergency room with all her paper bags around her. They held, she told him, all her worldly possessions.

In the morning he would be forced to move one of these ladies into his one remaining single cubicle on the female side. He could either put Mrs James in it so that she could die in peace without disturbing other members of the ward, or he could put Mrs Violet in it so that she could leave other members of the ward to die in peace. Sister officially had the last word. Sister would want Mrs James to have the side ward, but Mrs Violet would get it. She'd said she ought to be in it since the word go. Any patient who said something vociferously enough for long enough in any medical facility got what they wanted in the end.

Which brought him around midnight to his single female side wards. Euan forced himself to leave V.'s cubicle to last and to look dutifully at his other cubicle patient, but the excitement with the Indian diabetic lady was really all over now — her blood sugars were well down. V. He realized he didn't really have an excuse for having V. in a side ward. She wasn't like W. — whom Bob was pleased to refer to as his male nut, who squeaked like a cat, and that did disturb the other patients — she was absolutely quiet. She wasn't curled up, she just lay flat on her back; sometimes her arms were crossed, sometimes straight out by her sides, and she stared motionless at the ceiling. Physical examination of V. contributed even less than it had with W. Her pulse rate was rather slow, around 55 to 60. Blood pressure was not startling. Her central nervous system was unrevealing. She could move, reflexes were all present although some were difficult to elicit. On the sensory side she certainly felt pain. Euan realized that if he pressed a pin in slowly she was restraining a cry. By giving her a quick jab he broke her self-control and she let out a gasp. In fact Euan wondered why she'd been sent down to a general medical ward and not straight to the psychiatrists. He supposed they'd been considering a diagnosis like anorexia nervosa and that was sometimes regarded as primarily a medical problem. He hoped that wasn't the problem: he hated the idea of forcibly tube-feeding someone.

She would in fact talk, but only if forced to do so. When Euan had first questioned her she had just stared at him with her beautiful eyes and said not a word. So Euan, basing his surmise on the label on her wrist which had just read 'V. The Girl from Saigon', had put in for the overworked South-East Asian interpreter. She also was a long-haired girl — Thai, Euan believed — and two days later she appeared on the ward, came up to Euan and introduced herself to him.

'Good,' said Euan, 'come and speak to this girl V.'

'I have already spoken to her, Doctor.'

'What's she say about herself?'

'Very little, Doctor, but she speaks perfect English.'

'What!'

'You should have asked your nurses, they knew, Doctor.'

Euan said nothing and the interpreter smiled at him and then said mischievously, 'The Americans and the British have visited South-East Asia so extensively, Doctor, that many of us speak your language, you know. We detected that you would never learn ours.'

Euan went and looked at V.

'You can speak English,' he said. She very slowly nodded her head. 'The nuns told me I had a *flair* for languages.'

'You chose not to speak it to me,' said Euan. He tried to keep the anger from his voice. He should have found out from the nurses, he should have ... But then V. would not, he knew, be affected by his anger. She did, however, answer his question.

'Yes, Doctor, I chose not to speak to you.'

Miss V., *aet*. 18, was brought to me, October 8th, 1868, as a case of latent tubercule. Her friends had been advised accordingly to take her for the coming winter to the south of Europe.

The extremely emaciated look, much greater indeed than occurs for the most part in tubercular cases where patients are still going about, impressed me at once with the probability that I should find no visceral disease. Pulse 50, resp. 16. Physical examination of the chest and abdomen discovered nothing abnormal. All the viscera were apparently healthy. Notwithstanding the great emaciation and apparent weakness, there was a peculiar restlessness, difficult, I was informed, to control. The mother added 'She is never tired.' Amenorrhoea since Christmas 1866. The clinical details of this case were, in fact, almost identical with the preceding one, even to the number of the pulse and respirations.

I find the following memoranda frequently entered in my note-book: 'Pulse 56, resp. 12; January 1868, pulse 54, resp. 12; March 1869, pulse 54, resp. 12; March 1870, pulse 50, resp. 12.' But little change occurred in the case until 1872, when the respirations became 18 to 20, pulse 60.

After that date the recovery was progressive, and at length complete.

The medical treatment probably need not be considered as contributing much to the recovery. It consisted, as in the former case, of various so-called tonics and a nourishing diet.

Although the two cases I have given have ended in recovery, my experience supplies one instance at least of a fatal termination to this malady. When the emaciation is at the extremest, oedema may supervene in the lower extremities, the patient may become sleepless, the pulse quick, and death be approached by symptoms of feeble febrile reaction. In one such case the post-mortem revealed no more than thrombosis of the femoral veins, which appeared to be coincident with the oedema of the lower limbs. Death apparently followed from the starvation alone.

The want of appetite is, I believe, due to a morbid mental state. I have not observed in these cases any gastric disorder to which the want of appetite could be referred. I believe, therefore, that its origin is central and not peripheral. That mental states may destroy the appetite is notorious, and it will be admitted that young women at the ages named are specially obnoxious to mental perversity. We might call the state

hysterical without committing ourselves to the etymological
value of the word, or maintaining that the subjects of it have
the common symptoms of hysteria. I prefer, however, the
more general term 'nervosa', since the disease occurs in males
as well as females, and is probably rather central than peripheral. The importance of discriminating such cases in practice
is obvious; otherwise prognosis will be erroneous, and treatment misdirected.

In one of the cases I have named the patient had been sent
abroad for one or two winters, under the idea that there was a
tubercular tendency. I have remarked above that these wilful
patients are often allowed to drift their own way into a state of
extreme exhaustion, when it might have been prevented by
placing them under different moral conditions.

The treatment required is obviously that which is fitted for
persons of unsound mind. The patients should be fed at
regular intervals, and surrounded by persons who would have
moral control over them; relations and friends being generally
the worst attendants.

Old Ben slipped him another drink. He really made a first-class
waiter, looked the part too in his white coat. Everybody thought
he was one of the porters − indeed he wore porter's uniform
most of the time − but actually he wasn't a porter, he ran the
mortuary. Euan was chatting up Sally again. She was probably
the best girl he'd ever been to bed with. She'd stand in the
middle of the floor, legs apart, arms held raised against her
long black hair, and invite Euan to have a go. Euan would
thrust his hands into her cunt and she'd collapse on the floor
in the deepest orgasm he'd ever seen. She would be virtually
unconscious sometimes for five minutes or more and seemed
not to hear when he spoke to her.

Her conversation, though, now that their first sexual passion
was over, was beginning to irritate Euan. He started to tell her
about Ben. Very cool at first, about him being an ex-petty
officer from the British Navy. How his wife didn't like to go

out to work but liked to keep the house neat and tidy. She liked
Ben to be neat and tidy too. He liked a pint of beer with the
best, Ben had told him, but his wife didn't like him going out
in the evening. Sally listened politely, wondering why Euan
was so interested in Ben.

'Do you know what Ben was doing just before this party?'

'No.'

'Stuffing cotton wool up a stiff's arse.'

'Euan!' The predictable scream, wondering what the right
response would be.

'The pathologist wanted the liver, so to fill the hole and stop
the skin of the abdominal wall flopping about, Ben packed him
in with brown paper.' Sally decided that was funny and let
forth her very raucous laugh.

The story was nearly accurate. Euan had been to a P.M.
that morning and watched Ben tidy up afterwards. It was a
case of a young man who died in a hepatic coma. They had
wanted to preserve the liver. After the other doctors had
wandered off, Euan had remained behind to fill in the cremation form. At home (he meant in England) a cremation always
pleased Ben because an extra fee went with it. The doctors got
two or three pounds and Ben got some odd pence.

'It may not sound much, sir, but those odd pence in a busy
hospital, you know, they mounted up. Now on this ship, sir,
money doesn't mean much, does it, but I still feel pleased
when there's a relative about and we get permission to do a
burning.'

'Why's that?' asked Euan.

'It's the bodies, sir, so many of them. We shall have to start
burning soon or burying without the relatives' permission. It's
the superintendent, see, sir, he's a stickler: he reckons we
should hang on to the bodies while there's a chance they may
have relatives who'll want them.'

'Want their dead bodies?' Euan had queried.

'Yes, sir! But come and see; whoever converted this ship
knew we was going to have bodies.'

The P.M. rooms were right down in the bowels of the ship, you could feel the engines throbbing. Ben pushed through a door and Euan followed him. They were in the largest morgue he'd ever been in. It was all refrigerated and, on what seemed miles of shelving, there lay the bodies of the dead. They were packed tight one against the other on shelves about eighteen inches deep, so that sometimes a fat man's belly was pressed against the shelf above him. This is an intimacy, thought Euan, which some had never achieved in their lives. Lying there in their shrouds side by side, some of them looked as if they were holding hands.

'It can't go on, sir,' Ben's voice broke in, 'there's three thousand of them here already.'

Sally's loud laugh had caused several heads to turn. Among them was the fair head of Sheila and Euan caught her eyes looking at him (Bax 1976). Bob, who was also keen on Sally but had probably not yet had Euan's success, came over and joined their group. Euan backed off and slid over to Sheila's group. This time their eyes met for a moment and she introduced him to the man she was talking to, one of the consultant paediatricians. Isler from Switzerland, a tall, dark man of forty-five. He wrote a good book in the '70s (Isler 1971). He was telling Sheila how for a long time he'd thought of being a paediatric neurosurgeon, but then he'd seen that the succession was blocked and he'd decided to become a physician, not a surgeon. He smiled at Euan.

Euan had been to Switzerland. Basle. He started off about the breakfast on the station — the jam, black cherry, wasn't it? — so good. He kept, however, flashing glances at Sheila to see not whether she was listening to the story but whether she was attending to him as a person. Surely such basic biological signals should come over clearly, but he was sweating and nervous. At a moment when he judged no eyes were watching him he gently took her arm from behind above the elbow and squeezed it. He dropped his hand at once beside her but her hand found his and gave it a returning and friendly squeeze.

He talked faster to Isler. He was telling the anecdote wittily enough about nearly missing the train and the porter who, when bribed, had got them round the large queue of waiting tourists and on to the train. Isler was amused, smiled again and talked back.

Euan was actually thinking hard of something else. Not really thinking, but pumping with excitement about the girl beside him. Longing to take looks at her, doing it and finding that she was giving him a quick glance with a smile too. The images of Sally's dark hairy loins and familiar cunt had fled. Indeed specific sexual imagery was no longer on his mind. There was sweating. Wondering what he would say to Sheila when they were alone together. That night she would take him to her room. Then it would be a question of speech, of saying something. Although he knew he was talking well now, he was uncertain even though she was holding his hand whether or not Sheila was really impressed with him. Or whether that cool look she kept giving him in fact meant, how foolishly you talk. Perhaps then when they were alone together at last it would be best to be physical, start to strip her, if he dared.

Isler was asking the usual medical questions about career. Had he thought of paediatrics? Euan found his remarks about pursuing a policy of drift sounding even more foolish than they usually did. He suddenly developed a real interest in paediatrics. Yes, he'd always thought he was rather good with children. After he'd done some more medicine he might move across.

'Come over to the wards and O.P. some time,' said Isler, 'you'll find we are one of the busiest units on the ship.'

'But where do all the children come from, and the families I see camping out in the old hangars on A deck?'

Isler shrugged his shoulders, smiled slightly. It was quite clearly a subject he did not wish to discuss. There was a pause too in the bright gossip of the cocktail party and in the silence, for some unknown reason, the ship's sirens blared out a long blast, dying slowly and eerily away. Was it another emergency?

They all looked at the loud-speaker, waiting for a call on the intercom. But the speaker remained silent. Old Ben broke up the uneasy still by bustling round with refills for glasses which were being hurriedly emptied.

'All clear for more drink.'

'Plenty more where that came from,' he said to Isler, who smiled gratefully. When Ben had moved away he commented on his skills as a waiter, and Euan found himself telling the same stories he had told Sally about Ben. This different company made his account sound a totally different story. Sheila gave no raucous laugh and regarded him soberly, so he went on to give an account of Ben's naval background.

'He isn't a sailor now, then?' Sheila asked.

'No,' explained Euan, 'he was hired because he was a good mortuary attendant. In fact he told me why he left the Navy. "They started getting a lot of coloured recruits coming forward." Ben didn't like that. "I know Americans have been doing that sort of thing for years, sir," he said, "but black men in the British Navy! It wasn't right." '

Each of these outstanding young men asked himself the question, 'If I am going to be something, why not be something special?' Each answered by putting on the Navy uniform and becoming part of a heritage, once forgotten. The Negro has played a significant role in American history and in the growth of the United States Navy. Yet the achievements of black naval heroes have often been excluded or ignored. The story of Negro seamen doing their jobs has gone untold.

Their participation in the Navy began during the Revolutionary War when 1,500 blacks served their country as seamen, gunners and valuable coastal pilots. They were utilized without any distinction as to race, and, in exchange for their military service, were emancipated.

Negroes continued to serve well and in large numbers in both the Confederate and Union Navies during the Civil War. In a period of two years five of them were awarded the Congressional Medal of Honor. Robert Smalls was the first Negro naval hero of the Civil War. Smalls, a slave, was a stoker and later the pilot on a Confederate gunboat named the *Planter*. A bloodless seizure of the gunboat was led by Smalls who then turned the well-equipped vessel over to the Union Navy. For this heroic act Smalls, who later became a congressman, was given command of the *Planter* until the ship was decommissioned in 1866. A training camp at Great Lakes Naval Training Center designated for the training of the first Negro recruits for service in World War II bears his name.

Negroes continued to join the enlisted ranks of the Navy on a fully integrated basis during the Spanish-American War, and two more black seamen were awarded the Medal of Honor in 1898 for singular valor in combat.

During World War I the Navy first began showing partiality in its treatment and use of Negro personnel. Some 10,000 Negroes volunteered for Naval service during this time of crisis, but the vast majority were limited to a few ratings at sea and construction or stevedore battalions ashore. Fully integrated living quarters were maintained aboard Navy ships until 1920, at which time complete segregation became the order of the day.

Although these conditions continued to prevail during the early years of World War II, they did not prevent the Negro seaman from performing valiantly. Dorie Miller, for example, was a steward aboard the battleship U.S.S. *West Virginia* docked at Pearl Harbor on December 7, 1941. During the attack by Japanese aircraft Miller helped his mortally wounded captain to cover. He then manned a machine-gun, which he had never been trained to operate, and destroyed two attacking aircraft. He was awarded the Navy Cross for his bravery by Admiral Nimitz. In 1943 Miller was one of 700 men killed when a Japanese submarine torpedoed and sank the aircraft carrier U.S.S. *Liscombe Bay*.

By the time of the Korean conflict, the Negro officer and enlisted man were once again an integral part of all aspects of the Navy's operating forces. Among the officers who served with distinction during this period was Ensign Jesse L. Brown, a native of Mississippi. Ensign Brown was the first black man to win the wings of a naval aviator. For his service in combat, Brown was awarded the Distinguished Flying Cross and the Air Medal. On December 5, 1950, he was killed when his plane was shot down over North Korea.

Today the Negro is an active participant in all aspects of Navy life. The black officer can be found in any type of duty and in any rank from Warrant Officer to Captain. The Negro enlisted man is common in all ratings and in all pay grades within that rating. Racial integration is a reality on all ships and shore installations. Living quarters, recreational facilities and clubs on federal property are open to all personnel, their dependents and guests. In addition, the Navy has significantly helped to reduce discriminatory housing practices in many of the civilian communities surrounding its shore establishments.

Above all he is a dedicated American committed beyond the cost of hazards to the preservation of peace.

Euan's immediate wish now was that the party could end at once and he and Sheila could leave together. He began to pull her back a little from the conversation centred round Isler and they were almost on their own when the young Greek, Dmitri Spiropoulis, joined them. Euan almost regarded him as his oldest friend, as they had been flown together from Europe to join the ship. There was the eternal doubt as to whether any old friends survived.

'Looking forward to the Gurdurson wine?' he asked. Gurdurson was currently Senior Physician and took his social duties seriously. He entertained about a dozen junior staff to dinner at a time and tonight Euan had been invited. Before he could swear about this separation from Sheila she broke in, 'Are you two going? So am I.' They squeezed hands hard on that.

'He doesn't like you to be late,' Dmitri said, 'we'd better be off.'

'I must go and tidy,' said Sheila, sliding her hand from Euan's.

To Euan's annoyance Dmitri also said he wanted to visit his room, so they all three set off along the corridor to the elevator bank. Dmitri and Euan both bunked on G deck while Sheila, Euan already knew — he had at least found that out — was on F deck. They all got out together, still chatting, and Sheila moved on to the steep companion stairs to go down. Euan moved towards his door, even opened it, stood inside, waited until Dmitri had gone into his cabin and then shot out again and caught Sheila at the bottom of her stairs. They went to her room together and he took her in his arms. Her first words were: 'I couldn't believe it when you touched me at the party. Why hadn't you done it before?'

'Well ... ' began Euan.

'When I came into the bar two nights ago you looked away from me.'

'No, I didn't,' protested Euan.

'Can you bear the dinner?'

'We'd better get it over with.'

At least they were able to sit together. Dr Gurdurson had decided to do it romantically and they dined by candle-light. Euan was able to let his hand wander towards her. She was wearing those leather boots girls favour and he hooked a finger in over them and felt her leg just below the knee at the moment when Sheila was making some complicated decision about the vegetables. But above the board they hardly addressed each other throughout the meal; they talked obsessively to different neighbours but listened to the responses not of the person they were talking to but of each other. It was thus that Euan learned that Sheila was going on night duty tomorrow. It was a despairing piece of news because the night staff worked a 12-hour shift and it meant that their hours of meeting would be limited to the late afternoons. Only then, if Euan had finished his ward work and had no emergency admissions, might they snatch a few hours together.

Another part of his mind reminded Euan that this was, after all, only another casual affair, and what would one extra night more or less mean to that? He somehow felt that longer would be needed, he would need more time to make love properly than one quick night allowed. He risked a quick glance at her but she was not looking and he couldn't stare long enough to attract her attention without attracting others'. Perhaps when they left after dinner and he tried to follow her to her room she would do that act he was so familiar with: 'Sorry, not tonight, Euan, I'm so tired.' Then one was faced with the boredom of forcing the seduction or going away frustrated and irritated. Fuck her.

This fiction affected him when the whole party moved for coffee into one of the corners of the spacious A deck lounges. He saw Sheila sit down in front of a coffee tray and then set off to pee. He paused for a word with Dmitri on the way back and then found that Sheila had gone. He hurried out of the lounge again, about to make for the companion way to the lower deck, when he met Sheila herself coming out of the ladies' room.

'I thought you'd gone,' he said. She smiled and he pressed her back, a gesture which she paused to accept. They sat in separate groups over the coffee. Sheila was able to leave with the good excuse of a 24-hour stretch of duty starting at nine tomorrow morning, and Euan remembered that, although Bob had agreed to do his round tonight, he had to be up by seven to get a patient to theatre for a renal biopsy which was being done at seven-thirty before the general surgical lists began at eight.

When he tapped on the door Sheila opened it at once and led him back into the cabin. She stood looking at him. She had taken off her boots and tights but waited for him to touch her, which he did, pushing her back on the bunk and saying some usual abstract absurdity like 'You're marvellous.' She opened her eyes, looked at him and said, 'Do what you like to me.' Not just an invitation to make love to her, but an invitation really to invade her body. Naturally he took her at once, fast, not quite as well as he would have liked because excitement or nervousness robbed him of a really firm erection. It didn't allow him to be totally absorbed in the physical pleasure but left some of him doubting if the girl really genuinely responded to him so completely, or whether she said what she said simply to spur her lovers on: was she simply a type of very sexy, near-nymphomaniac girl Euan sometimes wished to encounter? Or did he really excite her in a unique way?

When the first burst of passion is over you find yourself still longing to stay in bed, wanting to talk, knowing that passion will resume whenever either one of you feels like it. Then the initial probing of talk is like the probing of the fingers which pull open the vagina, slide back to the anus and slip in there to pull that open to the lover. Or the fingers riding over the tip of the penis, pressing round its delicate opening and squeezing the bulb while the lover cries, harder if you like. Admitting the possibility of castration. While the girl, who feels torn asunder by her lover and bears pain as she is opened, makes no resistance if a cock is thrust crudely to her throat. All this precedes the probing of the fingers into the brain. The skull melts and the fingers are on the soft surface of the brain and they penetrate between the very cracks, the sulci, forcing them apart and burrowing down into the folds of another human being.

Talk is the weapon for penetration. It explores first the past, all the harm that previous failures have stored up. Wipes out the debts and injuries to others, leaving a tabula rasa on which to score up the new bond. As one gets older this investigation into the future is the more painful. The reliving of the failures of the past is nothing compared to the knowledge of the limits one can achieve, the knowledge that you can only offer a lover a limited repertoire of behaviour, a limited sort of enterprise, a limited bit of immortality that is existence beyond the relatively few moments of human passion. That currently is all the immortality I want. Some way to record, in some credible way, a statement about the love I bore and what it meant.

It is: that all the other possibilities of immortality, of fame if you like, are not worthy of anyone; whereas an understanding of the delight of our relationship, a passing of it on, that would have been worth achieving.

You will understand that I have passed on from the fiction I was writing. You will have identified the event, you know the evening to which I refer. You know that as the night went on and drunken with sleep I tried to say what was happening, I dropped again, into some sort of cliché: it was something like 'You are going to be the great passion of my life.' You will see through the trick I am using, projecting our experience back on to the younger people, hoping to give them the time we shall never have together, hoping too in the other loves I shall describe to kill the despair, the gloom we both feel, because there is no way we can meet.

Two days ago when we parted it was as if we were on a moving staircase. We were going down it together. We were rushed, but you stood by me and floated down. That is what I know you did, but in my mind I have this vision of you running down, your long hair mussed by me, your face flushed because only moments before we had torn ourselves apart. I am somehow stopped, you are rushing on.

You remember you said you had been drunk in the week and had wanted me terribly. I can't drink either — I begin to miss you too much and have to go out of the room. 'What did you do?' I said.

'What could I do, love,' you said, looking at me.

Acceptance of less than what we both want, you have some negative capability there, lady.

> A mouse lies quiet
> in an owl's beak
>
> A fox dies dumb
> in a dog's teeth
>
> God withdraws
> when his sons call

Neither of us believes in God, of course. But there is some malignant force which keeps us apart. The pleasure of loving is pulled apart by pain.

> Always at this time
> love comes down like sea mist

> Something to crawl behind
> imitating the pain call
> of a hawk on a pole trap

By the time you read this, my love, it well may be that the hawk will be dead.

3 Joint Consultation

These observations and experiences in a French colony, rarely visited by those of another nationality for whatever purpose, must be considered, from the start, as strictly superficial in respect of the country and its people. We simply touched upon the surface of things in this regard, devoting every attention to the game.

But if the reader — particularly should he care for shooting — chooses to ignore this preliminary warning and has the strength of mind to go through with the record of what was — to us — a trip of complete interest, he may be able to find some justification for what follows.

Our introduction to this partly tropical possession of France, their largest territory in this part of the world — I believe it measures three times the extent of the Home Country – was at Saigon, the capital of Cochin-China, four days out from Manila. Cap St Jacques, a sprinkling of government buildings, barracks and officers' quarters, is placed along the beach to the right of the river entrance, fronting the China Sea, and at the base of what appeared, through our glasses, to be a strongly fortified and deeply wooded hill. This town can be reached by motor from Saigon — some seventy kilometres up river; its architecture suggesting a French provincial city, which intensified my nervousness at the immediate prospect of a return to long-distant school and college French, barely improved by several visits to Paris where everyone, save the taxi-cab cutthroat, speaks our tongue.

The river, winding and rather narrow, nevertheless admits the largest liners of the Messageries Maritimes which can be moored directly against the waterfront of masonry at Saigon. To the south lies the famous and fertile delta of the Mekong River, a perfect rice-growing district, in which many tons — the greater part for the export trade — are grown. Cochin-China, thus, is not too hungry to ship rice which the Philippines absorb.

Saigon, one of the several Pearls of the Orient, also the 'Paris of the Far East', appealed to our practical sensibilities.

MOIS, ANNAMITES AND GENERALITIES

I have naturally had occasion to make frequent mention of the members of this simple and friendly tribe of aborigines, we being in daily touch with them and depending on their labour for our very life in the wilderness. They struck me as men worthy of more than the scant attention usually afforded by travellers to their beasts of burden. Not so, however, without the organized discipline called for in one's intercourse with the dwellers in the East. Individuals, in my limited experience, behave and think a lot alike in whatever corner of the world you encounter them. The trouble is that the various white races look differently upon the art of subjugation. The French point of view, on which I have already enlarged, is a bit too strict, the Japanese (you can never call them white, but these little brown chaps are a conquering race of modern days) go to the extreme limit with the peoples whose country they absorb. Their behaviour in Korea and Formosa gives the strongest evidence of tyranny. A party of Jap police officials from the latter Island are now touring the Orient primed with many questions on the difficult problem of the so-called 'wild men'. Our successful Philippine policy of pacification, which is based on kindness, schools, sanitation, entertainments and tact, is said to amaze but not convince these visitors. A Northern Luzon head-hunter is shown the folly of his habits by our constabulary and becomes almost a nuisance on the trails by reason of eager handshakings and desire to oblige the tourist. His cowardly bloodthirstiness has long been put aside, though such legends are still thrilling to our American cinema fiends. In Formosa, but a few miles north of Luzon — the two islands separated only by a turbulent strait and inhabited, I should say, by similar peoples — the Japs tame the mountain races by driving them off the plantations and putting up a barbed wire barrier, the approach to which is embargo! This was about all the reticent little Japs would give up — it seems enough. Your Japanese is the best seeker of information I know; when confronted with return questionings he absolutely loses the gift of human, or certainly English, speech.

The Britishers affect a sort of lofty attitude in the direction of their colonial inferiors; when taxed on the subject in a friendly fashion they proudly point toward India, emphasizing the leeway granted the blacks there, how much power they are permitted, and how hospitably they are entertained in London. I believe they are pretty well segregated on the home grounds and not given more inches than the law allows. My first impression of Eastern tendencies was in Colombo and Singapore, coming out from Marseilles. You have to say that the governmental regulation from a police standpoint — the casual observation a traveller makes in the streets — is excellent. I nearly died laughing at the bored expressions sported by Englishmen being dragged down to business in their rickshaws. Democracy to the winds! All they appear to think about is getting home on leave. As one person — and an Englishman, too, of humorous tendencies — phrased it, 'You can see him' — pointing — 'nipping into a fried-fish shop off the Strand to visit his old father, the proprietor.'

Our Mois were gentle savages, without any of the terror or suspicion of the visitor from the outside that is usually witnessed among similar wild peoples elsewhere.

Women wrap a piece of cloth from the waist to the knees and a short coat protects their shoulders and breasts. They possess more trinkets and also lavish them on the children. The female physiognomy is not a thing of beauty. Both sexes wear their hair long, generally bound up in a Psyche knot, a resting-place for a pipe or whatnot. Like all who have never known shoes, the feet are broad and hideous. In public the women coolies herd by themselves and remain entirely silent. But the men, Lord! what an uproar of talk. Millet seldom checked them in this much ado about nothing, I suppose on the theory that he must allow them some fun. Their conversation would run something like this: 'Coq de nig, cog tubig, cog donnai' — shouted often in the ear in front when it was too much trouble for the leader to turn around. It was precisely what Fred Stone used to call 'scarecrow talk' during his most clever work in *The Wizard of Oz*.

'It sounded very odd,' said Euan, 'something like "cock de nig".' He was going on to say she used a lot of 'cock' words but then thought that was rather an unsuitable comment to make to Van Thofen. 'And similar sorts of phrases — "cock tubig, cock don I." It's a strange sort of babble.'

'Probably her native tongue, nothing odd about that.'

'Well, I did ask the translator, sir, but she said that the Montagnards — somehow she thinks that's where this girl originates from — have hundreds of different languages just from one tribe to the next. They're not dialects ... '

'I'm not here for an anthropology lesson,' said Van Thofen. 'I accept she makes odd sounds but I don't think we can interpret that in any diagnostic way. Now ... '

Van Thofen had been irritated when he'd found on his female ward another patient with no history and, as far as he could see, next to nothing wrong with her.

'Why do they send us these cases?' he said. 'What's the receiving ward up to? This girl could have gone straight to Psychiatry.'

'I think they were thinking of anorexia nervosa, sir, and some people feel that's a basically medical condition.'

That's a shrewd blow, thought Euan; he won't like to admit that a case of anorexia nervosa should have been sent to the psychiatrists.

'I doubt if she should be a patient at all,' said Van Thofen, 'the ship can't take on the whole world. We must start refusing some of these so-called patients. Just because the whole world is breaking up we can't take on all the people who are breaking up too as patients. It will become impossible.'

Petulant today, isn't he, thought Euan. 'It could be a case of anorexia nervosa,' he persisted.

Van Thofen stripped back the covers, sat the patient up, sounded her, pushed her back and palpated her abdomen.

'Have we got any information about her at all?'

'None really, sir. She won't talk to me except these odd sounds, occasional words.'

'Anorexia nervosa, yes, yes, well I suppose that is a possibility.'

'She won't eat at all, sir.'

'She's taking glucose drinks well from my nurses,' Sister interjected.

Bitch, thought Euan.

'There's really no evidence that she's been refusing food for long, she probably doesn't like standard ship's rations. Find out from your anthropological friend what foods she'd eat in her own homeland. Get the ship's dietician to help you.' Van Thofen was examining her charts. 'Her weight's not bad for her height. She doesn't look anorexia nervosa to me. I should send her out.'

Bob, in the interest of pacifying Van Thofen, made one of his rare spontaneous remarks: 'She never looks at you, sir, won't communicate properly, perhaps she's autistic.'

'Rubbish!' said Van Thofen, 'it always has onset before the age of three.'

'We don't know how long she's been like this, and the paediatricians have had a great rush of cases. They think it's due to all the stress.'

'Stress, what stress?'

'Well, the stress in the world, sir.'

'We don't know if there is any stress; anyway it's an out-of-date view that stress causes autism. It's a communication problem. Trouble with integration of sensory input and output circuits.'

'Yes, but communication — I mean, that is the problem at the moment, here and everywhere.'

That finally got a laugh out of Van Thofen. How did Bob do it, Euan wondered. Bob kept going:

'The failure to integrate communications systems does itself cause stress. They feel that frustration causes the bizarre behaviour patterns. It's bad enough interpreting people's meaning anyway, but when one bit of your brain can't understand what another bit's doing, that must be really bad.'

'Yes, yes,' said Van Thofen, not following this train of thought and anxious to continue castigating his house physician. 'Well, let's consider autism. What do you know about autism, Euan?'

Euan always felt flustered and muddled with Van Thofen in this mood. He turned back to look at V. who was lying almost placidly, her arms crossed over her breasts, staring fixedly at the ceiling. It was strange, but for a moment he was reminded of Sheila the night before. He had woken beside her and seen that she was awake too, staring at the ceiling, but instantly she had turned and responded to him with welcome and love. Euan thought that he ought to know how to elicit such a response from V. if he were any good as a doctor. He wrenched his mind back to Van Thofen's question. Daydreaming of Sheila had called to mind an article on her table that he'd skimmed through (Clancy et al. 1969) late last night. 'The Diagnosis of Infantile Autism'. The useful thing about it had been the list of symptoms.

'Well, sir, she won't look at you.'

'Gaze avoidance — some people list that as a symptom, yes. What else?'

'She turns away from you, I mean, it's not only that she doesn't look at you but, well, you feel she'd fit into that category for young children of "non-cuddly".'

'It's hardly applicable at this age. One really doesn't expect one's adult patients to cuddle one.'

'There's her fragmented speech I was telling you about.'

'Ah yes, what did the interpreters have to say about her?'

'They say she can speak perfect English.' Euan tried to skate over that embarrassing episode. 'But she's aloof, sir, she acts as if she were deaf.'

'You mean she acts as if she's deaf to you. She must have spoken to the interpreters.'

'Perhaps it was fragments. I did hear her say an English word the other day — "depersonalization", she suddenly said. Even though she does talk to some people she communicates very oddly; one can't understand what it's all about.'

Sister, who had been leaning against the trolley with the notes on it, said suddenly, 'She talks to my nurses all right. It's my belief she doesn't like men.'

'Men, Sister?' said Van Thofen.

'Well, doctors anyway' — colouring under Van Thofen's glance.

'What has she said to you, Sister?'

'She asked for toilet things. And she asked where the shower was. She doesn't exactly chatter, but she'll answer direct questions if you put them politely.'

'Does she tell you why she won't talk to Dr Gregory?'

'She says she doesn't like doctors,' Sister smiled maliciously at Euan, 'young ones, I think she means. She says they're aloof and unaffectionate. They don't look at you or listen to what you say, and they talk back at you in an odd manner.'

'I don't believe she said all that,' said Euan, looking down at V.'s immobile face. Van Thofen looked at Sister and Euan quickly and grunted, 'All right.' He turned back to V. and spoke to her quietly.

'Are you really sick, my dear?'

'Yes,' V. replied. She rolled her eyes upward so that only the whites showed and then closed her lids quietly over the eyeballs.

The three doctors instinctively withdrew to the opposite corner of the side ward.

'Well,' said Van Thofen, 'I doubt she's anorexia nervosa — she's too placid, those patients have the nervous fidgets. But get Sister to tell her we'll force-feed her if she doesn't eat — that usually gets them going. Get Sir Maximov to see her too – he should be here tonight. He'll take them both off our hands. And we can get down to some real medicine. Now, how about that diabetic lady of yours, Euan?' He led the way out of the room. 'Do you think we'll be able to control her with oral agents?'

He doesn't think of anything except diabetes for long, thought Euan, trailing after him.

But Van Thofen paused outside the cubicle, tapping the card which had been slipped into the holder on her door. Name and diagnosis: 'V. Girl from Saigon'.

'Now that's not really a diagnosis, but I suppose it might be a clue. That place just might make it difficult to relate in an ordinary way. "Anorexia nervosa", "autism", "Saigon". We mustn't get romantic. Diabetes — I've always liked it, a good plain disease.'

The common denominator in all these patients is their disability to relate themselves in the ordinary way to people and situations from the beginning of life. Their parents referred to them as always having been 'self-sufficient', 'like in a shell', 'happiest when left alone', 'acting as if people weren't there', 'giving the impression of silent wisdom'. The case histories indicate invariably the presence from the start of extreme autistic aloneness which, wherever possible, disregards, ignores, shuts out anything that comes to the child from the outside. Almost every mother recalled her astonishment at the child's failure to assume at any time the usual anticipatory posture preparatory to being picked up. According to Gesell this kind of adjustment occurs universally at four months of age.

'The thing that upsets me most is that I can't reach my baby.'

'When he was one-and-a-half years old, he could discriminate between eighteen symphonies. He recognized the composer as soon as the first movement started. He would say "Beethoven". At about the same age he began to spin toys and lids of bottles by the hour. He had a lot of manual dexterity in ability to spin cylinders. He would watch them and get severely excited and jump up and down in ecstasy. Now he is interested in reflecting light from mirrors and catching reflections. When he is interested in a thing, you cannot change it. He would pay no attention to me and show no recognition of me if I entered the room.'

'The most impressive thing is his detachment and his inaccessibility. He walks as if he is a shadow, lives in a world of his own where he cannot be reached. No sense of relationship to persons. He went through a period of quoting another person; he never offers anything himself. His entire conversation is a replica of whatever has been said to him. He used to speak of himself in the second person; now he uses the third person at times.'

Every one of the twenty children has a good relation to objects; he is interested in them, he can play with them happily for hours. He can be very fond of them, or get angry at them if, for instance, he cannot fit them into a certain space. When with them he has a gratifying sense of undisputed power and control. Donald and Charles began in the second year of life to exercise this power by spinning everything that possibly could be spun and jumping up and down in ecstasy when they watched the objects whirl about. Frederick 'jumped up and down in great glee' when he bowled and saw the pins go down. The children sensed and exercised the same power over their own bodies by rolling and other rhythmic movements. These actions and the accompanying ecstatic fervour strongly indicate the presence of masturbatory gratification.

The children's relation to people is altogether different. Every one of the children upon entering the office immediately went after blocks, toys or other objects without paying the least attention to the persons present. It would be wrong to say that they were not aware of the presence of persons. But the people, as long as they left the child alone, figured in about the same manner as did the desk, the bookshelf, or the filing cabinet. When the child was addressed he was not bothered. He had the choice between not responding at all or, if a question was repeated too insistently, 'getting it over with' and continuing with whatever he had been doing. Comings and goings, even of the mother, did not seem to register. Conversation going on in the room elicited no interest. If the adults did not try to enter the child's domain, he would at times while moving between them gently touch a hand or a knee as on other occasions he patted the desk or the couch. But he never looked into anyone's face. If an adult forcibly intruded himself by taking away a block or stepping on an object the child needed, the child struggled and became angry with the hand or the foot, which was dealt with *per se* and not as a part of the person. He never addressed a word or a look to the owner of the hand or foot. When the object was retrieved the child's mood changed abruptly to one of placidity. When pricked he showed fear of the pin but not of the person who pricked him.

Even though most of these children were at one time or another looked upon as feeble-minded, they are all unquestionably endowed with good cognitive potentialities. They all have strikingly intelligent physiognomies. Their faces at the same time give the impression of serious-mindedness and, in the presence of others, an anxious tenseness, probably because of the uneasy anticipation of possible interference. When alone with objects there is often a placid smile and an expression of beatitude sometimes accompanied by happy though monotonous humming and singing. The astounding vocabulary of the speaking children, the excellent memory for events of several years before, the phenomenal rote memory for poems and names, and the precise recollection of complex patterns and sequences, bespeak good intelligence in the sense in which this word is commonly used. Binet or similar testing could not be carried out because of limited accessibility. But all the children did well with the Sequin form board.

There is one other very interesting common denominator in the backgrounds of these children. Among the parents, grandparents and collaterals there are many physicians, scientists, writers, journalists and students of art. Nine of the twenty families are represented either in *Who's Who in America* or in *American Men of Science*, or both.

It is not easy to evaluate the fact that all of our patients have come of highly intelligent parents. This much is certain, that there is a great deal of obsessiveness in the family background. The very detailed diaries and reports and the frequent remembrance, after several years, that the children had learned to recite twenty-five questions and answers of the Presbyterian Catechism, to sing thirty-seven nursery songs or to discriminate between eighteen symphonies, furnish a telling illustration of parental obsessiveness.

One other fact stands out prominently. In the whole group there are very few really warm-hearted fathers and mothers. For the most part the parents, grandparents and collaterals are persons strongly preoccupied with abstractions of a scientific, literary or artistic nature and are limited in genuine interest in people. Even some of the happiest marriages are rather cold and formal affairs. The question arises whether or to what extent this fact has contributed to the condition of the children. The children's aloneness from the beginning of life makes it difficult to attribute the whole picture exclusively to the type of the early parental relations with our patients.

Euan slept in Sheila's cabin and, a little after three in the morning, he was awakened in the most delicious way possible. Hands gently stroking him, a tongue licking him into an erection. When, after an hour, Sheila left again to finish her night's work, Euan got up and dressed too. He couldn't bear to stay in her cabin without her and it would later be more convenient to dress for the day in his own room. Once up, he didn't feel like sleep, so instead of going straight to his own room he went up on to the main deck and stood looking over the rail. All that romantic bit about tropical seas at night: the phosphorescence of the wake, the darkness of the sky, the glitter of stars, insects caught in the ship's lights — it was all true!

Crossing the flight deck, on his way back to his own quarters, Euan was startled to see a helicopter landing. It did not carry the markings of one of the *Hopeful*'s own helicopters. There seemed to be no one about to supervise the landing although the 'copter came down in a neat enough three-point landing. A hole opened in the side and a figure appeared who shouted and beckoned to Euan. He hurried across and answered, when he could hear the shouted question above the noise, 'Yes, we're the *Hopeful*.'

He was standing close enough under the open hatchway to hear the crewman's next remark and realize, inconsequentially, that the speaker was Australian.

'This is your bloody ship, boyo.'

At that a bearded figure, carrying what might have been a microscope case, appeared and seemed to fall down the short ladder which the crewman lowered on to the deck. The helicopter crewman hoisted two bags round and dropped them on top of the bearded man. He was struggling to get up from his doubled-up position on the deck but the two cases floored him again. The crewman turned and made a thumbs-up sign and the helicopter began to lift off again at once. But the man — who was rather fat, Euan now had time to notice — was not defeated yet; he managed somehow to leap to his feet and rush across the deck and shout out, 'Thanks for the lift, you bastards, thanks for the lift,' and he raised his two hands in the air, fists clenched, and shook them at the departing helicopter. It made a sweep back over the deck, and from the still-open hatchway a figure leaned out and shook a fist back, shouting some obscene farewell which was, of course, lost in the wind like every other message aboard the *Hopeful*.

Suppose, Euan thought, that behind us — some way behind

us – there is some inhuman figure, a God-scoop, picking up all the messages that we discard. He'd be a bit like Ballard's sound sweep, the man with the vacuum cleaner that swallowed all noises (1960). But this one, thought Euan, will do more than that. It will collect and file them in some system of its own. That would be a use for a God – the man who files the media's messages. Where would he put that last one? Under the letter F for farewells?

'You're a fucking bastard your fucking self, mate.'

Meanwhile the man was striding back across the deck. He had found a cap in his pocket which he crammed on his head, to shade his eyes from the moonlight, perhaps. He was six feet in height and wore no tie, a nondescript fawn shirt, light trousers and sandals. He had a tie, Euan realized, but he was using it as a belt to keep up his trousers. Despite his fat belly his face under the heavy beard was not paunchy, his upper lip was clean-shaven, he had brown eyes with which he seemed to glare at you. He talked fast, standing rather closer to you than most people usually stood. You could smell his breath which, fortunately, though tainted with cigar, was sweet.

'Pick 'em up, pick 'em up, if you've a will to help, pick 'em up.'

'I'd like to ... sir?'

'Do you know where my quarters are?'

Euan did. There had been some moving round and doubling up to provide the great man with two small cabins for his own use.

'Yes, I do ... sir.' Again the pause as Euan realized that he wasn't certain how you addressed a knight. They picked up the cases: one was enormously heavy and clearly full of books. Euan led the way off the flight deck to a lift. In the lift Sir Maximov Flint spoke again.

'You can call me Sur, Siree, Max, Maxy, Flint, Flinty – anything you like. Who are you?'

'Euan Gregory. I'm Van Thofen's H.P.'

But Sir Max was still thinking of names and made no sign of his acquaintance with Van Thofen.

'Do you know why I am called Sir?'

'I imagined you'd been knighted.'

'Of course not. Fool! Me, take honours from some left-over nineteenth-century relic? No, no; I was christened Sur by my father — a wise Bavarian humorist.'

'Christened it?'

'Yes; the pastor objected but my father, who had been in the East, told him it was in memory of a Burmese servant called Sur that he'd had, who had saved his life when his canoe capsized in the river and a crocodile bit off his leg. He had got only one leg by that time so the pastor believed him. Do you believe that story, my boy?'

'Which?' asked Euan. 'Your father's story or all that you've just told me?'

'Cautious boy, there are two stories there, you're right, mine and my father's. Now my father said the Anglo-Saxons would inherit the earth and so that's why he christened me Sur. He meant the Anglo-Saxons would always be snobs and they'd die intestate, which they have. Ah, now, talking too much as usual. I could have changed my name to Sur by deed poll, you know. Well, that's all I'll ever tell you about my name, so I'll shut up.'

By this time even the slow flight-deck lift had descended and they were struggling along narrow corridors on their way to Sir Max's cabins. Euan told him a bit about the ship's layout and asked him if he wanted guiding to the Captain.

'No, he'll find out I'm here in good time.'

'They like to de-brief anyone who comes on board. What is going on in the world? Can you tell us? I mean, is there a war?'

'Several, I should think.'

'But I mean, is it a blow-up?'

'It's all in a seething confusing mess, a lot of people are sick and ill. Very few people are really healthy. There's plenty of work to do. What's happening tomorrow?'

'Yes, but … '

'No, I'm not a historian, a politician, a social scientist, a camera or, least of all, a journalist. I make no attempt to record the mess. It simply isn't worth it. I'm concerned with the sense I can make of my pie and the future. What's going to happen tomorrow? Shall I come on your round with old Offal?'

They bundled into the two tiny cabins. There was an inter-communicating door which seemed to occupy most of the space in both rooms. Maximov jerked his cases open, threw clothes about and suddenly produced a whisky bottle. Euan had stood there, uncertain whether he was wanted, but was pressed to a toothbrush-glass of the Scotch. Sir Max wandered round stuffing his books on to shelves, under the bunk, into any sort of place. He came across six copies of his classic intro-duction to psychiatry, *The Open Body and Its Friends*. He took a copy, signed it with a flourish, asking Euan what his name was again, and presented him with the book. Then he sat down, pulled his chair close to Euan and said, 'What other psychia-trists are aboard?'

'Kline.'

Kline! Yes, the prospective analyst was aboard. Moreover he had brought with him Coma — his most famous female patient. Coma, the million-year girl, the first and most famous forward analysand. She had been a classic neurotic. Massive mood swings dominated her personality. Sometimes she sat for hours in the corner of a room like an inconveniently placed statue, then, late at night, she would become manically active, call her friends on the telephone, talk to them for hours and then, when they hung up on her, dramatically slash her wrists. She had numerous liaisons with men who despised her, told them she was a masochist and then went to solicitors with stories of assault when they tried to beat her.

Coma went through psychiatrists like a dose of salts and finally came to Kline. It was at a time when Kline had become increasingly restless, realizing the uselessness of traditional analysis as a therapeutic tool. He had been wondering whether it had anything left to offer as a research tool by way of provid-ing fresh insights into human nature. On the face of it, Coma was the most unpromising material to offer these fresh insights.

She had been analysed again and again. The feature of such studies was the essential lack of analytical material. She had had a strikingly dull childhood, with loving but not too devoted parents in Iowa City. She had had no separation experiences. She had been through all the stages of penis envy or whatever branch of theory was believed in, and where she had not had the experience she had been taken through it by a competent analyst. There was no more analytic material to dredge from her past. What was Kline to do?

It was then that Kline had his moment of brilliance. It was not the past but the future which contained the seeds of Coma's neurosis. Kline settled her on the traditional analytic couch and asked her to tell him not what had happened to her, but what would happen to her in the future. Traumatic event after traumatic event poured out of her troubled brain. She described the incident in her late fifties when, wearing the most up-to-date Parisian fashion on a visit to Brasilia, she was taken for a nun. By that time in South America the Catholic religion had been identified for the evil thing it was and Coma was seized. She was bound across a gym horse and ritually raped by representatives of the government, the city authority, the armed services, the people's party and then by those members of the diplomatic corps who wished to demonstrate their solidarity with the new regime. But this was only one of the incidents contained in Coma's future. She knew all the disasters of the future and it appeared she was going to be present at most of them. It was not surprising that these events cast their shadow not only over Coma's future, but over her past as well.

Kline found the material deeply disturbing and his own training did not provide him with the emotional reserves he needed to meet the situation. He realized that, instead of his patient reacting to the process of analysis and consequently to her analyst, he, the analyst, was affected by this disastrous material from the future. He felt insecure and threatened, and looked for some prop or support. It was then he realized that a transference was taking place, but again not the traditional one.

He himself, the analyst, was undergoing a strong positive transference to his analysand. It was a dangerous position for a psychiatrist to be in.

Kline, Euan explained to Sir Maximov, was aboard the ship and officially appointed as emergency psychiatrist. From time to time he was lifted off in a helicopter to a deserted planetarium, to some terminal beach. There he had to argue with some relict of civilization who had chosen to occupy the area and who, the ship's officers felt, should be removed from the vicinity. Sometimes he was successful in persuading them to come away but on other occasions the victims eluded him (Ballard 1964) and Kline left with an added dimension to the depression which had over-mastered him since Coma's future had become synchronous with his own.

Sir Maximov was of course familiar with the details of Kline's early involvement with Coma, but was anxious to learn details of the latter stages. In particular he wanted details of Coma. A very ordinary girl, Euan opined; of course nobody would attempt to have an affair with her, but she remained an attractive blonde. She had shed all traces of the neuroticism which had engulfed her and had become a placid, pleasant girl. She was the local expert at deck quoits and Euan, who liked the game himself, played with her regularly. Coma usually won.

'But what about Kline, then?' asked Sir Maximov. What did he do with all this prospective material he had collected about Coma? How did he spend his time? What was he doing with Coma now? He gave no reports or case conferences, so little was known about the present stage of his research. In particular it was not known whether he had been able to generalize from Coma's specific accounts of her future to some less personal details which would fix the temporal sequence of events. The opinion of the ship was that Kline was now so obsessed with Coma that he was unable to make any objective assessments of his or the general situation.

'Kline's positive transference has become overt,' Euan told

Sir Max. Recently Euan had had a glimpse of Kline's disorganized involvement with the analysis. He was seeking some way out of his dilemma. Euan had courteously escorted Coma back to the quarters she shared with Kline. Euan had opened the door to allow Coma through and Kline swung round in the swivel chair from his desk. Coma ran to him and nestled on his knee.

'Coma,' Kline murmured, 'let's get out of time.'

The year saw the tightest money conditions in the memory of any living banker and witnessed the highest interest rates in contemporary banking history. Both the shortage of lendable funds and the extraordinary level of interest rates were the direct result of Government policy designed to contain the United States' growing inflation problem. Unfortunately, too few people in this nation realize that the commercial banking system is simply an instrument of Federal monetary policy. As a result of this misunderstanding, large segments of the press, of the nation's lawmakers and of the public have tended to be critical of the banking system. We urge our shareholders to take an active and informed interest both in this issue and the related question of the one-bank holding company concept now being argued in the halls of Congress.

Despite the problems of tight money and high interest rates the year was a banner year for your corporation on many fronts. I am pleased that this annual report tells of another record year for your company. Over the past five years our resources have increased from $16.3 billion to $25.6 billion. During the same period, net income has risen from $2.74 a share to $4.43. Naturally I am proud of this record personally. More important, however, the record of the past years is a tribute to the group-management concept under which your bank operates. It is also indicative of the depth, the strength and the competence of the senior management of the bank and of the loyalty and dedication of the 33,000 men and women who make up the team.

During 19xx, the Bank engaged in a number of relatively small, but interesting activities. We entered into several real estate joint ventures during the year through the holding company. We have a $5 million equity representing an 86% ownership in the Decimus Corporation. This corporation is in the business of computer leasing systems, software programming and consulting services relating to data processing. We also made a minor (under 5%) investment in Envirotech Corporation which specializes in the production, sale and service of environmental control equipment. Perhaps the most important single feature of the holding company was the access it gave us to the commercial paper market.

NEW BUILDING DEDICATED

A highlight of the year was the dedication of a 52-storey World Headquarters in the heart of the financial district. Hundreds of spectators and dignitaries attended the ceremonies. The whole complex, including the bank's glass-enclosed Main Office now under construction, is bounded by California, Montgomery, Pine and Kearny Streets.

The bank now occupies about one-third of the 1.5 million square feet of office space. The remainder is tenant office space, most of which is already leased.

To introduce the building to the staff outside, the bank held a series of tours and receptions prior to the dedication. In four weekends, over 12,000 bank employees and their families visited the new building.

The huge plaza, fronting one side of the skyscraper, was designated 'A. P. Giannini Plaza' in tribute to the bank's founder.

A. P. Giannini Plaza, a spacious 290 by 140 feet and paved in flame-finished carnelian granite, faces California Street. It was conceived to offer a large area of open space among the business district's buildings and is landscaped with trees and plants. The west end of the plaza contains a massive black granite abstract sculpture by Japanese artist Masayuki Nagare. It weighs 200 tons and stands 13 feet high. Art authorities have described it as 'one of the most important works of art in our time'.

When we first planned for our new headquarters building we expected only a modest return on our investment in dollar terms. We felt that intangible returns in the form of prestige, community goodwill and employee pride justified a modest operating profit. However, it now seems certain that, in addition to these intangible benefits, we will realize a dollar return on our investment in the building fully comparable with the return on other long-term bank investments.

INTERNATIONAL GROWTH CONTINUES

Expansion of our international banking activities continued during the year. Most of our new foreign branches were opened in countries where we already had one or more branches, usually in cities ranking second or third in economic importance in their respective nations. Several new branches were established in principal cities as additional branches in these metropolitan areas. Adapting to changed conditions or requirements of the host countries, our Lagos Branch in Nigeria was converted to a wholly owned subsidiary, while our subsidiary in Uruguay was converted to a branch. We opened branches in three countries where we previously had neither facilities nor affiliates, increasing to seventy-five the number of countries and territories in which we have direct representation. Among our thirteen new overseas branches were the first branches of any American bank in Lyon, France and Manchester, England ...

On a consolidated basis, income before securities transactions, after provision for loan losses using new Federal accounting rules, reached a record high of $153,810,000, or $4.48 per share. This was an increase of 12.6% over last year's comparable figure of $136,355,000, or $3.98 per share.

Deposits rose by $668,699,000 to reach $22,171,314,000 at year-end. Loans increased by $1,247,584,000 to top $14,600,000,000. Resources rose to nearly $25,600,000,000 …

So huge were the anticipated proceeds from the sale that our appointment was made only after the State had consulted with the Federal Reserve System, the Treasury Department and the financial experts across the nation. The transaction required considerable money market expertise to assure that the paying in and investment of the funds did not disrupt the nation's already strained money markets.

Thus it was both gratifying and challenging that our bank was selected to do the job.

In anticipation of the billion-dollar magnitude of the sale, it was necessary that our Bank Investment Securities Division, at the bank's own risk, begin accumulating U.S. Treasury securities in advance of the sale. This was done in order to preserve an orderly money market following the acceptance by the State of the successful bids. In the credit squeeze only banks of our size and experience in the money market could have handled this massive yet delicate assignment.

Adding to the excitement was the Bank's chartered commercial jet airliner, poised at an international airport for flight to the nation's money centers in a race against the clock. At the end of the day, when the State's cash register on stage had rung up more than $900 million in high bids, our jet, carrying bank couriers with checks amounting to 20% of the successful bids, dashed non-stop to New York to make immediate collections.

This flight, as necessary as it was dramatic, enabled the State to earn approximately $45,000 a day in interest which otherwise would have been lost for several days if conventional collection methods had been used. Our race against the five time zones caught the imagination of the financial world and the public and captured a great share of national and international news coverage. Perhaps no other event could have more graphically demonstrated our bank's capability in the money markets of the United States.

After his famous midnight words 'Your nurses are asleep, Doctor', W. (or Bill, as they'd taken to calling him) began to talk, but it was not talk that was easy to make much of. He lay on his back, smoking as ever, and muttered words which streamed up towards the ceiling. Euan bent over him and listened.

'1966 ... 11.4%. 1967 ... 11.9% ... 1968 ... 12.8%. 1969 ... 13.7%. 1966 ... 28½ billion. 1967 ... 28½ billion. 1968 ... 34 billion. 1969 ... 34½ billion.'

Euan turned to Bob: 'You were right, I think he was a banker,' but then W. shook his head and started on something else.

'Mondays. Newcomers! Report to the Director! Nice work from Masius. Benson tired as usual. Beans, limping the stuff out. Will they really survive? Brisk venture in the beers by J.W.T. and some lovely carpet work by Crawfords.'

'Well, what on earth's all that, then?'

'God knows.'

They were waiting nervously by the bed. Sir Maximov was coming to consult on the case, as promised. Euan was busy going over his notes again. There was still, of course, no history but there were all the investigations to report, virtually negative. Some of the hormone levels a bit low — bordering on significant. There was something about high lactate levels and Euan was trying to remember what the story was about lactate levels and anxiety states. He asked Bob anxiously.

'I shouldn't worry, old bean, don't think Sir Max is all that keen on the biochemistry stuff himself.'

'But that's what he is.'

'Was — he's switched now — you know he says biochemistry is the detail and not the substance. Neurology — I heard him at the party last night.'

'I congratulate you,' said Sir Maximov as he came in,

followed by a clutch of other people who had somehow assembled. Bob and Euan looked at each other. Sir Maximov was smiling at Euan. 'I was just looking her over myself, heard her speak. I love those long-haired fair American girls, they're cool, very cool — you find there's a lot underneath.'

He turned to Van Thofen to allow Euan to recover from his embarrassment.

'Ever made love to an American girl, Johnnie, or doesn't your nation go in for love — I was going to say illicit love, but it's all the same thing.'

Van Thofen shook his head slightly, made no comment but merely indicated the figure on the bed.

'This is the man we're worried about. Tell us about him, Euan.'

Euan launched forth into the absent history. Sir Maximov listened quietly, occasionally queried a figure, asked for the hormone levels to be repeated to him. Then he went and sat on the patient's bed.

'I hope you'll excuse my examining you,' he said, and delicately elevated an eyelid to look at the conjunctive.

'His haemoglobin, sir … ' Euan began.

'I know, I know,' said Sir Maximov, 'but never forget he may have had a bleed since he came in. Now then, help me up with him.'

He sounded him thoroughly, went over heart and abdomen, got him to blink to a bright light but got no response to pinprick, insisted on doing a rectal examination.

'Tight,' he said, but made no other comment. Euan wondered if he thought the prostate was normal in size. He had himself, but he'd found it difficult to feel.

'I should stop him smoking,' said Sir Maximov. 'It's mere self-indulgence on his part. He decided not to kill himself, so we shouldn't aid him. You've done a very thorough job as usual, Johnnie. Now let's go and see this girl of yours. We can discuss them both together.'

Both Van Thofen's teams were there, and an assistant

assigned to Sir Maximov, plus a sister and a staff nurse. The peaceable quiet of an ordinary Monday round, thought Euan, had somehow turned into — well, not quite a Grand Round, but one with far too many people on it for his liking. He hated these great treks of white coats up and down wards; everybody chatting away, not looking at all at the patients who were not of interest medically, indeed shunning the half-curious, half-scared looks the patients threw at them. When they arrived at V.'s bed he forgot his nervousness and pitched into his tale.

Afterwards they all went and perched round Sister's office, consumed coffee and began the case conference.

'Well,' began Van Thofen, 'suppose you tell us, Sir Max, why the man won't respond to your therapy.'

'Why did I do a rectal, Euan?' asked Sir Maximov, apparently ignoring Van Thofen's opening crack.

'Well, I suppose you wanted to feel the prostate — I mean, the low hormone levels, perhaps some sort of prostatic repression ... ' He tailed off.

'Nonsense. My therapy failed; why could that have been?'

'I don't know,' said Euan.

'Well, the first one's obvious: he might be a homosexual, in which case you were using the wrong sex nurses. That's why I did the rectal.'

Euan made some sort of puzzled noise.

'Homosexuals,' boomed Sir Max, 'never have piles *and* you can dilate their sphincters easily because they get buggered a lot. Now that's the sort of thing you'll never get taught in a medical school.'

'Well, was he a homosexual?' asked Van Thofen.

'I don't think so,' said Sir Max, 'which means he's gone so far that ordinary young nubile women — image women, you know — can't get through to him. We'll have to find him something really exciting.'

'You mean you think Maximov therapy could bring him out of the state he's in?'

'I'm sure it will, but I need you to suggest who should administer the therapy.'

'There's a physiotherapist who won a beauty contest and once had a screen test to become a film star.'

'No, no, no, I said nothing imagey. You're stupid, the lot of you. Put W. in the same cubicle as V.'

'But she can't give him Maximov therapy — she's not trained.'

Sir Max laughed. 'She may not be now but she will be — just leave them alone together.'

'But ... ' — there were streams of 'buts' from all sides.

'They're patients — you can't put female and male patients in the same room. It's — it's not ethical.'

'What about the nurses?'

'What will Sister say?'

'What about Matron — she'll have a fit.'

'It's my opinion these two patients should be nursed in the same cubicle,' said Sir Max, and he got up briskly, beckoned to his assistant and left the office. There was a long silence. Then Van Thofen got up, looked, said, 'Yes, do it,' and walked off after Sir Maximov out of the ward.

4 *Transference*

Bob was somehow on hand to supervise the move of 'Bill' (the nurses had given him his nickname) into the special side ward that had been prepared for the two silent patients.

There had been interminable discussions between Day Sister, who was in charge of the two wards, Matron, who felt that such an unusual concept of mixing patients must involve her at an early stage, and Euan. Euan had said that it didn't seem to him to matter whether the pair occupied a side ward on the male side or the female side. Matron pointed out that there were difficulties, whatever Sir Maximov Flint implied. One of the couple would have to use lavatory facilities which were normally exclusively the prerogative of the opposite sex.

It occurred to Euan when she said this that he had seen or heard of neither of the patients visiting the toilet. He concluded they must go some time, as there had been no reports of incontinence. Admittedly neither patient was eating yet and their fluid intake consisted only of the half-hourly sips of glucose drinks which the nursing staff pressed on the patients. Yet he was sure he'd seen a normal urine report on at least Bill; not yet, he thought, on V. but then the female side were always slower at getting urines. Had Bill said anything when the nurse asked him to provide a urine specimen, or simply walked to the toilet and performed, handed it to the nurse and gone back to bed again in complete silence?

Euan realized that although he was nominally in charge of the patients on C deck medical wards, things went on in them which he, the doctor, did not know about. Nor could he easily find out. He could not ask, 'Nurse, did he just wee when you asked him to?' It would imply that he didn't know whether or not his patient would have performed that function for him. Yet clearly Bill had done it for the nurse, so it should have been even easier for the doctor to get him to do it. But supposing, when Euan asked him to wee, he refused. Perhaps he should put it to the test. What would it prove? That Bill the patient did not like doctors, that would be evidence of some negative emotional response. But why should W. or anyone else for that matter dislike doctors particularly?

All these thoughts were going through Euan's mind while Matron was going on about the lavatory question. Euan realized that he had not been listening; fortunately Sister was recapping the argument. It was as well he'd kept out of it as there were some signs of disagreement.

'Do you really think, Matron,' Sister was saying, 'that I couldn't prevent male patients on one of my wards raping a girl while she was on the way to the lavatory?'

'Now, Sister, I did not imply or use a word like rape. I just feel that on the ladies' side the patients will know instinctively how to behave towards a man on the way to their lavatories, while the men might interfere, well, not interfere, but not be so tactful towards a female patient using their (male) lavatories.' Matron, of course, got her way and Euan and Bob were wheeling the Man from the West to this side ward on the female side.

Bob's appearance at this moment was rather a surprise to Euan. Bob had affected a total lack of interest in Bill ever since the old man had called in Psychiatry in the form of Sir Maximov. Euan was coming to realize that Bob's abrasive manner actually concealed a very kindly person. It was a pity he adopted this tone of voice and manner because the patients found him unsympathetic. It was simply that he'd never learnt how to talk to people. Yet Euan realized more and more that Bob was a most conscientious doctor. He was always quietly checking that Euan had done everything he could for the patients and Euan found additional nursing instructions written in when he was checking the nursing reports. Now he was telling Euan to be careful and not let Bill's arm catch on a wall as they wheeled his stretcher out of the side ward, but at the same time commenting sardonically on Sir Maximov's management of the case.

'What will happen, Euan, you'll see, is that this guy will get better, start talking that is, in a couple of months or more and then we'll have Sir Max trotting round telling us he's achieved a cure. But he'd have done that anyway and what sort of a new man will we have? I tell you, I've met some of these businessmen who've had psychotherapy.'

'We don't know he is a businessman,' said Euan.

'Of course he is,' said Bob. 'Any rate, what happens to them? They have the breakdown because they think the world's a big and nasty place. O.K., it is — we know that now, sure enough — but you look at them in twenty years and then you'll find out what the cure's about.'

'Well, what will this guy be like in twenty years?'

'Same as he was before he had his crack-up. A cool, no-nonsense, unscrupulous tough businessman — only, and this'll be the difference, he'll tell you he's sensitive. He knows what it's like, he understands your problems. He'll even claim that he's doing things not for money. He'll be an accepting, apologetic, totally compromised bastard whom people'll respect because he had a nervous breakdown.'

They wheeled the trolley into the side ward. V. was already in her bed. The beds, on Sir Maximov's instructions, had been placed side by side with nothing between, but they were not, and this again had been carefully laid down by Sir Max, actually touching. There was a gap of about six inches to a foot between them. V. lay arms crossed on her chest as usual, looking up at the ceiling, and she betrayed no interest in the new arrival in her ward. She lay under a sheet only and was wearing a ward nightgown several sizes too big for her. Looking at the coarse cotton Euan realized that it was the same material that had been used for the shrouds which covered the bodies in Ben's enormous store. V.'s stillness, too, increased the illusion that she was dressed not for the rituals of love which Sir Maximov had planned, but for the ritual of death. Surprisingly, just as Euan had this thought, V. slightly moved one arm, adjusting the sleeve a little perhaps. That movement brought back a curious episode in the post-mortem room. Euan had been helping Ben slide a body back into the morgue when he had been startled by a similar apparent movement of the dead body's arm. Euan had jumped back with an involuntary cry and Ben had exclaimed, 'God bless my soul, it's one of my mice. I'd forgotten I'd let them out.' He'd dived a hand up the sleeve and pulled out by its tail a wriggling white mouse. Once caught the animal sat quite still in Ben's hand while he admonished it.

'Now then, my little darling, don't want you getting froze to death.'

He walked over to a table and Euan saw at the back of it a small cage which he'd never noticed before. In front of the cage another white mouse was roaming around.

'Supposed to be a pair,' said Ben, 'only they 'aven't 'ad any kids yet so I reckon the dealer sexed them wrong. Pretty little things, aren't they,' he said, shutting them up in the case.

Bill's nightwear was no more elegant than V.'s. Old, faded, striped-cotton ward pyjamas which had lost their cord and were tied with an old-fashioned bandage. It was all that type of bandage was ever used for now, as far as Euan knew.

A small table lay opposite the end of the bed and there were two vases of flowers on it — well, not really flowers. Everlasting carnations, they were called. No fresh flowers ever reached the ship. Artificial ward flowers were part of the fitting-out equipment, and the sisters moved them from patient to patient, trying to create the illusion of new arrivals of fresh flowers. Euan noticed that there were no chairs and made a note to ask Sister to move some in. Bob was regarding the table.

'Pity there's not a crucifix,' he said, 'then they'd really feel they were here to celebrate something. Which way up would you put it, Euan?'

'Put what?'

'The crucifix, of course. They'd need it reversed — Black Mass is celebrated on the naked body of a woman.'

Euan realized that he felt and probably looked fairly shocked. He couldn't in consequence think of a retort to Bob's remark and shifted the conversation hastily back to the prognosis.

'What will V. be like in twenty years?'

'Someone's wife, maybe three kids, in a bungalow-type house somewhere in America.' Bob glanced at Euan but Euan made no comment. Bob had a wife and three kids and, as far as Euan could make out, he'd just walked out and left them to join the hospital ship. 'Listening sympathetically when old Bill gets in from the bank or whatever it is. "You know that new office complex we put up just to provide a service for our workers, well, it's a funny thing, V., but for some reason it's making money." "It's a beautiful building, Bill, you should be proud of it." "It *is* aesthetically pleasing. Personnel were right. The employees like it. It attracts recruits." That's how it will go, Euan — you follow them up in twenty years.'

'Huh,' said Euan, 'you've been listening to too many of Tafteria's crazy souped plays. We don't even know if there are any banks — or personnel departments.'

CONFIDENTIAL

To: Personnel Dept.: Senior Staff Only
(To supplement Personnel Weekend 354)

In the last five years employees joining the company with higher education have fallen by an alarming 50% annually. If present trends continue we can envisage a situation within five to ten years when the company's activities will be seriously handicapped by a shortage of management personnel in many middle-grade managerial posts. In twenty to twenty-five years the company could simply cease to exist because of the absence of senior direction. This situation presents a challenge to all members of the personnel sections.

RESPONSES

All personnel sections will review existing arrangements to visit schools, colleges, universities and all places of higher learning. Visits should take place on a very regular basis. Contact should be at three levels: (1) senior academic staff (2) career advisers or career counsellors (3) students.

SENIOR STAFF

Purpose of these contacts is to informally image-build for the company. Teachers in scientific faculties should have attention drawn to the company's research activities. While no major help can be given to fund research activities, small grants for additional assistance or gifts of old company equipment may be made to smooth the course of university sponsored contacts. Within humanities, draw attention to company's practice of grants, sabbatical leave to staff wishing to complete post-graduate work. Great emphasis should be laid on the company's belief in the positive use of pleasure by its employees.

If friendly personal relationships are established it may be possible to have academic staff draw company's attention to particular, suitable students. Provided intellectual achievement is fair, there are now so many varied opportunities within the company that there is practically no graduate who cannot be fitted into the company, provided the man has the right personality. The recruit must be capable of becoming genuinely loyal, personally devoted to the company. Loss of graduates who leave after only three or four years with the company and who never develop these qualities is another aspect of our senior staffing problem.

CAREER COUNSELLORS AND ADVISERS

Quite junior academic staff are often in charge of career

services. Sometimes social workers may run these services. In schools they are often the responsibility of counsellors with a social work training. In general these groups have a view of business which is confused and unhelpful. Do not attempt to change basic attitudes, but try to emphasize the distinctiveness of our company. Do not emphasize its diversity, but draw attention to specific activities of the company with which they may be familiar, such as ...

Staff in these positions are often poorly paid. They may welcome gifts in kind. Personnel staff are aware of the company's rule in these matters.

STUDENTS

Very many students are now openly hostile to the company. Again, do not attempt a direct confrontation. Formal presentations of company activities on career days should be made by out-of-town staff who should not attempt to make personal contacts with the students. Local staff should concentrate on personal contacts with local students. They should emphasize their own interest in people and their enjoyment of work with the company. Personal commitment to the company need not be overstressed at this stage.

Once good contacts have been established within the student body, shy and less overtly active students should be freely approached. Company is advised that there are many students who will respond to the opportunities the company can offer them. Do not emphasize the company at first, but rather commitment to the *society we are living in*. This should be your clarion call. Many students do not actually want to see our existing society destroyed. There is too much in it for them.

THE INTERVIEW

Over the last years there has been a subtle change in the proper conduct of an interview with a prospective employee of the company. Most young people of the right calibre have many possibilities of finding employment. Few of them are initially interested in working at managerial levels in industry. Company personnel staff must realize that they (and the company) are often the real subject of the interview. While not failing to establish the company's prime position and authority, at the same time they must be open and yielding to the candidate. He must feel the company has no secrets.

Traditional bargaining elements in the company's position no longer seem to have the same attraction as they used to. Thus offers of free material goods (cars, houses) as an initial lure to the candidate may no longer be the most appropriate opening. Some candidates may in the long run respond to these pressures, but initially they may lead the candidate to sheer off and perhaps apply to another group. Candidates today need to feel that the company is going to be involved with change, not only within the proper sphere of the company's activities but in wider social and political spheres.

Attention should be drawn to the company's interest in meaningful political activity of its employees. Widespread emphasis should be laid on the company's broad social programmes for its workers. Opportunities for management staff to be involved in these programmes should be stressed. The role of the families of candidates must be fully discussed. Many potential company wives will no longer accept purely social roles.

WOMEN IN THE COMPANY

Woman's role in our society is changing. Company policy is to offer equal pay and equal opportunities to female employees. Nevertheless the position of company wives who are not working but caring for young children needs careful consideration. Attention is drawn to our document 'The Working Wives of the Company'.

Pleased with his performance on Van Thofen's consultation, Sir Maximov wandered along to the Psychiatric Unit to which he was formally to be attached. Hurst, the child psychiatrist, and Banerjee, the Indian who despite his American training now used trance therapy as his main therapeutic tool, were the only two consultants in the small meeting room. They were eyeing each other covertly over cups of coffee. Not much chance of communication between those two, Maximov thought, as they greeted him. After he had accepted Hurst's quietly spoken but genuine pleasure at his joining them and Banerjee's more fulsome remarks, there was a silence and Maximov wondered what would interest both of them. He asked after Kline. His enquiry produced a torrent of abuse from both of them.

'He's like some of Banner's patients,' Hurst complained, 'in a bloody trance the whole time. You can't get a word out of him — and he's supposed to be running the department this quarter, it's a . . . '

'Oh no, no, no,' Bannerjee interrupted, 'not a trance, surely, oh no. More of a retreat, I would say — backwards, I would say, into some sort of childlike psychosis. One of many varieties that our friend here finds so difficult to treat.'

Hurst ignored this attack and went on: 'Well, at least I try to treat them. I don't think Kline's seen a single patient this last month, apart from his sortie with the chopper when he claimed to have sorted out a mad American on an atoll. He claimed he used a new form of therapy. Telling him the future held the same terrors for everyone.'

'The million-year therapy, he calls it. Tell the patient we'll all be the same in a million years,' said Banerjee.

'Well, I wish he'd try some sort of therapy on the patients. There's more than enough to go round. He could set a clinical trial if he liked, to see if it worked.'

'You are forgetting his one permanent patient, Coma! It worked with Coma, Kline maintains.'

' "Coma, oh Coma," ' drawled Hurst, 'she's his fate, he said. Fey,* he says to me. "Oh Coma!" '

*'Fey – the state of those who are driven on to their impending fate by the strong impulse of some irresistible necessity.': Sir Walter Scott in a footnote to *The Heart of Midlothian*. There are two further notes on 'fey' in the same author's *The Pirate*.

Maximov went along the corridor to Kline's consulting room, tapped quietly on the door and went in.

The great analyst was alone, sitting swivelled away from his desk and staring blankly at the wall, a cigarette with a long ash between his fingers. Coma was not in the room. Maximov took two or three paces forward and then stood waiting. Slowly Kline swung his chair and his body round and, starting at the feet, he began to look slowly up Maximov's body. Suddenly he identified his visitor and jumped up and took him by the arms, giving him a great bear-hug.

'Maxy, Maxy,' he shouted, 'you here, you here, oh Maxy.' Then abruptly he sat down again and took up his previous position.

Maximov pulled a chair from the wall and sat down too. He thought to himself, I'll wait one minute and see if he speaks again; but that was too long for Sir Maximov's patience and after half a minute he began:

'What the fuck's sake's going on with you, Klingy?'

'Nothing,' said Kline.

'Everybody says that you sit here doing just that.'

'What?'

'Nothing.'

'Oh.' Another pause.

'How's Coma then?'

Kline looked up. 'You've never seen her, have you? She's ... she's ... oh, she's marvellous. Her innocence, her skin, her mind, her body, oh, she's ... '

'Christ, you have got it hard. Does she love you?'

'Love?' said Kline. 'How can I — her psychiatrist — talk about love. It's transference,' he said, 'transference. Overt transference, at that. But it's the wrong way. I'm transferred on to her.'

'Good for you, boy,' shouted Sir Max, 'good for you. What I've been telling you all these years. Don't worry about patients loving you. Give 'em a bit yourself. Love.'

'Don't use that word, Maxy, don't use it ... Any rate,

what's the future? That's my problem. What's the future?'

'Whose future?'

'Mine. Mine and Coma's.'

'But you know all about Coma's. I mean, you've published it all.'

'Before I loved her! What am I going to do? Where am I going to be?' A pause and then: 'She says they'll brand her breasts. Now it's almost as if she wants it.'

'Well, you clever sod, you've cured her. She can accept all the pains the world's got to offer better than the rest of us, by the sound of it. You're with her. Look at me, haven't had a regular for ten years, since Mary died ... a poor old bachelor... '

But Kline wasn't going to listen to Maximov's soothing domestic tales. 'It's me I worry about. It's me. What am I going to be doing when they torture Coma, where am I going to be? Will I just be standing by?'

'Can't Coma tell you? Doesn't she know whether you're going to be with her?'

'She knows that I'll be there. At least she says she thinks she knows I'm there. But the future's mistier now she's no longer neurotic. She's not obsessed with it any more and I can't even get her to concentrate on what's to happen when we get off this damn boat. "We'll be together, of course," she says. "You are my lover." Fancy a patient saying that to her psychiatrist. Not "I am your lover", no, that would be straightforward transference, but this is the wrong way round. It's a reverse transference, that's what I call it, an overt — it is overt — an overt reverse transference. How long can it last, though?'

'What does Coma say to that?'

' "For ever, my lover," she says. "For ever, my lover," but then what am I doing when she's tortured? A man will brand her, she knows that, with his initial between her breasts ... think of that, between her breasts. And now she says, "I don't mind him doing it, he really needs to." The initial ... my God, my God.'

'What initial?' asked Maximov.

'The one between her breasts. She knows the letter, she knows the letter ... K. She says it's a K.'

Maximov thought about that for a bit and then offered: 'Well, there are other men whose names begin with K.'

'I know,' said Kline, 'I know, but she told me originally that her torturer was her lover, that's what she couldn't understand, but now she says she loves me so much that she doesn't mind what I do to her. What am I to do?'

Kline moaned aloud and at that moment the door opened again and large blonde girl bounced in. Maximov, having read of Coma in Kline's original publication on her, had always thought of her as a thin-faced frail girl, but if she had ever been thin her cure had seen to that. She was a big girl, blonde hair falling in curls over her face, big breasts, lovely chunky buttocks. She had been playing deck tennis and she was wearing a short white garment that wrapped round her. Hearing Kline moan she took no notice of Maximov but bounded over to Kline, sat on his knee and swung the chair round so that she could lean back on the desk.

'I had a lovely game,' she said. 'You should play, K., instead of sitting here all day. What are you worrying about now?'

'You, my love,' said Kline, moaning slightly again.

'Oh Kline, don't worry, I'm all right,' said Coma, unbuttoning her tennis slip so that her breasts were exposed and pulling Kline's head on to them.

'This is getting worse and worse. I'm off,' said Max, getting up with a snort of irritation. His eminent colleague took no notice of Maximov's departure but buried his head in Coma's breasts.

'Coma, Coma,' Kline murmured. 'This transference, it's killing me.'

All you need is love

There have been many efforts to interpret the phenomenon of transference, and while most psychoanalysts publicly prohibit all physical reactions, there are a few who have admitted overt expression. When Freud (1924) introduced the term 'transference' he defined it as the displacement of affect from the patient to the psychoanalyst. He insisted that such transference was entirely an emotional expression and should not be physically shown, but he was not able to distinguish between the nature of transference love and that of romantic love of one partner for another in a mature sexual relationship. Eventually Freud was forced to admit that 'one has no right to dispute the genuine love which makes its appearance in the course of analytic treatment'. Karpman (1948), an analysand and trainee of Freud, and under whom I had some of my training in 1927, emphasized the need to allow the analysand full expression both verbally and physically. As I have pointed out elsewhere (McCartney 1956) love, or transference, is primarily dependent on need, and is based on the possibility which a person offers to the lover for a fuller unfolding of his or her feelings by being in reality with that person. In the transference neurosis, that person is the analyst, whether male or female. If the patient is to work through to emotional maturity, the relationship will have to be heterosexual, for the analysand will hate his or her analyst as long as he or she is still open only to a child-father or child-mother relationship which limits all reactions to frustrating experiences. The patient will hate the analyst even more if, because of countertransference, the analyst actually behaves like one of the formerly hated parents and censors his appropriate reactions.

The female analysand begins to love the male analyst as soon as she becomes aware that she has found someone for the first time in her life who really understands her and who accepts her even though she is neurotic. She loves him all the more because the analyst permits her to fully unfold her real emotions within the safe relationship of the transference. In none of his writings does Boss put a limit on the extent to which the analysand should be allowed to go in expressing her needs.

Alexander (1963) pointed out that 'unfulfilled needs, no matter what their nature may be, whether hunger for food, hunger for love, curiosity, or the urge for mastery, initiate groping trial and error efforts which cease when an adequate behavioural response is found. Adequate responses lead to the need for satisfaction which is the reward for the effort. Rewarding responses are repeated until they become automatic and their repetition no longer requires effort and further experimentation.' He personally told me that he allowed the analysand fully to express herself. Every psychiatrist has seen the need of some patients to show affection physically, and in forty years of analytic practice I have found that 10 to 30 per cent require some overt expressions. This 'Overt Transference' may be defined as a visible, audible or tangible muscular or glandular reaction to an inner feeling. These patients not only want to think or talk about their relationship to the analyst, but also want to experience the newly discovered possibilities in the language of their emotions, as expressed by the body.

Meyers (1963) states that 'the psychopathology of the female pelvis is essentially sexual' and that physical pathology may result from frustration, although more frequent and more varied coitus will not supply an answer. 'The psychology of the woman depends on the functioning of her pelvis, which she uses as an organ of communication. Pelvic activity can have meaning only if it is using a language that is familiar to the partners in question, and is a channel for the expression of love. The woman uses her pelvis to receive and give that which is most precious to her, and she can consequently be transported to ecstasy or be tortured by a tantalizing frustration. Not all organic pelvic pathology needs to be surgically removed, for most chronic functional conditions such as discharges, menstrual distress and irregularity may have an emotional background. Many of these problems are corrected by simply allowing an opportunity for ventilation of the details, and an injection of hormone may convey more therapeutic value as a ministration by a trusted doctor than as a replacement of an endocrine need.'

Wilhelm Reich (1949) pointed out that 'the goal of analysis is to crystallize out the genital object libido and to liberate it from repression. The analyst therefore should let the overt evidence of sexuality develop without interference until it is concentrated without ambivalence in the transference.' He emphasized that 'the ultimate end of the transference is to concentrate all libido in a genital expression'. I have talked with his students and analysands and they related that he required each to disrobe and to respond to their instinctual needs. He physically manipulated the patient to appropriate response, concentrating on the erotic zones until the orgasm was reached.

As stated before, if a mature personality is to develop, then only a heterosexual response should be elicited. If the patient needs to be taken through an Overt Transference, then the analyst should be of the opposite sex, for a homosexual response is immature, neurotic and adolescent. If the analysand is a male and the analyst also male, then the patient's treatment should be shifted to a female analyst when overt expression shows itself. In selected patients the analysand may be able to work out his needs with an objective surrogate, in 'free love' or with his wife. It is not so easy for a female analysand to find a surrogate, and so the analyst may have to remain objective and yet react appropriately in order to lead the immature person into full maturity. It is of no import whether the woman be single or married, as long as she is beyond 'the age of consent'.

The patient may lie on the couch, sit in any chair, walk about or even sit on the analyst's lap. If the patient wishes to have the analyst also sit on the couch or hold hands, the request may be made and I will respond appropriately, although I will ask the patient to analyse and explain the need.

The therapist must realize that Overt Transference is in conflict with most of the firmly defended positions of conservative society, and that for this reason he will be exposed to criticism, sarcasm, contempt and slander, because the theoretical and practical application of this treatment is rejected by the social order and vigorously condemned by most religions. In order to gain this emotional maturity, the patient must find an active relationship in the living presence, for without this reality relationship, the patient can never adequately fulfil the demands that adaptation requires and the patient will therefore remain in a life of fantasy. The therapist, thus being a vessel of expression, cannot put restraints upon the patient that would appear to be demanded by moral and social standards. In working through the transference neurosis, the therapist should allow himself to be reacted to as though he were someone from the patient's past.

The therapist should not mistake the erotic demands of his female patients for those of mature women, in spite of the fact that such actions often appear to be evidence of mature sexuality. Such genuine maturity is difficult to attain, and if the analyst is not ready to open himself to an analysand sufficiently to be able to live up to the demands that Overt Transference will put upon him, he had better refer the patient to another analyst who is capable of meeting the demands of the patient. The patient may improve in an amazingly short time with an emancipated therapist. For the last twenty years, I have allowed full overt expression. Of the female patients who underwent psychoanalytic therapy about 75 per cent made good adjustments. The time involved extended from 30 to 309 analytic hours, with an average of 89 hours, covering anywhere from 8 to 159 months. Of the adult women analysands 30 per cent expressed some form of Overt Transference, such as sitting on the analyst's lap, holding his hand, hugging or kissing him. About 10 per cent found it necessary to act-out extremely, such as mutual undressing, genital manipulation or coitus.

There was a very long silence — much too long for W. Women bear silence better than men. W. smoked, of course, and this provoked an action. V. had risen from her bed and then gone round to the small table where W. kept his ash-tray, picked it up — it already contained five or six cork-tipped stubs — and took it from the room. She came back with it cleaned and emptied and placed it by his bed. W. smoked on. He had stopped muttering that curious series of numbers and comments which had disturbed Bob and Euan and finally it was he who started talking first.

'In New York I worked for a man who used to say . . . I'll tell you that later. I drifted there, went there deliberately. Eventually after all those successful jobs I'd done, after all those successful marriages, ménages à deux ... Anyway after, and I'll tell you about that later, after that is my life in the Navy, bank, philharmonia orchestra, industrial engineering, advertising, big businessman, Senator, when I had failed or succeeded in all of those there I was, a drop-out in New York, not a young drop-out but an old one. Not really fancying the garret life, cold cheap food, nothing much to do, the hours of boredom in dim-lit bars talking. Once you have had money, been busy, eaten good food, lived in comfort, had space, books, radiograms, tape sets, indoor swimming pools, horses, what is it like going back to urban nothingness . . .

'The people will tell you they don't want it, that Hollywood luxury, the mink, champagne, blonde Marilyns dancing by the pool, deep-set eyes staring into yours, palaces, castles in the mountains. But they want it all right. It's just that some of them have the conscience to realize that there are not castles in the air for all of us, only for a few, and so they aim for something less, something drab, rights for the people to own one overcoat even if it is the identical design for all of us.'

All this and more poured forth from W. before he paused. He lay silent for half a cigarette, possibly waiting for some response from the girl at his side, but V. lay as still and silent as she had for the previous hours. W. didn't think she'd even turned her eyes towards him.

'I suppose you must blame the doctors that I'm talking at you. I had gone far away from reality. Here I am touching it

again. Nothing has changed for me in the world at all but
their drugs have made it bearable. They've made me accessible
again. It's not treatment — it's pollution. Like they can prop
up a cancer victim now, keep him alive for months and months.
Or people who've been in car crashes. They have to deliberately unplug the heart-lung machines. A pathologist told me
about one once, when they opened his skull the brain had
liquefied, it ran out on to the table. Mine's like that inside,
I'm still all to pieces inside.'

Still nothing from V.

'Well, any rate, there I was at long last in New York. You
might say, why New York? I mean, why not Rome, Paris,
London, San Francisco? I was still living then, attempting to
live, and I give you the reasons I gave myself then: although
the problems may be — are — worse, there's more excitement,
more involvement, more enthusiasm. In New York you meet
people and you feel they really are trying ... Trying to do
something, make contact. There's an atmosphere of things
going on all the time. Freshness even, or so it seemed to me
then. They may seem conventional statements to you. That
was what I thought anyway. Friends who understood me. All
that. America, where the decline and fall is finally going to
take place. And if you're going to make anything change,
that's where you've got to start.

'Any rate, niceness of friends and all that, I had to take a job
of course and being an older drop-out it's much more difficult.
They think maybe you won't take the long hours, that you'll
get them into trouble for not paying you enough. You'll join a
union and all that. So it's very hard. I started thinking, manual
work, and I went down, walked to the docks. I thought they
must want men there. Perhaps they'd think I wasn't strong
enough any longer. I actually watched, hung around all day.
Actually there wasn't much lifting that I saw. Every docker
seemed to have his own little fork-lift truck. I was only in the
warehouse, not actually on a ship, and they all looked fat and
overweight.

'There were all sorts of jobs, too. The sampler, I think one was called, sort of customs guy — went round crashing open crates, taking a bit out. What I wanted to know was, did he ever give it back? Otherwise, Italian silk scarves, Finnish glass, English books, Spanish lace — what did he do with it all? I never found out. But I did see there were no drop-out type jobs. It was all sewn up, if that's the word, by the unions. Longshoremen's union or something. Getting in on that when you'd been a boss yourself, they'd have found out about me. Wasn't a hope.

'So wandering about town, looking for the washing-up jobs, cleaning rest rooms, all that. Even then, being older, they'd say, what experience have you had? With the kids they didn't bother, they knew they hadn't any, but they reckoned I should have had.

'So what experience had I had? Thought about it and one day went and said, yes, I was good at cooking. I was, too, I was the best short-order chef in New York; I could fry in two pans at once and I remembered all the orders in turn easily as they shouted them across the shop at me. And I could work any hours. The place I worked was mid-town, about 50th Street. It was a block away from some of the big hotels and we took part of our money from them. Their coffee shops were so expensive that people came out to eat in ours. Then midday of course there were the regulars, office workers, the poor tourists, and then all night there were just the odd guys dropping in, a few regulars who worked late. Ham and eggs. Sunny side up or over. Hamburgers and so on. French fries.

'All this is clearly of very little concern or interest to you. It's gone on so long because the remark I wanted to repeat was ... made by the man who owned that coffee shop, He was a Jew, of course. Father came from Germany, I think. He'd saved and saved to get that shop and he worked. I worked, but he was there all the time. It didn't seem to me that he'd ever had any time to do anything else but he had somehow. In the slacker periods, mid-morning, afternoons, he'd tell me about it all. Philosophy of a Jew from Brooklyn. I used to kid him he should write a book. He'd spotted I was literate pretty quickly. Any rate, about women — girls, I should say — he had of course a wife and kids of his own — of girls, though, he'd say, "Never refuse an affair. You won't get the chance of many so never refuse an affair." "When did you ever get a chance to have an affair, you fat Jewish slob?" I'd shout at him. "You sweat after money too much to have affairs. When do you have time for affairs?" And he'd just smile at me, ignore all my shouting. "Never refuse an affair," he'd say. And again, "Never refuse an affair." '

It was like a record then that had stuck. W. went on and on repeating it, reversing it: 'Never refuse an affair. An affair never refused. Refuse an affair never. Never an affair refused.' But after some time he got slower and slower, the words became more and more drawn out.

'Nev ... airr ... rrefoooose aaan affaaaaire ... affaair ... ' — he almost sang it out — 'aff ... a ... a ... air'. He had stopped smoking for all these verbal tricks — 'refooo ... se ... ' — but his voice finally faded away into complete silence. Breathing only could be heard in their small side ward; then:

'Is it offered?'

After a little while V. got up again and walked round to Bill's side table.

'I don't mind you smoking,' she said, 'but I can't stand the smell of stubbed-out cork-tipped cigarettes.'

An Affair with the East

It is not what everyone in this crazy country thinks. It is what we think. What we know. You have been valiant these last few weeks. You have kept your promise* and now we are out of those wilds again I feel like jubilating. Have a glass of cham-

*S. had agreed not to attempt to make love to her while they were in the 'wild'.

pagne and we shall drink to the health of the He-he Mois and be glad we are still above our six feet of earth. An hour later we entrain for Saigon.

The impulse of the Asian night is strong. Hovers on heavy wings in the purple shadow; drifts insidious fragrance from flowering trees.

Facing each other our hands come together. Ten finger-tips. Pressing — pressing — in tense contact. Subtle electric currents pass through them, thrilling, exquisite, compelling. I am still standing struggling between romance and common sense. Why not snatch a flower when it beckons? A strange exotic flower; something different. Passion flowers. Mountain peaks. The old urge for experimentation lures. Suddenly I lose the Occidental objective view of the East, cease to be the observer, the alien surveying the Orient as a background for his Western reaction; lose that sense of 'racial superiority', however well or ill deserved; I am assailed by a desire to toss intellectual conceptions to the tropic night and melt into the feel of the East, to be one with its sensuous body, its bare feet padding the soft earth, its flexing muscles made for amorous play, flowers in the hair, naked bodies caressed by vivid coloured sunsets and hot languorous dawns. After years of Oriental travel tonight I feel Asia lift its curtain. I want to cast off so-called civilization, let conventions go to the soft winds. The East is wooing me like a lover, ardent yet subtle, beckoning deeper and deeper into the violet shadows. A dangerous mood — is this the way S. feels — is this what has charmed him and the occasional European exile one meets in outposts — that young man, blood brother to the Pnongs, in the Moi jungle? The sentient, unhurrying, unashamed body of the East, silently, carelessly wrapping its warm arms around my spirit, unheeding, indifferent to the fabric of science, psychology, all the isms of written civilization. It snares the primitive senses and beckons to its bed of hard teakwood or woven bamboo or leaf-strewn earth — it invites me, without lust to the rich secret of life, the incense of nature's beauty without evasion and hypocrisy which are the chains of civilization. Drink it if I have the courage — the dark spreading grip of the jungle might not let me go!

Sensing this hesitation, the sensitive soul of the man shrinks a little. He too values romance more than passion.

5   *The Crucifixion Disease*

The Gibraltar Sequence

Very cautiously the big atomic-powered hospital ship was
creeping up towards Europe. They had swung back from the
Pacific, for no very good reason really, and cruised slowly up
the coast of Africa. They had kept well clear of South Africa
itself and not even seen a sight of the famous Table Mountain.
From Angola they had picked up a group of dying and sick
children who appeared to have been in a Catholic orphanage,
but no adults were available to tell them how the children had
been deserted. They had been standing or lying on a quayside
as a picket-boat came in from the hospital ship lying further
out. They were dressed in rags, looked half starved and did not
know how they came to be where they were. They each clasped
a tightly rolled scroll in their hands and were reluctant to
release them. The doctors gently prised them from their hands.
Each child held a Catholic baptismal certificate but none of
the children answered to the name engraved on the particular
parchment they held. They shook their heads when called by
the listed names and shouted aloud strange unchristian names
like Xuna.

Further up the coast they had again sent a party ashore and
found a small African town functioning quite normally. They
had been able to purchase fresh fruits and even to replenish
the ship's vast storeroom with some tinned foods that the locals
were happy to sell them. But there was no news. Tafteria
reported all wavelengths dead. They had hoped that from
South Africa some stations would still be broadcasting and the
constant radio search had been intensified. There was only

one which was on the air. It was broadcasting over and over again obscenities and swearwords in Afrikaans. The sequences were never repeated in exactly the same order but were interspersed with short abusive speeches addressed to the Kaffirs. The listeners decided that the messages were being generated by a computer. Did the programmers hope to attract some reply? The *Hopeful* did not know what reply to make so they transmitted their call signal only, but there was no response.

Now, as they came on past the Equator and ever closer to Europe, the air became alive again. Atonal music, bunches of static, half-sentences about budgerigar care, cake recipes, origami instructions for making parts of the human body in paper (like heart and kidneys). Tafteria was busy again. 'News!' she would shout, and rush out of the wireless room with her rolls of paper full of bizarre messages. Finally one message dominated all the rest. THEY ARE USING US it said. It came in from all over — Dubrovnik, Montreuil, Danzig, Oulu, Narvik and finally Gibraltar which lay ahead of them. WHAT FOR they cabled back, but no reply was vouchsafed.

The Rock then as evening was coming on. Very slowly they slid in, ready to turn and flee if they were attacked. They had swung round in a big arc from the Atlantic to approach from the north-west. The Captain wanted to have a good look at the airport. All eyes were on the runway which stretches out into the sea. Would a plane speed out to investigate them? But no, the runway was not in use, a great plane lay crumpled and crashed on it.

Beyond the runway lay Waterport Wharf and the North Mole. There was some sort of construction work, it looked like, going on. There were what appeared to be huge arrays of rather small derricks mounted all along the quays. They were short, say sixteen feet high, had an upright piece about two feet long, reaching up above the side arms stretching out about four feet on either side. Curious shape. Cruciform, when you stared at them and thought about them. Crosses. They were crosses.

'Something to welcome us,' said Sir Max. 'To remind us of what we've always been proudest of in our own civilization.' Glasses were raised and trained on them now. Men, dead men, were attached to them. The ship dropped anchor outside, not far away from the end of the runway; the Captain was not going into that harbour. There were men attached, nailed to all the crosses along all the quays. They blew a long blast on their hooter and waited. A host of birds flew up from the crosses. Crows will pluck out the eyes of living sheep. What will the scavenger gull do to the dead human being? No one human moved on the shore.

They lowered some of their motor boats and volunteer groups set off to examine the crosses. Some of the men might still be alive. On board the ship's crew and staff crowded the rail, watching in silence as the boats plied in and tied up at Waterport Wharf — where the Tangier boats used to dock. Row upon row of men looked blindly down at the shore party. Some of the younger doctors felt they should listen to the hearts of the victims to check they were dead, but they had no ladders and they couldn't reach up the ten to twelve feet to their chests. The older staff merely pointed to livid changes in the feet, the dried blood round the nails in their feet.

By now it was quite dark and a small party decided to go and look for other humans. They followed the road up into the town. At first all seemed deserted but as they came to Main Street a little old lady came scuttling down Crutchett's Ramp. They didn't mean to grab her but she shrank against the wall in terror, screaming, 'I was only going out to try to get a little tea.' They hastened to reassure her and tried to explain who they were, but fear overcame her and she hurried back the way she had come, still clutching the empty envelope she had hoped to fill with tea.

But they became aware that there were inhabitants about. The hotels were empty, the banks and offices were shut, but some of the little shops along Main Street showed a little cautious light — candle-light. Some of the inhabitants were there,

shut into their houses, doing nothing, not coming out to welcome them but present and alive. After a while they began to
knock on doors, summon people out and try to find out what
had happened. There was an unwillingness to talk, a with-
drawal, a sliding away even when a well-known neighbour
appeared as well. The details of what had happened had to be
wrung out with direct question after direct question.

'Who were they?' 'Did they kill all the men?' 'Why did
they do it?' 'Where did they come from?' 'Where have they
gone?' To all they had less than clear answers. They were men
in grey suits — respectable men, they were. Some of them
had their wives and families with them. Gibraltar being a nice
place they said they'd brought the families along for a bit of a
holiday. Nice people they were really, when you got to know
them.

'Why did they do it?' Hard to say. They said they had to.
It was their job and they'd been told to. They left just one
man alive — old Harry — he has wooden legs and they said
they didn't fancy hammering through that wood. Any rate
he's nearly dead. 'All men are dogs,' he (Harry) says.

They did it very quickly, very efficiently, you know. They
had guns and so on if they needed them but there wasn't any
shooting. Three sons I had, God bless them. I don't know where
they've gone. Drove off in their cars and vans as soon as the
job was done. They said they had a lot of work to do and
didn't see themselves getting a proper holiday all year. Poor
souls. On their way to North Africa they were. Or had they
come from there?

If there was a pause in the questioning, 'Is that all then because if you don't mind I'll be shutting up and going to bed
now. Goodnight then, goodnight.'

The ship had nothing to offer. There are no medicines for
the dead. But they decided that in the morning they could at
least remove the crosses and arrange burial for the dead. The
psychiatrists said the inhabitants were in a state of shock and
if the crosses and bodies were removed some more normal

form of mourning might develop. They felt the ship should stay under the Rock and help the inhabitants work their way through the mourning process.

Around three in the morning lights and fires on the shore awoke the ship. Everybody tumbled out on to the deck to stare at the shore. Someone soon after dusk must have driven round and sprayed each cross and corpse with petrol. The night watch had suddenly seen a glimmer of light near the bottom of the North Mole and then with a great flash of sound the flames had swept round and every cross was suddenly burning brightly. Many of them had been tilted crazily forward so that the bodies hung over the sea and, as the flames took hold, there was added to their roar and noise the hiss and splash of burning flesh and wood falling into the water.

Soon drifting across the water to the ship came the smoke. A smell first of petrol then of roasting meat. People turned away, covering their faces, and fled down to their air-conditioned rooms. None of the medical staff argued when the Captain took a policy decision without consulting them. He abandoned Gibraltar. He pulled his anchors and sailed at once. The fires sank below the horizon, the stench was blown off the ship as it pulsed on through the night into the Mediterranean basin.

In the morning they were clear of all land but steaming east fast. Bob and Euan breakfasted together and then went up on deck before going down for their daily ward work.

'Tafteria had it wrong again,' said Bob.

'What do you mean?' Euan asked.

'Those messages she kept getting, you know, "They're using us." That's not what they were saying. What they were saying was, "They're crucifying us." She can't put that down to static. It was her deaf Welsh ears.'

'Yes,' said Sir Maximov, who was up on the deck breathing deeply the fresh morning air, 'they were telling us about a disease process and we didn't recognize it. We ought to have done, it's been well known for years.'

'What disease?' said Euan.

'The crucifixion disease,' said Sir Max, 'it can start in early infancy.'

The Psychopathology of Everyman

Human infants are provided with powerful innate release mechanisms through which they command adults to attend to their vital needs. Since human infancy is so protracted and so dangerous, these commands elicit biological responses in adults of a most powerful kind. Cataclysmic breakdown of this inter-action is at the core of child abuse. 'His crying,' said a mother of a battered baby, 'his crying seemed to follow me round the house, I could not stop it — and I could not escape.'

The breakdown, the paroxysms of violence, are always followed by denial and confabulation, epitomized by 'it did not seem to be me that did it'.

This denial and the fantastic explanations offered for the injury meet, nearly always, with collusion by the spouse. This compulsive denial of the obvious is shared, with relief, by doctors and social workers. 'I cannot bear,' said one such, 'I cannot bear to believe that anyone could do such a thing.'

The Psalmist knew this behaviour. 'Blessed shall he be that taketh thy children; and throweth them against stones.'

So why were we, in the modern West, so long delayed in our acceptance of the syndrome?

I think it was no historic accident that recognition came after Hitler's war. We had been forced to see, unwillingly, that a whole nation of ancient Christian civility could suddenly degenerate into a frenzy of barbaric cruelty. This led many to admit that there lay buried in the common humanity of all modern men a violent beast awaiting release. Be that as it may, denial is a universal feature of the syndrome. Denial leads to recurrence. The paroxysm of violence generates its own return.

Either side, or both, may have defects which set the scene for the explosion. Henry Kempe has taught us, and our own experiences echo his at every point, that a common pattern of parental rearing can be discerned. The parents were themselves unloved children, children to whom nothing was given, but much was demanded. In some cases they had themselves been battered. They now expect from their own infant that he should, from birth, love them unreservedly — he must in particular never excite in them that disquiet which drives adults to respond to infantile crying.

When repeatedly abused children are watched they show a diagnostic behaviour pattern. I have called it 'frozen watchfulness'. They make no sounds. They keep quite still. They look you in the eyes but they give out no facial signals. They have learned not to ask, by cry or word; not to demand, by approach or flight; not to influence, by smile or frown.

Frozen watchfulness, that end-product of repeated abuse, declares an adaptation to a world where a loving and loved adult unpredictably and without warning is transformed into a brutal aggressor — and then immediately reverts to good mothering once more ...

Both parents came from families where violence ruled and had done for generations. Fear and anger bound the two together. Their other children were dirty and unmanageable. Their house, their persons and their biographies would excite disgust in all of us.

But that was four years ago. Now the whole family is a stable and loving unity. Cleanliness and kindness and a sort of simple courtesy are what strikes one in them all. The change began when they, at a crisis, learned that what they did had not cut them off from the rest of humanity.

The psychopathology of the Battered Baby Syndrome is basically quite simple. It is part of human nature itself. It is the psychopathology of Everyman. If *we* can grasp this then, like the parents of the blind baby, perhaps there will be hope for us too.

The Roman poet Catullus knew that this dilemma was universal. I will English what he wrote: 'I love-and-hate, and if you ask why? — I don't know. But that's how it is, and it crucifies me.'

Kline seemed less depressed than anyone by the Gibraltar scene. He had, he explained, been expecting it.

'Coma's been telling me about it for years,' he said. 'People are capable of being infinitely nasty to each other. That's all there is to it. I don't know if it's right to call it a disease either. I mean, after all — hammering the nails home — it's something we'd all do if we were told to and offered enough money by a respectable organization. I mean — all in the interests of science, they'd say. We'd all do it if we were told to.'

A group of psychiatrists were drinking their mid-morning coffee and enjoying the Mediterranean sun.

'Come off it, Klingy,' said Sir Maximov. 'Don't try the tough act. We know you can't contemplate one person getting hurt. Isn't that right, Coma my darling?'

'He is learning to bear the thought that one day I shall be hurt. Isn't that so, darling?' But Kline had turned away from them, his moment gone, he was walking drunkenly away and Euan guessed that he was probably crying.

'He needs to do some work,' said Sir Max.

'That is certainly correct,' said Banerjee.

Kline's colleagues trapped him into work by simply assigning some of the new patients to him that very morning. Kline was back in his consulting room, sitting there gloomily as ever, when a junior nurse tapped on the door and walked in with some notes which she put down on Kline's desk.

'Your patient's here. I'll send him in.'

'Er, wait ... ' Kline was starting, but the girl (she had been instructed by Banerjee) had already opened the door and the patient who had been sitting on a chair outside immediately came in.

Taking up the case notes with a grunt of irritation or perhaps more exasperation, Kline looked up at his patient. A fattish middle-aged man walked slowly across the room. As he turned his head Kline saw that one ear was packed with cotton material. 'Bugger,' thought Kline, 'deaf.' He grunted again and looked down at the notes. Sure enough he found that the patient had been referred to psychiatry by the oto-laryngologists. There was a brief note signed by the African surgeon Arbace:

R 40 db loss   L? 40 – 50
Man seems mad. Talks of 'A Man at Trenton'.
Mad. → Psychiatric O.P.

Kline motioned the man to a chair. Then with an embarrassed shrug he indicated Coma, who was sitting reading, 'One of my research assistants.' He had a faint worry that this was unethical but felt he could hardly ask Coma to go. His mind wandered off and he thought that although she was his lover she knew nothing really of how he worked. He should have explained medical procedure to her and then she would have known to leave the room when the patient entered. She had shut her book and was looking at the patient intensely. The patient had looked at Coma but could not meet her gaze and swung back to look at Kline.

'John's the name, isn't it?' said Kline, glancing down at the notes. 'You look rather tired.'

John was a big man. He was wearing heavy dark cloth trousers and a waistcoat that looked like part of some uniform. He had a chain diving into a waistcoat pocket and Kline guessed he worked in a public utility service.

'Yeth,' he said, 'I am tired. I overlaid thith morning. I had to take a little of my bithmuth. It wath that man at Trenton,' he said.

'The man at Trenton?' Kline queried.

'Yeth, the man at Trenton!'

'Tell me about it,' sighed Kline.

John was a railway guard, as far as Kline could make out, or a conductor. The trains to Philadelphia stopped at Trenton but the platform at Trenton was too short, so the last two coaches weren't opposite the platform. If you wanted to go to Trenton you had to travel forward.

'Thome of them never did,' said John. So John had to go back into the coaches and shout out, 'Anyone for Trenton, not thith coach for Trenton.'

John, who had been telling his tale fairly quietly, jumped up at this point and began shouting, 'I hate them. I hate them. Not thith coach for Trenton.'

'Whom did you hate?' asked the puzzled Kline.

'Telling them to move forward if they wanted Trenton. I hated it.'

As far as Kline could make out, what happened was that there was some hard-headed tough-looking guy who'd maintain that they'd never told him which coach he should be in at Penn Station in New York. There would be cursing and swearing at John:

'What the fucking hell's this line coming to! Why the fuck can't they run it properly! Carry my case forward, you fucking little conductor.'

'I had to do it, you see, it was my job. Get the men for Trenton up from the back two coaches. Not thith coach for Trenton,' John shouted again.

'Was it because you've got a lisp that you minded having to go and shout out?'

'Of courthe not,' said John. 'I've alwayth had a lithp. It was becauth of the men. What they thaid to me about changing coacheth. I hated it.' He stood up again and shouted three or four times, 'Not thith coach for Trenton.' Then he collapsed back in his seat again, pale and sweating, as if badly shocked.

'Other men, you know, thometimeth they'd thtart arguing for me. "Thith man'th juth doing hith job, treat him with thome thivility." And then the otherth would shout at him. I didn't like that either. I juth wanted them to get up quietly and thenthibly and walk two coacheth forward. I mean, why were they like that? You're a thychiatritht, why were they like that? Why were they like that?'

'I don't know,' said Kline. 'Perhapth when they were children ... ' finding himself imitating John when he was under attack.

'They were children,' reiterated John, 'But why were they like that?'

'Well ... ' began Kline.

'You don't bloody well know,' said John. He jumped up again, paused for a moment to look at Coma, then shrugged his shoulders and stamped sturdily out of the room. They could hear him walking away down the corridor shouting out: 'Not thith coach for Trenton.'

Kline, looking rather shyly at Coma, was anxious to explain his failure. 'I can't think what to do for him, these cases of hysteria, you know, are ... are very difficult.'

Coma put down her book and stood up. 'I shall go and tell him,' she said, 'that I'm stuck in the two back coaches. I want him to come and help me get off this bloody boat at Trenton. See you in Philly, Klingy — when I get there.' She kissed him wetly on the mouth and went out shouting, 'Conductor, conductor! I want you.'

Later on that afternoon a perspiring John, rigged out in faded blue shorts and a rather dirty singlet with the Stars and Stripes printed on it, was observed having a lesson in deck quoits from Coma. Kline was strutting up and down beside them. He knew nothing of the game — any games for that matter — but he called out advice to John from time to time. He exhorted him to play harder, sounding like a master from an expensive private school. 'Good show! That's the way. Get some of that weight off!'

Sir Maximov joined them and Kline boasted proudly: 'Look at this for psychotherapy. Deck quoits! It's a discovery.' But when Coma took John in to change he was back in as black a mood as ever.

'He's mad, of course, mad as he always was. I know nothing about it. You know nothing, Max. What can we do? How can we start when the whole world, huge groups of people, are mad? It's nothing to do with us. We are to do with sick individuals. People who come to us when they are ill and in trouble. But what we're getting now — we're getting whole groups of totally mad people. Those people this morning, Maximov. The men crucified, Maximov. That's nothing,

Maximov. That's a straight old-fashioned way to die. What you
don't know is about the women. I know. Coma's told me. It's
much worse than any crucifixion scene you can imagine. The
way they treat the women, Maximov. And I love women, Max.
I love them. They will do more than crucify them. I will do
more than crucify. Do something about that, Max.'

Lieutenant A. is dead. His funeral oration was unanimously
summed up in a comment, 'Too bad, but he deserved it.'

Who was this man? Adored and hated by his men, abhorred
and yet admired by the other officers, he stalked around the
battalion, a neat and elegant silhouette, with the narrow face
of a vulture, pointed ears and round grey eyes wherein, at
times, shone cruelty, irony, obduracy and lust.

A born freebooter, a pirate made for blood and slaughter, he
did not join the Army by vocation but out of sheer necessity.
In this twentieth century only a military career could provide
him with an occasional outlet for his pent-up passions.

What was known of his past? Only what he chose to tell, a
few remarks here and there in the course of conversations
rolling eternally on the subject of his war experience. Life for
him seemed to have started with the outbreak of war in '39.
He was eighteen then and had joined up immediately. He was
in a tank corps during the retreat and never saw combat.
The tidal-wave of the exodus carried him to Lyon. Then came
the occupation, the Resistance, Spain, finally North Africa
where he stayed over a year. He enjoyed telling us how he
helped to burn a *douar* (nomad settlement) where several cases
of plague had been discovered. A battalion was sent to encircle
the tents while they were being drenched in gasoline. The
inhabitants who tried to escape the inferno were shot on sight.

Sometimes he would recall the Italian campaign where the
women did not need to be coaxed. It took a lot of the fun out
of it, he remarked regretfully. Then on to France and Germany.
Through one country after another his story added up to one
long trail of rape, torture and slaughter.

I could not tell whether this show of cynicism and cruelty was feigned or real, I could not discern where the truth ended and where the myth began.

As time went by, however, in the course of battle it became apparent that A.'s personality fitted his own description. This was no travesty, he really was the cruel, cold-blooded torturer to whom human life meant bloodshed.

On March 8th, 1951, during operation 'Pataugas', a few miles from the Seven Pagodas, D. saved A.'s life by killing the woman he was raping. Indeed, unnoticed by him, she had managed to extract the lieutenant's Colt and was preparing to use it when D. walked into the hut and nailed her to the mat with a shot from his rifle.

A. quietly finished his business over the corpse whose stiffening fingers still clutched the weapon. Then he thanked D.

Sgt. R. spoke of the days back in 1948 when he was in Cochin-China under the order of Lt. B., nicknamed 'the Moi' because of his fondness for hunting wild buffaloes while clad only in a loin-cloth.

An anecdote of B.'s always found an appreciative audience: the scene took place in a Delta village in the course of operation 'Lemon-Tangerine'. The company had just taken it and the men were going through the usual routine. A group of ten or twelve soldiers had discovered a very beautiful young Vietnamese girl whose legs were paralysed. They all raped her.

Then it was that B. appeared. His organ was famous in the company for its size, and he pretended he could not find a woman to fit it in this damned country.

One of the men hailed him: 'Hey there, B! We've opened the way for you! You might try now!'

Before his court of admiring spectators, B. exhibited his specialty and, in his own words, all but 'twisted it' in fact 'almost broke it' in the ensuing process.

At this point of the tale someone always interrupted with a loud laugh: 'And do you know what he did then?'

An expectant silence reigned.

'He b ... her.'

More laughter. R. kept the ball rolling: 'I had a friend who would first f ... the girls, then he would shove the cannon of his machine-gun where his tool had been and empty a clip into them. The dame's stomach would burst wide open.'

After a while the lieutenant, kept awake by our shouts and laughs, would start yelling: 'Turn those lights off!'

That is how we quietly spent our evenings in Ban-Mo.

'I liked the idea — the marriage idea — I mean, some didn't from the start but I liked it, tried it two or three times. It wasn't to be a closed thing, it was to be an opening up, it was to provide one with a firm base from which one could operate. First there was the physical bit — that seemed easy — an almost beautiful thing. You had let me into you and so once we were married, once we were fixed permanently together, there could only be expansion. I saw your body as something that now was mine to explore, feel and touch. It would be a pleasure to you but if there was something I did to you which you didn't like, which felt unpleasant, that also would be a pleasure for you because you would let me do it. Make me do it to you over and over again so that you'd train your body to enjoy my desires.

'In the same way I looked forward to your exploration of my body. I longed to be lying there passive while you thought out tricks with your hands to make me squeal and squirm beneath your touch. There were things I couldn't bear. Immediately after I'd come — drained out a full load of sperm — desire would leave me and although I could bear you stroking my back, if your hand moved to my penis or even more took my balls in a firm grip, I would jerk away from you to protect myself. I couldn't help myself. But this was something that you would have overcome.

'How would you have done it? I wondered, Maybe you would have let me take you with your legs up and with a subtle hand gently squeezing me throughout, and then when I came you would just have refused to let go. You'd just have held on to me firmly. The first few times you might have kept your hand still but then one night, deeply roused, you'd have insisted on continuing your gentle play. Or maybe it would have been more violent than that. Stretching me out across the bed you'd have lashed my limbs securely to the four corners of the bed and then mounted me and ridden me off. And when I came you could have laughed and just gone on playing with me as I twisted and strained beneath. The laugh would have been soft and kind, not cruel, a laugh knowing that deeply it was my pleasure, that my body should be trained to submit to your whim.

'But it was not like that, love, ever. When I came to your bed late from my books you were not waiting for me. You never came down to drag me to you. You accepted me if I came at a time that suited you but late in the night when my hand sought your crotch, my vulgar thumb pressed into your ass or my teeth clicked at your nipples, you turned away from me, closed your legs and shrugged me off your firm back. I was lost. I thought you were mine. Should I then take you violently? That was no good, you cried or fled from the bed and I hated tears. Or wait till the morning. I couldn't bear to have you leave me without a deep embrace from which it was agony to stop. But you could have been too sleepy to talk about it the night before and away next morning briskly to some expedient of the day.

'Then I had thought too that there would be moments during the day when a touch of me would be essential, when your hand would be in my trousers and I would be dragged despite the children, visitors, postmen, the insistent ringing of a telephone, to somewhere where I could quickly thrust up to my full depth and we could both abandon ourselves to ourselves. I had wondered whether our physical contacts would lead us later to to share with our friends our sexual pleasures, but that I didn't mind about, I wanted you to guide my body and I had hopes that you would have had thoughts, things to communicate on this and all else that was hidden behind your grey eyes.

'Later in the night you would be riding me leisurely, my erection by this time a little willowy, and hands would be idly stroking my flanks. Your long hair would be falling down towards me and I'd open my eyes and you'd ask me something trivial and we'd start talking. I did manage to tell you a bit about my past, all that weary mother stuff that the Freudian prostitute hungers after but it's the present and the future that should mean something to you. And was it because of something in my weary past or in yours that we never made it, we never really found out about our own creativity, we never got our two sets of thoughts fused and frozen in one direction? Surely two people should think and feel better and wiser than one.'

Bill paused.

'V?' he said. And waited.

'The men would come for me. I would be just lying about. If it were hot, naked maybe, perhaps reading, perhaps thinking, listening to the radio. I wouldn't go out because they wanted me to be there. Where could I go? What was there to do? They'd say, "My God, V., why do you go about naked all the time?" I'd say, "It's very hot, why are you wearing clothes?" Then they'd look at me and I'd know what they were thinking, "What a body," "What a snatch," — I learned their language — "Just let me get my hands on that." But they wouldn't at once. They were all tense, turning aside, and they'd say, "How's about a drink, baby," and I'd say, "Maybe," and they'd say, "You're a strange girl, V." And I'd go — because I knew that's how they liked it — and get them glasses with ice in them and they'd pour the whisky into them and I'd stand in front of them, lift my glass and look at them and they'd say, "Jesus, baby!" and grab me then.

'Once, I remember, he pulled me towards him fast and the whisky spilt all over me and yet he pulled me still and the whisky went all over his clothes. When he'd fucked me he dressed again, swearing about it: "Fucking bitch, fucking whisky all over my fucking clothes," and he slapped me hard on the face and went out. And I cried, not because it hurt but because I had done what I thought he'd wanted and it had been wrong somehow and he had gone out hating me.

'Sometimes, of course, it wasn't fast like that. Sometimes although we both knew what they wanted they'd sit down with their whisky and talk for a bit and they'd try and talk to me, they'd say:

' "Where do you come from then, baby?" and I'd say, "Up there," waving my hand, "a village in the mountains." "Oh yeah." "I'm a Moi," I'd say. Once only did I ever get beyond that, once one of them said, "What's a Moi, baby, when it's at home?"

' "It's what the others call us," I said. "Moi — it means savages."

' "Savage girl, are you, baby? What's it like back in the village then?"

' "I don't know really," I said. "I was orphaned when I was seven when my mother got killed, and then the nuns brought me up."

' "Oh yeah, the nuns ... " And that embarrassed him, to have me having to do with nuns, and he said, "Now me, I come from Cedar Rapids, that's a place I'd sure like you to see ... "

'That was mostly what they wanted to talk about, what it was like at home. Often they'd show me photos of their wives and kids, shyly at first, and when they saw I didn't mind: "This is Marge before we had any kids." A smile was all the response they seemed to want.

'After the family photos they'd find it even more difficult to start with me and so I'd lean against them, slip my hands inside their shirts, stroke them. They'd love that and then my hands would stray down to their groins and I'd pluck their penises out. Sometimes I'd let my lips and tongue stray over their firm erections, nibble them up into a stiffer erection. Once a boy moaned out, "Gee, Marge never did that." And I thought, why not? What sort of people were these Marges — why didn't they find out what their lovers wanted from them? Simple things which it was easy to do for them. Pleasant always to yield one's body to another's loving desires. Maybe, I thought, these Marges desired something from them only, didn't really love, didn't desperately want, as I always wanted, to be really involved with them, tied up deeply in a passion surrounding, overwhelming us both. Make it impossible to break off loving — and part abruptly at the end of an hour or more. Depositing green dollars on the chest — which I didn't want — maybe coming again, maybe not.'

A lot later he showed her the poem (Hollo 1963) about the girl who wanted to go to Cedar Rapids.

> She said: I am stranger born I can never make love
>   to people I know
> This is the last time I'll speak to you
>   please give me the fare to Bergen or Cedar Rapids
>   and that's all I ask of you darling she said
>   adjusting her seams

'Yes,' she said, 'that was it, that was what they'd have been like, those women who come from Cedar Rapids.'

'You should meet the men.'

The Men from Cedar Rapids

Who were the men who seized supreme economic power and 'built up the country' while enriching themselves? How did they build, how did they use their power, and how did they have it sanctified by tribunes and magistrates, churches and schools? How much did they further progress? And how much catastrophe?

Their deeds, in the last analysis, were determined by economic forces, we must remember. Hence we have tried in so far as possible to write of them without anger, to paint them as no more 'wicked' than they or their contemporaries actually were, though we are aware now of living in another moral climate and in the midst of a new generation which carries the vast and onerous social responsibilities bequeathed to it ...

I had hoped my boy was going to make a smart, intelligent businessman and was not such a goose as to be seduced from duty by the declamations of buncombed speeches. It is only greenhorns who enlist. You can learn nothing in the army ... Here there is no credit attached to going. All now stay if they can and go if they must. Those who are able to pay for substitutes do so, and no discredit attaches. In time you will come to understand and believe that a man may be a patriot without risking his own life or sacrificing his health. There are plenty of other lives less valuable or others ready to serve for the love of serving.

The son, like John Rockefeller, Pierpont Morgan, Armour, Gould and the other gifted young entrepreneurs who were of proper age, sent substitutes to the draft armies and as a rule found ways of displaying their patriotism without risking life and limb.

Behind the army lines there were lucrative tasks to be done in short order. Bankers and investors must raise a million dollars a day in money for the war government; goods and produce must be multiplied; woollen cloth must be manufactured in place of cotton; rivers of pork must flow from Chicago; the new free lands of the West must be opened up quickly for productive use; the iron trade must be developed for wartime needs; railroads, which quickly proved their great usefulness in the immediate war area for troop movements, must be extended across the continent to unify the country; coal and minerals of all sorts must be dug from the earth; innumerable oil wells must be opened; farm machines must be fabricated to replace a million men in arms.

The father of Pierpont Morgan was lauded for upholding unsullied the honour of America in the tabernacles of the old world. 'While you are scheming for your own selfish ends, there is an overruling and wise Providence directing that most of all you do should inure to the benefit of the people.' A wise Providence doubtless directed him upon a venture in war munitions, on the sensible ground that carbines were as keenly demanded as bags of coffee several years before. He needed the sum of $17,486 in order to purchase the carbines from the very same government at Washington whose armies in the West clamoured for guns. This paradoxical situation was caused by the fact that the carbines in question were found by inspection to be so defective that they would shoot off the thumbs of the soldiers using them.

The elder Rockefeller went further than this:

'I cheat my boys every chance I get, I want to make 'em sharp. I trade with the boys and skin 'em and I just beat 'em every time I can. I want to make 'em sharp.'

His mother would punish him, as he related, with a birch switch 'to uphold the standard of the family when it showed a tendency to deteriorate'. Once when she found out that she was punishing him for a misdeed at school of which he was innocent, she said, 'Never mind, we have started in on this whipping and it will do for the next time.' The normal outcome of such disciplinary cruelty would be deception and stealthiness in the boy, as a defence.

This harshly disciplined boy, quiet, shy, reserved, serious, received but a few years' poor schooling, and worked for neighbouring farmers in all his spare time. His whole youth suggests only abstinence, prudence and the growth of parsimony in his soul. The pennies he earned he would save steadily in a blue bowl that stood on a chest in his room, and they accumulated until there was a small heap of gold coins. He would work, by his own account, hoeing potatoes for a neighbouring farmer from morning to night for thirty-seven cents a day. At a time when he was still very young he had fifty dollars saved, which upon invitation he one day loaned to the farmer who employed him.

He was given to secrecy; he loathed all display. When he married, a few years afterward, he lost not a day from his business. His wife, Laura Spelman, proved an excellent mate. She encouraged his furtiveness, he relates, advising him always to be silent, to say as little as possible. His composure, his self-possession was excessive. Those Clevelanders to whom Miss Ida Tarbell addressed herself in her investigations of Rockefeller told her that he was a hard man to best in a trade, that he rarely smiled, and almost never laughed, save when he struck a good bargain. Then he might clap his hands with delight, or he might even, if the occasion warranted, throw up his hat, kick his heels and hug his informer. One time he was so overjoyed at a favourable piece of news that he burst out: 'I'm bound to be rich! *Bound to be rich!*'

6 *Therapeutic Problem*

At isolated moments V. now interrupted W.'s monologues, although mostly she would listen to them courteously enough. He even kept talking now when Sheila and Euan were in the room. They identified two topics: his personal life – his love life – and his public life, his place in society. But for V. this distinction did not hold; her work – her public life, what she'd had of it – had always been work of the most personal kind, and a distinction such as Euan and Sheila made within W.'s discourse did not occur to her, it was all one and the same related theme. She began to see it as a film. She'd seen some of those big American films, 'The Creation', 'Exodus', and she knew the formula. She gave the film a title in her mind – 'Ways of the West'. She knew it was rather a bad film.

'I was of course extraordinarily blind about you.'

'Not about me,' interrupted V. briskly.

'It's the same with all women,' W. insisted. 'My blindness consisted in believing that you had any desire to be loved in the way I meant it – I wanted it. But one day you actually told me about it – not wanting me, that is. We were in bed, somewhere hot, and affectionately enough – because we had not made love the night before when you'd known I wanted to – you crossed into my bed. It was very hot, the bed squeaked abominably but finally we made it in some sort of way and I collapsed off you on to the other ·bed to let the sweat dry. There was a little breeze and when I felt cooler I went over to you, took you in my arms and tried to express some sort of thanks for your generous gesture. There was a relaxed feel

in the air and you felt communicative on the subject and
startled me by telling me that for you the magic, the excitement
had mostly gone from our love, and what was it like for me?
Was it the same as when we first met? I hardly knew how to
reply. I knew the magic had gone and I'd spent the years
trying to bring it back so it was different ... in a way. But for
me ... in a way ... it was the same. So, "Yes," I said, "it's the
same." You repeated what you'd said, even described a bit
how you felt when we first met, but then you said, "I don't
mind. I didn't expect it to go on like that. No excitement, no
magic now, but I feel I know you better."

'I doubt if I can explain to you why that sounded so terrible.
It was that you didn't mind — you had accepted the idea of
settling for a non-magic, non-exciting relationship and you
said you didn't want anything different. You liked the security
of it, you liked knowing me, you said. *Knowing* me when I had
spent the intervening years trying to pull something back,
rekindle our excitement.

'When you first said lovemaking was becoming a routine
and why did we do it every night, I was amazed. We naturally,
I thought, aroused each other but I gave the matter some
attention and came up in my mechanical way with the solution.
It was a technical problem, you were bored with my technique.
So I started varying it. Most innovations you'd resist at first
and end up by saying you quite — "quite" was your word —
liked them. So we explored the suck, the bugger, I even beat
you occasionally. You quite liked that if I did it on the right
occasion. I'd even been downtown and had a look at some of
the shops and wondered what mechanical contrivances might
help. But I held off, somehow those pink and vivid red dildos
looked cool and uneventful. I didn't concentrate entirely on
the physical side; I tried to think of things we liked to do
together, wondered about working together, but the whole
business was casual for you. I thought perhaps we should start
reading books aloud to each other. We had cousins who did
that sort of thing. You weren't concerned. Told friends we

had a good marriage. I remember you came in one morning from a coffee party and told me you'd had a long chat with E. about us. E. had said it was just the same for her. Peter was wanting it all the time. You'd obviously had a laugh about us. Poor old chaps, just interested in the flesh. I watched Peter more carefully after that.

'But that incident ought to have made clear what you later told me. You did not care, you didn't miss or want my passionate love, you were quite happy to settle down. I had been wasting my time trying to re-arouse something you felt couldn't be re-aroused, you were happy in yourself, all passion spent. It was over, fini, and my years of trying to recreate it were a waste of time. It wasn't that I couldn't stimulate you, you did not want to be stimulated.

'I suddenly understood what had happened to my father as the waves of depression hit me. You know that some time when I was about five or six he'd switched off and been totally depressed and withdrawn until he became senile. At last I knew what had happened to him. He'd married that girl — I'd seen her photo — with the long brown hair, the soft eyes, the kind look, and thought, at last I'm home. For he was very shy, you know, and that approach must have been difficult. Well, of course, my mother in ten minutes was involved with babies, the linen, cooking, women's committees, all her and several of his relations, and he was like a boat that was half launched but never finished, capsized under the waves and stranded there barely visible until the seas at last got him and he was finally submerged.

'I stuck it out. Suburbia was what you wanted and that you had. I found us a nice house in a suburb, it could have been Paris or Surbiton, upstate New York — I commuted by air — or the whole of Los Angeles. Any rate I settled in, did all the things you wanted at home and went for a regular job. I thought that doing like that — like my father — I could submerge too, put up a periscope from time to time for a drink, but otherwise call it a day. I took a regular job as an industrial engineer, cut down sex to once a week, played cards ... waited until I was washed up here from a deserted strand ... '

It was his first pause. V. broke into it, and for the first time he heard her laugh. Deep laugh and:

'You took it all very seriously.'

'I am serious, it was serious. It is serious.' More laughter.

'I was lying there,' she said, 'not looking for anything more than food, lying under those men, like you I suppose, only worse for them, they were fighting a war. I wasn't worried about relationships. I never thought that sort of thing existed. I received their thrusts, raised my legs so they went deeper, enjoyed the moment of orgasm. Tried to be kind to the men afterwards, didn't understand their women who gave them all this trouble but really just felt thankful it was easy for me to eat and that I was no longer trodden down in the orphanage by those black beetles of nuns.'

'But didn't you want something ... more?'

V. just laughed. She got out of her bed, walked over to his, put her hand so that the fingers were all along his jaw, looked into his eyes and laughed again.

'Tell me about being an industrial engineer,' she commanded.

'Oh that,' said W., 'that was my big move ... '

The Big Move

After all those sensitive decisions in the executive's life that we have been discussing, there comes at length one that towers over all the others. It is supersensitive. It is the key moment in his career. It is 'the big move'. For some it is the decision to leave a company where your progress is blocked and join a company where the age and inclination of those in power seem to indicate a chance for you to move to the top. For others, it is making up your mind to go into business for yourself. This was the case with me, and that decision cut short the years of searching for the right path.

After leaving behind the champagne cider plant (as a matter of fact the place burned down), I joined a certified public accountant who wanted to add an industrial engineering consulting service. There I planned to prove my theories and, incidentally, began making a fortune.

That was my 'big move'. Like that of so many other entrepreneurs, it was only the prelude to decades of turbulence and toil, and again like many other ventures, it was immediately followed by pure panic.

THE GRASPING OF THE GOAL

If a man is truly successful, this is an exceedingly difficult stage to define. What is success? Where is the peak of the mountain? Perhaps it's better not to know.

Nevertheless, in retrospect, a man may be said to have reached his goal when he becomes the chief executive officer of a great corporation, after all those years of planning and struggling. Or, somewhat more realistically, the goal may be said to have been attained when the man has put in five years as chief executive officer and the company still hasn't gone broke.

The entrepreneur, perhaps, never reaches a goal at all. By the time he completes one project there is already another one that is occupying his mind. Eventually, however, we all look around us and find that the concerns of a lifetime have begun to be replaced by a whole new set of concerns. And this may be the beginning of a new and even finer phase of the life of an executive.

THE AFTER-LIFE

These days it is not at all uncommon to find a successful businessman turning to another career when he is in his prime. Norton Simon became so interested in art collecting that it became almost a vocation, after which he turned, by some progression of logic, to politics.

Other executives go from company to company, attempting to repeat their success and, perhaps, reliving their youth. And some seem to go on doing just that indefinitely. It should be noted, in this connection, that most professional corporate managers do not make huge fortunes. Charles E. Wilson had amassed $3.5 million when he left General Motors. Robert McNamara left Ford with only $1 million. This is wealth but not, by today's standards, great wealth.

At various times I have tried to alert the business community to coming dangers, such as the balance of payments crisis which has now arrived; and I have tried to alert the nation in general to unhealthy trends such as the drift away from free enterprise.

But business, national and world affairs are also fun. And they are the finest of all amusements for an executive who has long since grasped the major goals of life.

World Affairs: The Piraeus Piece

The *Hopeful* had planned to go up into the Gulf of Lyons and visit some of the towns in the South of France. But Marseilles had been one of the towns that cabled and no one really fancied another crucifixion scene. They had heard nothing, however, from Greece or Turkey so the ship now plunged on towards Athens. Hoping that there some shore contact would enable them to determine what was happening, and to define more precisely what the ship's own role should be in their daily dealing with what the psychiatrists were calling 'the Crucifixion Disease'. The patients suffered, they said, from an obsessional neurosis — an unavoidable urge to crucify people.

The ship's move, however, was an ill-conceived one because it led to almost direct confrontation with the crucifixion men. Piraeus has many quaysides and harbours twisting and tumbling along the Attic coastline. They anchored again off-shore among the fishing boats, not far from the quayside where the boats for Aegina and the other islands left. It was before dawn, and light was just beginning to come up but on shore they could see lights and flares; hammering and screams became audible as soon as the anchors were down and the engines stilled. Again the large shore-boat was lowered and the anxious decision taken to send in an exploratory party. Their boat crept in as the light grew. The flare torches dimmed as the light grew stronger but when the boat was still fifty yards out, they were hailed in a cultured mid-Atlantic voice: 'No closer or we fire.' The clatter of a gun and bullets whistling among the vedette's masts. They sheered off back to the hospital ship and waited, watching, as the sun came up and the trees of crosses sprouted on the shore.

They realized they had arrived as the job was being finished; the crosses were mainly up. Beyond them they could see a line of grey cars protected by armoured vehicles. There were men on top with machine-guns. Beyond that some sort of barrier had been erected across the street pinning back a crowd of women, some older men and children who stood silenced by the menace of the guns mounted on the cars.

What should the doctors in their ship do? Could they intervene or should they just watch? It was a role they knew well — one of sustained hopelessness. Watching the young girl with leukaemia, the attractive dark-haired lass with the carcinoma of the breast, the upright 55-year-old with the lung cancer hacking his life out. Negative capability, a doctor called it, being aware and doing nothing. Keeping some sort of hopeful face towards the future. The *Hopeful* loaded its boats with emergency teams, blood, cardiac resuscitation units, all the the paraphernalia, and waited.

Now the men in grey had completed their task and had silently withdrawn to their cars. They set off, rattling away south down the road to Glyfada Beach and along that rocky shore to Sounion. No doubt to offer some sort of oblation at the famous temple on that rocky promontory.

As soon as they moved all the ship's boats tore in towards the shore. Long before they were on shore there came the howl from the crowds as they crushed down the barriers and rushed forward to the crosses. As the doctors, nurses and orderlies climbed ashore with their little battery-run resuscitation trolleys, women rushed at them, wailing and weeping. Their arms were almost torn out as they were pulled or pushed towards this or that cross.

Although Euan spoke no Greek he could understand well enough, he found. The women with their weathered faces, their long black dresses, their headscarves, tears pouring down their faces, crying: 'I have lost my son.' They crowded round the *Hopeful's* staff, pressing up against them and preventing them from getting to work. What should you do when you did get to a cross? Pull the cross down first? Which was difficult — deep holes had been cut for the bases and still-soft concrete had been pushed in round them. Or climb up and wrench out the nails and lower the man down — and then what? What was the modern treatment for crucifixion?

In the '50s a German Professor of Anatomy crucified some of his medical students. He didn't use nails but bandaged them to their crosses. They lost consciousness very quickly — that not being a good position for breathing — and the respiratory distress led quickly to cardiac embarrassment. Many of the men were already dead. Dying of shock, perhaps, in the initial moments. But others could be resuscitated. They were far too many to take on board the ship so treatment was given them then and there on the quay. Packets of O blood were rushed ashore and, with the patient lying on the quayside and relatives acting as willing drip-stands to hold the transfusion bottle, blood was poured into them. The stigmata were sutured. Antibiotic cover and passive tetanus immunization were pumped in. Hearts shocked back into action.

These were not the only cases the doctors had to treat. Women had been savagely assaulted, children struck by falling masonry. As soon as it was known that doctors were on shore people crowded round them with sick and dying relatives. All sorts of diseases seemed rampant. Euan suddenly realized he was examining his first case of leprosy. The whole ancient seaport became one massive hospital.

What impressed itself on Euan during the long day was the noise. The continual shout, jabber and almost hysterical scream of people involved in a disaster. The clangour was incessant and it formed a background to the quietly spoken words which he exchanged with his nurse and with his orderly. 'Have we some catgut? ... I think I ought to put a couple of sutures through this muscle belly ... Yes, give him a shot of morphia ... Scissors, please ... ' And occasionally: 'Please, please, please stop scream-ing.' Towards sunset long blasts of recall were blown by the *Hopeful* sirens. Euan sent his orderly and nurse off but was still there himself it seemed hours later.

A woman had carried a four-year-old child up to him and pulled back a shawl to show him swollen glands in the axillae and groin. Euan began to palpate them, even in his fatigue curious to know what the cause of the swelling was. But then he glanced at the child's pasty face and realized there were no respiratory movements of the chest wall. He took his stethoscope and held it for the statutory minute over the precordium listen-ing for the faintest evidence of heart-beats. There were none. The child was dead. He looked up at the mother and said, shaking his head:

'He's dead, dead, dead.' And shook his head hard at her. But the woman thrust the child at him shouting the two words of spoken English she'd learnt:

'Doctor, doctor, medzines, medzines.'

He seemed to be pressed back against a wall himself and he was unable to escape and he had to reach out with his hands and push the woman and her burden away from him. He managed to turn her round so that now she had her back against the wall but in some way she managed both to hold the child and cling to his sleeve. He looked round at the many bystanders for help, but they looked on with uncomprehending eyes. He turned back again to the woman, shaking his head again and wishing he could remember the Greek word for death.

Suddenly someone pushed firmly through the crowd, reached forward and took his wrists from behind in a firm grasp and pulled him round to face her. It was Sheila. Euan felt embarrassed to face her because he realized that he too had been and still was crying. The tears rolled down his cheeks. Sheila wiped his eyes with her hands, bent forward and kissed his lips. She said:

'Come on, Euan, we're leaving. The ship's packed with patients, there is no more we can do on shore, we must give up and go where we can work.' He allowed himself to be led away.

'The dead,' said Sheila, 'are not our patients.'

The woman with the dead child made a feeble attempt to follow them. He heard her stumble a few paces after them, a final cry of 'Doctor, medzin' and then the excited sweating crowd separated them finally.

The hospital ship turned back south from Athens and began wending her way down through the islands, uncertain whether to attempt another landfall within the Mediterranean basin. At dusk a group of medical staff had come out from their wards and operating suites and were standing, not speaking, apart to allow the wind to catch and cool and freshen them. Some noise, movement suddenly caught their attention and they all turned. There, outside her wireless station, crying silently, stood Tafteria. In each hand she held sheaves of opened cables and as they turned towards her she thrust out her arms and shook the cables like leaves, demanding with her action that they should pluck them from her hands.

No one moved. They looked at Tafteria. She was not tall but was hugely proportioned. Great shoulders, huge bosom, thick waist. Her hair, which was white, she kept rather short. She wore thick-lensed pale-rimmed glasses and it was difficult to decide whether her rather too orderly teeth were all artificial or not. Normally her warm but spinsterish personality led people to tease her about the deficiencies of the communications section. Now no one said anything, awed by the tears that streamed down her face. After a moment they simply came forward, took a cable each and moved away to read them.

They all bore the same message. Indeed they had guessed the message. THEY ARE CRUCIFYING US. They passed them round and the assortment of addresses rang in their heads: Beirut, Budapest, Ostia, Smyrna, Port Mahon, Bizerta, Sevastopol. All the same message: THEY ARE CRUCIFYING US. Euan was reminded of MacBeth's attempt years before to describe this event with his sinister poem game 'Fin du Globe' (1963) in which complex and meaningless postcards had been presented from all over the world.

Too complex, thought Euan now, too complex. Ends can always be put simply.

Tafteria, her hands empty, still stood there crying hopelessly. Sir Maximov moved over to her, placed his hands on her shoulders and shook her slightly.

'Go back inside there, Tafteria,' he said, 'and send a message to God: WHY HAST THOU FORSAKEN US? Got it? WHY HAST THOU FORSAKEN US.' Tafteria looked at him, nodded and went to do his bidding.

Later in the evening they were strolling the decks when suddenly Tafteria was before them again. This time she was her usual sharp self.

'Your prepaid reply, Sir Maximov,' she said, thrusting the cable at him and retreating into the wireless station at once.

'Quick work,' said Sir Maximov, taking the cable and slitting it open, 'must have been a hot line.' He read it and passed it over to Euan. It read as follows:

JESUS CHRIST ALIVE STOP WONDERFULLY WELL STOP WONDERFULLY HAPPY STOP IN PARADISE STOP ENDS

The message was unsigned. Sir Maximov took the paper back and tore it into small pieces and let them float slowly over the side.

'Been there a fair time too by all accounts. Wouldn't mind it myself. Not bad really for just nine hours on the gallows.'

On the Gallows

The war here — and it's a bitter, inglorious war, which is gradually engendering fierce hatreds on both sides — may go on indefinitely. You have to see it to realize it. I have just been thinking of the chap you sent here and who departed outraged! And I don't mind telling you he had hardly seen a thing. It's Defoe, or Fenimore Cooper, or anyone else you can think of, but in real life! After an attack the other day, our partisans hurled themselves on the dead rebels, slit their stomachs open with their daggers and ate their livers while they were still warm. What do you make of that? These were Hoa Haos who were then on our side; though they have since deserted with their arms and baggage, after killing some of their white officers. I had just been nominated to join them. Lucky, as usual! All this reminds me how useful a camera would be. There are sensational photographs to be taken here, but a Leica is out of the question, since the climate would destroy it in six months. But if you could find me something small, smaller than 6 x 9, with which I could take photographs, I would be grateful.

Don't be anxious, this isn't a real war, merely a Western, a sort of succession of bancos, for we live as if we were playing baccarat.

I shan't be giving you any news when I tell you that the situation here is very far from being resolved or, indeed, that it's far from satisfactory as yet. We're expecting a big attack on the part of the V. from day to day. It will probably be better mounted than the last as they will have benefited by their previous experience. Anyhow it will be interesting to see what happens. I have made arrangements to be recalled to my unit at once should there be some little job for me in the business. Clearly, nothing at all may happen, all the same the V. would seem to be compelled to attack soon because of the weather, which is bad for aircraft at the moment, and also because our defensive works are nearing completion. There is also the army we're reorganizing. All these reasons must tend to make action imperative for them. Nevertheless, though the V. have undoubtedly made good the losses they suffered in the last battle and are probably even stronger now than they were then, the unknown factor is still China.

I've recently been to Hue by a mountain road within sight of the sea. It's very like the Esterel. I set off, alone and happy to be so, to visit the palace of Bao-Dai, which is unfortunately much damaged. It's a sort of monastery, five kilometres square, surrounded by walls and with a multitude of enclosures within. If you let yourself dream and give your imagination free play, there is a great deal of pleasure to be derived from the peace that reigns over these old, deserted buildings. With an effort, you can recover the atmosphere that inspired Pierre Loti. Yes, I like this country; apart from its filth, its diseases and its hypocrisy, it has a sort of poetry one can understand, a kind of animality. The women are attractive because of the simplicity of their dress, the regularity of their features and their frail appearance, though, as everywhere else, this does not apply to the majority. My feelings about this country remind me rather of La Fontaine's fable in which a bird explains to the eagle how beautiful his children are, and the eagle eats them because he thinks them ugly. You see what I mean? It's merely that I see this country through rose-coloured spectacles and I can't help it.

I even enjoy the operations, though they are utterly exhausting. If you can forget the cutting grasses, the leeches, the mosquitoes, the sweat and the stifling climate, you can live like a character in a novel. The other day, for instance, when we were looking for a Viet post, we came to the crest of a hill and in the valley below lay the tomb of one of the emperors of Annam. It seemed to me a wonderfully solitary place in which to be buried, since it is cut off by twenty kilometres of almost impenetrable jungle, unless you go there along the beds of the streams. I wish I could find words to make that landscape live for you;

I can still see it in my mind's eye. Imagine a circular amphi-
theatre and within it a rectangle surrounded by fosses full of
water in which grow green plants, while here and there stand
trees with astounding red flowers; from time to time, the loud,
mournful cry of a bird breaks the silence. I went down with
my men and crossed the fosse, sometimes losing my foothold
and almost drowning. Breathless and exhausted, we rested for
a while on the farther side before going on. There was a magnificent staircase, worthy of Versailles, bordered by stone ele-
phants and a variety of gods. We climbed it in silence, while
lizards fled from under our feet. Some hundred and fifty yards
farther on we reached the main wall, in which stood a ruined
door with heavy iron-work. I'll spare you a description of the
labyrinth of the interior courtyards in which we nearly lost
ourselves. In the end we reached a bare cellar, some sixty feet
square, with a plain rectangular tombstone in the centre. After
the rest of the decor, only simplicity such as this could prevent
one being disappointed. Do you see what I mean? With some
difficulty, I found my way back to the entrance door. I had
missed the view on coming in. It was magnificent. Before me
lay the great staircase with its gods, the fosse and, on the hillside
opposite, directly in line with the corners of the steps, two huge
columns I had previously failed to notice. And exactly between
the columns rose a mountain peak on the horizon. You felt you
could walk down the steps, pass between the two columns, and
with the mountain peak on the horizon to guide you, march
away into the infinite. I have just read my letter over again
and I am far from pleased with it, but I'm busy this morning
and, after all, you have other things to do than dream of land-
scapes in this part of the world. All the same, all this adds up
to something I know does interest you: the fact that, in my own
way, I am happy here.

I found in a Viet pack a book that had probably been
captured in an ambush: *La Dignité Humaine*. It was a lucky
chance, for the book is worth reading, though I had never felt
like tackling it before these present conditions. The articles

you sent me interested me; it remains to be seen how long it will take the predictions of global war to be realized, if they ever are. To tell the truth, I don't much care. As far as I'm concerned, it will be merely another edition of the 1940 business with, this time, a better comprehension of what's going on and greater opportunities for effective action. I shall survive or I shall be killed. In any case, I can promise you that there will be no question of my being sent to a salt mine. You need have no fear of that, for I've made up my mind.

Bill now gabbled away most of the time. This and that: ship's gossip, what it was like to be alive again, what was happening, what was he going to do? He was prepared to discuss the world situation endlessly with Euan or Sheila. Euan enjoyed these arguments and discussions and Sheila would take part at first. V. would be silently listening or doing something with her hands — she always had things to do — and Sheila would drop out of the discussion and lean back, her long white coat falling open, her stethoscope swinging in her hand, and she would stare fixedly at V.

Euan and Bill would become uneasy and their talk would drag to a halt. Once he said to V., 'I talk too much,' and began to cry in an incomprehensible jerky way. V. slipped out of her gown, went to him, wrapped him in her arms, held his head against her breast. She looked distantly over W.'s head and said to Euan:

'Do you know how to treat unhappiness, *Doctor*?' She emphasized the 'Doctor'. 'It's not done by talk, you know, *Doctor*.'

Euan felt forced into some defence of his profession.

'Well, there are depressions and anxiety states, and there are a lot of really good drugs now that really do affect depression, you know. Perhaps I should ask Sir Maximov to let me give W. some.'

It was not the first time W. had cried like this. He'd done it quite often recently. And of course he'd been crying when he first came in. And really when Euan thought about it he might have started off with something like librium and if that hadn't worked, why, he could try the mono-amine oxidases or the tricyclics. He was remembering the answer he'd written in his finals on the treatment of depression — he fancied it had been rather good.

V. had led W. to his bed, had lain him down and was gently stroking his body. She was looking over at Euan and interrupted very precisely his thought.

'Well, Doctor, which of your drugs do you think is appropriate in our case, Doctor?'

The sneer she was able to put into 'Doctor' suggested to Euan that she despised the whole profession. Euan recalled the thrill which he'd felt when he had realized that he could say 'I'm a doctor' when asked what he did. 'Can I see the doctor?' 'Doctor will see you now.' But with V. he suddenly found himself longing to lose that appellation which he had worked so hard to acquire. He found he wanted her to recognize him not as a doctor but as a person. He thought he must ask Max whether he thought it was right or wrong for a doctor to want to have a personal as well as a professional relationship with a patient.

Euan couldn't understand V.'s exact attitude towards him. She had embarked, he noticed, on a most complex reading schedule and huge fat books lay by her bed; recently he had surreptitiously inspected them and discovered that they were works on psychology. The classics, Freud and Jung, Deutsch's study of female psychology, as well as people like Ronnie Laing. But when he asked her what she thought about them she shrugged her shoulders with disgust:

'They seem very overrated, Doctor,' she said. 'This is simple but entertaining.' She held up Darwin's essay from *Mind*, on 'The Life of an Infant'. Personal biographies — they might be the thing.

Prowling round V.'s room a few days later Euan noticed a pile of case-notes in their brown folders. Thinking that a nurse had carelessly left them there, Euan picked them up and looked at them. To his astonishment he saw that the names on the covers were not of patients but of the medical staff. Sir Maximov Flint. Euan Gregory. Robert Sandler. Sheila Braun. Van Thofen. Gurdurson. There were files on all of them and flicking one open he saw notes inside.

'What on earth are these?'

'You keep notes on me, Doctor,' said V.'s precise voice, 'why shouldn't I keep notes on you? Would you like to read your own file?'

'No, no!' Euan found himself exploding violently.

'Look at Sheila's then,' said V., handing him the folder. Euan took it. He was torn between curiosity and a certain feeling that he was prying. It was a long time since he'd felt any reticence (if he ever had) about jerking open a patient's case history and rummaging through it, but these were notes about people he knew!

Sheila

PHYSICAL EXAMINATION

A tall girl, long hair well below her shoulders, fair to blonde in colour. Thinnish face but not too skinny. Nice white teeth, second upper incisor a bit crooked but not enough to matter. Eyes — how can you remember colour of eyes? — but I think pale blue. Slender but surprisingly well covered when stripped off. Big breasts which would flop around, probably likes having them sucked. Even at the height of her women's lib phase wore a bra. Pleasantly fat belly with belly button rather buried. Fair pubic hair. Good long slender legs. Good back, one or two moles on it. Loves having the bottom of her back stroked. The nape of her neck, too.

FAMILY HISTORY

American by birth, parents first-generation Americans. Father of Greek parents, mother of Finnish. Grandparents did not approve of that marriage. Born and brought up in St Louis with two siblings. Father making money, mother living the busy housewife's full social life. Classic American upbringing à la Spock, well described over and over again.

PERSONAL AND SOCIAL HISTORY

She had the ambitions of an American girl: marriage, home, children, family. But also the beginnings of some other imaginings. She had thought that after college she would go to medical school. Suddenly when she was eighteen there was a tall handsome stranger liking her. Taking her to Princeton Ball. He'd done the business course there, seemed assured, knew everything. He was vaguely well connected in the family way. Proposed to, married. Big wedding, lots of money spent, lots of nice presents.

Twenty; married, living in Grosse Point, Detroit. Husband something connected with the car business. Pregnant, a messy miscarriage four months later. Suddenly very depressed. Doesn't want a baby or miscarriage again, stops enjoying intercourse with husband. Coffee mornings with young wives, meets women's lib speaker. Becomes founder member of Detroit women's lib chapter. Supporter of many radical causes. Helps draft-resisters and deserters across the border into Canada. Writes articles for women's page in *Detroit Free Press*. On the pill, sleeps around.

Attempted reconciliation by husband. Taken on business/vacation trip to Europe. Elects to stay in Salisbury, England, while husband doing business in Birmingham. Drives small car round English villages visiting pubs to try and radicalize the people. Tries to inflame ruddy-faced working-man against pigs, finds he is village policeman. Flies precipitately back to America. Breaks from husband. Accepting a little alimony on the promise that he'll never see or touch her.

New York, women's lib scene, thinking about transcendental meditation. Travels widely as speaker, much enthusiasm for her. Trips to college campuses all over America. Admired by many girls, finds herself stripped off with several, at different times and the same time. Orgasms but wishes she was with a man. Picks up some for one-night stands, likes the balling. Starts work on her book *The Open Woman and Her Friends*. Is sent as a visiting women's lib speaker to Samarkand. Utterly unresponsive audiences baffled by her ideas. Returns to New York depressed.

Working on *The Open Woman*. Decides she knows little or nothing about women. Starts studying their reproductive system. Women seem to be designed to bear babies. Re-contacts medical school she had been thinking of going to years ago. Reads medicine — starts off with a major interest in obstetrics. Finds it mechanistic. Begins to lean towards paediatrics.

FUTURE HISTORY

This hospital ship. She is trying to love Euan Gregory. Does he know how? Does she know how? Can they communicate? Will they connect?

Seeing People

We cannot so easily perfect our schemata of people as of those of apples or socks. As we know only too well we do not all agree about what we see and we often fail to predict correctly a person's behaviour. According to their past experience and future intentions one person sees a policeman as a kindly figure who safeguards his passage across the road, another sees him as an enemy who may send him to the law-courts.

Apart from differences in interpretation according to the schemata employed in perceiving people, there is a further source of confusion; in interpersonal situations the observer influences the other persons he observes. The way in which I look at a table does not affect the table; whether I look at it with a frown or a smile the image it throws on my retina will be the same (though, as we have seen, the information I get from it may well be different, according to my state as I interpret it). By contrast, whether I look at my son or my husband with a smile or a frown certainly does affect them, and consequently changes the image which the light rays coming from them make on my retina (or on anybody else's for that matter).

Similarly, the policeman referred to above may in fact behave differently if he believes that the observer needs help to cross the road because of infirmity or because of inebriation. So intimate and indissociable are the relations between the participants in the perceptual act that in some cases we can be said to make our predictions come true, as when he who thinks himself unloved behaves in such a way as to make it difficult for anyone to love him. Such a person is caught in a hopelessly closed vicious circle, because his schemata of people's behaviour are continually reinforced by receiving confirmatory information; he cannot be presented with contradictory information until his own behaviour influences people differently. Small wonder, then, that in personal relations the information we obtain from a given visual pattern is not always such as will lead to the most effective way of behaving, even when it does allow correct prediction.

EYE CONTACT AND DIRECTION OF LOOKING AS STABLE INDIVIDUAL DIFFERENCES: William L. Libby

Identified four ocular responses by an interviewee to specific questions: (a) maintaining eye contact, (b) breaking eye contact before completion of question, (c) direction of look-aways at or after end of question — up vs. down, and (d) direction of look-away — right vs. left. In fifty-two male and fifty-two female undergraduates, each response proved markedly reliable in terms of inter-O agreement, intra-S stability, and temporal stability. Directional responses were more frequent — Ss tending to look up rather than down, left rather than right. Ss with more social experience and women tended more to maintain eye contact. Implications of directional responses for personality assessment in face-to-face communication are suggested.

ROMANTIC LOVE AND RECIPROCITY: Philip R. Kunz

1647 college students were asked to supply an ending to a story chosen to invoke responses relative to the concept of love or reciprocity. Endings were coded, and the results indicate that when analysis is made for sex differences, females respond with reciprocity to a greater extent than males. Comparison of marital status demonstrates that the married students respond with reciprocity to a greater extent than the single students. The single students are found to be more romantically inclined than the married students. The study demonstrates that reciprocity becomes significant in some situations and directs a non-romantic response.

THE SWEETHEARTS' EXPERIMENT: John Beloff

A common assumption is that telepathy between emotionally linked persons, such as sweethearts, is above what may be termed 'average'. Many investigations have agreed with this assumption. There were twenty boy-girl couples who took part in this study of ESP, which was carried on similarly to other such investigations. The number of 'hits' scored did not exceed chance expectations. It is concluded that mutual attraction between two persons does not insure telepathic rapport.

7 *Family Planning Clinic*

A strange set of circumstances brought us to the country of the Mois, which lies between South Vietnam and Laos, and is outside the area of official administration. We crossed this land and suffered physical hardship on our journey, yet the months we spent there were, in the main, a happy time. We made friends among its inhabitants; one of us found love. Unhappy? No; their horizon was so limited that they were unaware even that other people lived on the far side of the mountains. All the same, I did not forget that they were women.

(I'm sorry for any man who has never known the intense excitement of surprising his victim and killing it at his own chosen moment. This momentary relapse into a beast of prey, when the instinct of domination reaches its climax, is a necessity to anyone who has not been completely tamed by civilization.)

Our recent companions silently disappeared one after another, leaving us alone with the newcomers, who looked at us with large soft black eyes, full of lively intelligence and a certain mischievousness. Their oval faces were light-skinned and their waving hair was dressed high round their heads; their natural grace and elegance marked them out from any of the women we had met so far. Instead of the straight sarong to the knees they wore full skirts reaching to their ankles, but their superb torsos were as bare as those of their companions. The enchanting impression they made upon us seemed to be reward for our long and arduous journey through the jungle. Y. became lyrical.

'You often find the most delicious fruit hidden in the heart of the mountains! This ravishing trio must surely be the last survivors of an exiled noble family, or of some lost civilization.'

When the young woman let my friend take her long slender hand in both of his under the very eyes of her father, I had no further doubts about their mutual desires. But how could Y. achieve his ends? Any possible solution seemed the purest lunacy. To carry the girl off to France could only make her miserable; she needed the freedom and sunshine of her forest life. And if he should stay and allow himself to be absorbed into the life of her tribe, how could he fail to compare this rudimentary and almost barbarian civilization to the subtle refinements of life in our lovely faraway country?

When we were alone in our room, Y. at once broached the burning question.

'As you see, my dear G., I'm caught at last. Mi-Lane — that's her name — has got me in her net and I don't see how I can escape. So I suppose I shall end my days here trying to share in the life of this tribe. I'll come with you as far as the end of your journey, then I'll leave you and return here. No sermons, please.'

Instead of the usual wild tea, we breakfasted on fruit, a sort of guava jelly and cakes made of honey and maize, after washing ourselves in hot water. In spite of the fresh innocent high spirits surrounding me, in spite of the sun which turned the matting on the floor to cloth of gold, in spite of the thrilling awakening of all nature from its nocturnal sleep, I could find no pleasure in anything — only fresh reasons for regret and gloomy thoughts. Smiling faces surrounded me, beautiful eyes looked teasingly into mine, but I wouldn't yield to them; and I withdrew into deliberate isolation.

I would never grow old among these Mois. I wouldn't live, pale as an albino, muttering words which no one understood, an outcast from my own land, among these bronzed and muscular warriors, these women with breasts modelled by a divine sculptor.

What had Mi-Lane done to bewitch him so thoroughly? How was it possible that the level-headed Y., who was usually immune to all but passing attractions, and who was so in love with life and liberty, should be ready to tie himself to an uncivilized woman — almost a barbarian in fact?

I cursed that girl with the burning eyes and the body like a Tanagra figure for abusing her powers by snatching my friend away from his proper setting and his own race. Of course she loved him, but not enough to give him up for his own sake. Perhaps he would change his mind when the moment of parting came?

The sun was still hidden behind the high mountains which separated us from South Vietnam. Not a cloud in the sky, the day would be fine and hot. A few light wisps of mist still hung over the little river which mingled its murmur with the song of birds, the cries of monkeys and the rhythm of the pestles pounding rice. From all the surrounding hills an orchestra of living things sent up a hymn of greeting to the sun — trumpets, fifes, bells, cooings, miaulings and trills in the most astonishing cacophony.

I too felt a longing to express my happiness at being free and strong, my own master, with this boundless empty space around me. I sang as I walked, sang out of joy at being in this wild country, out of joy in my quivering senses, joy at being in Laos, joy because my life stretched before me — life for whose beauty and variety my adoration grew with every day that passed.

I turned my back on the gurgling stream, though in my exalted state I had felt tempted to swim across it; I crossed some little fallow fields fringing a rocky slope and took a path leading towards a wooded hill. Soon afterwards I was among the trees. The cries of the *tou-ou*, a grey bird as big as a thrush with a long tail, echoed as if in the aisles of a cathedral. Here I found my little world of creeping, climbing friends, some armed with wing-cases, others with antennae or stings. I tried not to crush their tiny bodies with my boots.

I said good morning to the death's head spider, lying on his dew-spangled web waiting for his breakfast of dragonfly; and to the little ant, hurrying off to work so busily. Let her beware of her enemy the white ant with her deadly mandibles! The lazy centipede lay on my path waiting for me to tread on him; I moved him out of the way with a piece of straw. I wouldn't pick the beautiful sapphire-coloured flowers of the orchid, ravishing though they were. The agile squirrel, hiding behind a tree-trunk from that great coward the green chameleon, need have no fear of me.

Here we were in Laos, that promised land, that earthly paradise!

As night fell, the sound of singing accompanied by stringed instruments was heard from all over the village, and the singers collected on their verandas in groups. In the light of the torches the red, blue, yellow, orange and purple sampots, accentuated here and there by a white scarf, looked like bunches of flowers. It was a Court of Love, a singing contest in which young men and girls exchanged declarations and mocking replies. The winner was the one who left his adversary speechless. Lost in the emotion of the moment, I saw faces draw closer and gentle kisses exchanged, as they laughed and sang while the twanging strings hid the emotion in their voices.

A tall European dressed in a tropical suit was advancing rapidly towards us with a look of surprise on his face. I showed him Y.'s letter which he read carefully. His face became grave, he closed his eyes and said dreamily:

'Another of them!'

I refrained from asking what he meant, but I imagined his was the desperate cry of regret of a man who hadn't been brave enough to realize, as Y. had, a vocation to which he was profoundly attracted. There was something in him of the explorer, the apostle, the pioneer, the idealist and the man of action, yet here he was leading a bourgeois existence at the edge of the forest, with his wife, his servants and his documents. Like me he had chosen a comfortable armchair and illusory satisfactions rather than liberty and the free gift of his life to the tribes who would have accepted him as a brother.

The Brave Vocation

Euan detected in Sheila at this time some degree of strain. He saw it when she took to coming on ward-rounds naked. He saw it in the hours she spent with Ben helping to wash the bodies in the mortuary. He saw it in her fascination with Coma. Sheila followed the million-year girl with her eyes whenever they met, she sat cross-legged against a wall in Kline's study and watched her yield herself to the psychiatrist. Euan saw that Sheila was fascinated by the tranquillity of Coma's new personality which allowed her to offer a completer love to Kline than Sheila felt she could achieve with Euan.

Mostly he saw it in the wild abandon of their own loving. She insisted on bringing to their bed his previous lovers and made him copulate with them while she embraced them. When he withdrew she moistened her fingers in semen oozing from the girl's vagina and touched it to her lips. She begged him to beat her, threw herself at him demanding that he should use her body, 'Use it,' she would moan. As he drove deeply into her Euan found himself distracted, trying to analyse what sort of relationship the beautiful girl was seeking from him. But she would feel this slackening in his erection and cry at him, 'Work, work harder!' He knew that in some aspect of their affair he was lacking. She felt he was failing to abandon himself totally to her and failing to take her wholly.

'I want to be annihilated by you.'

After a night of emergency work when he collapsed on to the bed with exhaustion, she would brutally shake him awake, saying:

'Take your energy from me, not from sleeping. You must never be too tired to love.'

Sometimes when he failed her in one way or another she'd jerk away from him, wrap a gown round herself and sit isolated in a chair smoking and glaring at him. If he tried to move towards her she would order him to lie still:

'My eyes and my imagination will do what your body fails to do.'

At the same time she threw herself fiercely into her work and expected Euan, who besides helping Sir Maximov now had a post with Isler, the paediatric neurologist, to involve himself with her work as well as his own. Sheila was working for half her time on a research project which Hurst had set up with the psychotic children. An attempt was being made to use a conditioning therapy with them, but the difficulty was the identification of what rewards should be given to the child. Sheila's task was to make behavioural observations and identify for each individual child what gave them pleasure, and devise a way for this pleasure principle to be used as a reward during conditioning therapy. Euan found himself watching Sheila as she watched the children, trying to establish what reward would enable him to achieve a lasting relationship with her.

Once he asked Sir Maximov whether he knew what Sheila really wanted, but Sheila overheard his question and swept into the room before the psychiatrist could speak. Euan was afraid she'd be angry, but she was cool, smiled at Max and said:

'How are you going to talk your way out of that one?'

'I shall say to Euan that whatever you want from him, he must find out for himself, because you want him to reach your position by himself.'

'And what is my position?'

'It is paradox. On the one hand you want to be totally free to do what you want, think what you want, love who you want; at the same time you want to be totally bound to Euan, physically moulded by him, your thought dominated by him and all your social responsiveness obsessively involved in him.'

'Do I?'

'Yes! And,' Max went on, 'I've not finished yet. You want both situations to last for ever. You are seeking — and I hope you find — that modulus — the arrangement for totally satis-fying living — that modulus which is adult love. That is what you are looking for. If you find it — that *modus vivendi* — tell me about it. It will help me with my lecture.'

'Coma and Kline have found it.'

That was true; Kline at long last seemed to be coming out of his depression. Euan had even asked him the other day how he had rationalized his dilemma over Coma. What was he going to do about the branding? What was the solution?

'There is no solution,' Kline had replied. 'If she can bear to be branded by me, I can bear to brand her. There are some things that just have to be borne with feeling.'

'But do you think you actually will brand her?'

'How can I say?' said Kline. 'What does it matter? Where will we be in a million years?'

Kline's latest contribution to psychotherapy was his Million Year Theory. He maintained that patients were only anxious, depressed or whatever it was because they felt there was no end to their troubles. What you had to do was to take them forward a million years. He asked the patients: 'What will anyone feel about your problem in a million years?'

'There is only one answer to that question — nothing,' said Kline. When you had established that, all you had to do then was close the gap between now and the future — a million years hence. Then the patients could say, if nobody's going to worry then, why worry now?

'Then I make love to the million-year girl, Coma, and I'm all right,' said Kline.

Coupled with his belief in his patients' mortality Kline believed that living with Coma would give him everlasting life.

'I shall make love a million ways. We will experience all the sorts of living and loving. It may be that we will shut ourselves away for a year together and simply look at each other. Not even touching.'

Kline's extravagances with Coma may seem fictional but he uses, you see, the same device that you have selected in order to see that the passion that exists between us does not fade. You remember the single room.

Being shut in one room alone together you had had the idea suddenly that intimacy between us should cease. Physical intimacy. Guilt about your other obligations was the reason for this decision. But we had had the physical bit. There was a lot of exploratory work to be done, we had still to find the time to work away at each other's bodies, prise them apart, open them to each other, but there was no occasion for concern about how this would go. We knew it would be O.K. That first contact *(vide supra)* had established that, so your decision left us back-chatting to see what else we would dredge up. We had that series of light sleepy conversations.

You initiated these conversations rather fast, afraid that I would try to seduce you. Frenetic talk about the group of people we were with. We were both interested in the behaviour of groups and the way individual behaviour influenced the whole behaviour of the group. So we discussed our colleagues. The doctors, the Pickwickian one from the West and the rather manic character who told us tales of Indian princes who were his friends. The pure scientists who were there, phlegmatic as ever. They were worried whether their present course of action/ philosophy was appropriate to the position in which we found ourselves. Faced by impending catastrophe, one associate of yours was ready to abandon his biological science which clearly could only tackle small aspects of the major problems the world faced and look for holistic solutions. He had indicated a desire to join a commune.

In the discussions I of course countered this Platonic Hegelian argument with a classical Aristotelian/Popperian Knight's move in defence. You thoroughly approved of this and as I spoke I had the welcome feeling that you admired my marshalling of the argument. The encounters with this group of people reinforced, therefore, your feelings about me. By discussing the group and its behaviour you insisted, in fact, on our intimacies because remarks you sleepily made would

match, of course, my own. For my amusement I shifted the
discussion, which you didn't really want me to do — for fear
of increasing our intimacy — on to another subject.

The book you were reading was *Felix Holt, the Radical*;
I told you about the descriptive elegance of the start and you
read the book all night while I was turning over aching for
touching. Detailed discussion of books needs mutual reading
together, we flitted over titles but our opinions juxtaposed.
Avoiding physical depths, serious discussion about any topic,
least of all anything of our relationship, you hoped this light
conversation would keep us apart. The reverse: our surface
glitter was too similar for either of us to doubt that our roots
were powerfully intertwined. You would have been better
trying to end our relationship by fucking me out and trying to
propose that there was only one parameter where we related
and that this one was sated.

Behaviour Patterns of Groups

Assemblies of people which are not as haphazard, anonymous
and amorphous as crowds, but are more enduring, structured
and organized, are specifically called groups in a narrow sense.

In organized groups, people can retain their individuality
and, at least, the possibility of independent thought. At the
same time, organized groups have enabled men to reach
heights of achievement which are unattainable by purely individual effort. The progress of civilization and the advance of
human culture would not have been possible without the aid of
co-operative group life. Unfortunately, this applies also to
progress in the art of waging war and to advance in developing
the destructive power of weapons.

This transition of group antagonism from disciplined rivalry
to organized gang warfare was experimentally induced and
studied by M. and C. W. Sherif (1953) in the microcosm of a
boys' holiday camp in America. There were twenty-four boys

in the camp of about twelve years of age who had a similar social, cultural and educational background, and were free from obvious psychological disturbance.

At the beginning of the experiment, the boys did not know each other. They were allowed three days to get acquainted. During that time, they all slept in the same hut, engaged in any activities they chose and associated with whom they liked. On the third day, each boy was asked to state the activities he particularly favoured and to indicate which companions he would choose for each of them. In this way a sociogram of friendship choices was obtained.

On the morning of the fourth day, the boys were told that the camp would be divided into two groups so that boys favouring the same activities would be together. In fact, the groups had been chosen by the experimenters with the idea of putting boys who liked each other into different groups.

The two groups became known as the Red Devils and the Bull Dogs. They were kept physically separated for the next five days as far as possible. They now lived in different huts, ate at different tables and engaged in different activities. On the fifth day, friendship choices were again obtained informally. They revealed that the two groups had become stabilized. Most friendship choices were now for in-group members and no longer for the boys selected in the beginning, who were now members of an out-group.

It also became clear that feelings of loyalty and solidarity were stronger among the Bull Dogs than among the Red Devils. Each group had come to refer to the other in derogatory terms, but their official relations were friendly, even if somewhat formal. For instance, when some Bull Dogs of high status paid a visit to the Red Devils, they were cordially received and entertained.

After the new friendship choices had been obtained, the next stage of the experiment began. The boys were told that, to comply with a general request from them, a series of competitive games would take place. Each group would receive points of credit according to its success at games and its efficiency in carrying out camp duties.

This point system was rather flexible and the experimenters planned to manipulate it in such a way that each group would receive approximately the same number of points until nearly the end of the contest in order to stimulate and sustain the hope of victory in both groups. However, because of their better teamwork, the Bull Dogs were generally victorious in games, and this caused a spirit of frustration among the Red Devils. The first sign of this frustration was that the leader of the Red Devils behaved vindictively against some low-status members of his group.

During the next stage of the experiment, it had been intended to engineer a number of incidents which would give the impression that one group played deliberate tricks on the other. However, only one of these incidents could be staged. It proved too effective. One morning, the two groups were told that they had shown too much aggressiveness and hostility against each other. It had therefore been decided to hold a party in the evening to let bygones be bygones.

The experimenters saw to it that the Red Devils arrived at the party of reconciliation a few minutes before the Bull Dogs. They found cakes and ice cream on the table, but half of these refreshments were battered, broken or crushed. When told to help themselves, the Red Devils naturally picked up the more appetizing half.

When the Bull Dogs, on their arrival, saw the mess that had been left for them, they protested. They felt inclined to throw the cakes at the Red Devils, but decided against it on the ground that the cakes would still taste good. They hurled insults at the Red Devils instead.

This was the start of open hostilities. The next morning the Red Devils deliberately dirtied the breakfast table because it was the Bull Dogs' turn to clean up. The Bull Dogs were furious. Instead of clearing the table, they messed it up further and pinned slogans on the wall which insulted the Red Devils.

At lunchtime, it was the Red Devils' turn to feel enraged. Open warfare broke out. The groups began to throw food at each other. When they started to throw table knives and saucers as well, the staff intervened and the fight came to a temporary halt.

In the afternoon the groups threw apples at each other and two windows were broken. The staff had to separate the boys. A short while later, the Red Devils raided the hut of the Bull Dogs and stole some apples. The Bull Dogs retaliated with a similar raid.

The Red Devils could not sleep that night. At two o'clock in the morning they got up and tried to break into the hut of the Bull Dogs. A staff member stopped them. At six o'clock in the morning they tried again and were again stopped.

The experiment was now broken off and measures were taken to amalgamate the two groups by fostering a spirit of solidarity in competition against an outside team which was specially invited for that purpose.

The war in miniature had come to an end.

The Group Called Despair

Somewhere about midway between Crete and Sicily, the *Hopeful*'s officers saw the first boat they had encountered in the Mediterranean basin. Off Africa they had seen some small fishing vessels in the distance but no one was fishing in the Med. This ship too had probably been some kind of fishing vessel. She was half-decked with a small cabin forward of the main-mast. She had an engine but she was not running under power. She had a sail, not fully hoisted, and it flapped idly in what wind there was. There appeared to be no one at the tiller.

People could be seen lying about in the ship but no one moved as the big hospital ship approached. They hove to and the Captain bellowed at her through his loud-hailer. Suddenly a figure staggered up, took off her blouse and waved it at them. She made no sound. The *Hopeful* lowered a boat and a couple of doctors went over with the sailors. The sailors were always apprehensive of infectious disease and the Captain, particularly, was sure they were going, one day, to hit a major small-pox infection on their travels. The doctors tried to explain that their vaccinated and revaccinated crew would be immune anyway, but now the Captain was expostulating again to Van Thofen whose month it was as senior physician:

'I'm not having them aboard until they are cleared as free from infection. They might have smallpox. You can't be too careful.'

Van Thofen smiled, pulled at his small imperial but dutifully despatched two of his junior colleagues to have a preliminary look at these new patients. Soon enough they shouted 'no infections' and the caique was pulled alongside.

There had been rather more than fifty people in it. Their main problem had been a shortage of water (and food). They were suffering from exposure, dehydration, sunstroke — what you like. Several of them were dead. The girl who had waved was reasonably coherent after she had had a drink.

'I had a water flask of my own,' she said, 'kept me going.'

They seemed to be a largely American party. At least that sort of American group which includes a Maltese who'd been at Buffalo for at least five years, two Egyptians who had made it into San Francisco and the usual assortment of sons and daughters of middle-European Jews. Then there were those who had joined the group in Europe, the usual Scandinavians, Englishmen, etc. The men were mostly bearded, rather tall, their clothes now in rags but giving evidence of the remittance money with which they had travelled. The girls equally ragged but more variably dressed: ponchos, long skirts, jeans with gay patches — you know the mixture. Mostly their hair was long, their necks beaded, their feet bare and rather dirty.

'A bunch of bloody hippies,' said Bob, leaning over the rail beside Euan, watching as the vagrants were lifted out of their boat and brought aboard the *Hopeful*. 'Hippies are all right,' said Euan. 'They're friendly sort of people.'

'Depends what sort,' said Bob. 'Some of these will turn out to be radicals as well and they'll turn the boat upside down.'

'Most of them are really quiet people — like old-fashioned religious people. I expect they were planning to go to Katmandu or something like that when the Crucifixion Disease caught up with them.'

When the boat was empty Bob and Euan went down into it to have a look at it. Not that there was much to see — dirty boards, empty petrol cans, bedding rolls which had not yet been moved. They wandered forward towards the cabin. The mainmast was mounted just behind the cabin and round its base there was a low circular seat. Bob and Euan became aware that this seat was not empty. On it sat a little fair-haired girl, four or five years old, wearing pyjamas. They felt rather than saw that she was phocomelic — she had virtually no arms — possibly flippers at the shoulders.

'Thalidomide baby?' queried Bob.

'They don't make the stuff now,' said Euan. The child had been watching them, unmoving but following them with her eyes. Euan crouched down until his face was level with hers and smiled at her. She smiled back. He made some non-committal remark to her but he realized she wasn't English and couldn't understand what he said. Euan stood up again, wondering uneasily what to do. Behind came the smooth mellow voice of Hurst, the child psychiatrist:

'All over the world,' he said, 'you'll meet lovely little blonde girls like this one, wondering what the hell has hit them.' He gathered her tenderly into his arms and carried her up on to the *Hopeful*.

Later Euan and Sheila encountered Ginny, the girl who had waved, in one of the A deck lounges. They found her trying to feed a pair of caged white doves.

'They belonged to Iain,' she said, 'but he's dead and I don't know what to do with them.'

'Let them go,' said Sheila, 'they'll find somewhere safe to land if anyone will."

'I'll have to think about it,' Ginny replied.

Euan found his guess about the destination of the group had been correct. Ginny and a group of her friends had been on their way to Katmandu by truck, but it had broken down irretrievably and they all found themselves in a Youth Hostel outside Genoa. There were other groups in the hostel; one party had been planning to go down from Genoa by boat to Palestine but, of course, no boats were running. Someone had come up with the idea of buying a boat and getting out of the trouble that way. Everyone in the hostel had joined the scheme and pooled their dollars. Between them they had collected a large sum of money with which they had purchased the boat — a Spanish vessel named *Los Desperados*. It had been abandoned by its owners and the harbour-master in Genoa, who had a passion for greenbacks, had gladly handed it over to them. So, with the crucifixion men on their tails, the party had set forth.

Harry had done most of the organizing. He'd organized strikes of telephone operators in New York so he knew what it was all about. It was then that their troubles had begun. Harry had told Richard and Tony to see to the water tank. They'd probably only about half filled it.

'I guess they still had some grass,' said Ginny. 'Because, boy, were those boys stoned when we set out.' Nobody had found out about this or their other problems until later, and nobody had checked how much water was drunk daily.

'We were a great, a really great group when we set out,' said Ginny. 'Boy, did we have some fine times together. You know some of the boys, they really made you feel.'

'Feel what?' asked Euan. 'Sexy?'

'No, no. We all felt together. You know when you get in a real group of people, I mean, you know, a *real* group with people, with *the* people all together. You know. Why, then things really start happening. Well, you know, it was like that on the *Los Desperados,* it really was ... to start with.'

As far as Sheila and Euan could make out, the first sign of a water shortage had been when the flow from the tank got slow and someone looked inside and saw there was practically no water left. Somehow in the period before that (and this amazed the *Hopeful*'s sailors) they had managed to navigate themselves down Italy and were somewhere south of Sicily when the water shortage hit them. Some people had wanted to head back to Sicily for water but others said, 'We'll get there O.K.' The argument had not been resolved when the engine spluttered and failed. What was supposed to be a pile of spare petrol cans turned out to contain heavy duty oil. The sail had been lifted but nobody really knew how to sail and they had drifted in the direction the wind had blown them.

'So,' said Ginny, 'it was a happy thing when you came by. My stars had said it would be a good day. Something hopeful will happen, they said. How about that! Do you think the Captain will take us on to Palestine now?'

'Well,' said the two doctors, 'we'll have to see.' A good nondescript medical reply.

The statement by the emergency-room doctors that the boat was free from infection turned out to be not strictly true. While they were busy re-hydrating their patients the staff observed little specks on their hair which, when pulled, stayed put. The sign of the crab louse. He is a friendly fellow. He looks terribly evil when he is magnified. There are two varieties: the body louse, *pedicularis pubis* — and the head louse, *pedicularis capitis*. There's a strange thing about them: the body louse breeds thickly in the pubic bush and the armpits but won't move to the head, at least he'll get as far as the eyebrows, even the eyelashes, but he won't go up into the hair, whereas *capitis* is the opposite, he sticks close to the head. The company from the caique were variously infected. Some had the body louse, some had the head louse, some had both, few had neither.

This knowledge slightly spoilt the drink that Euan and Sheila were enjoying with Ginny that first evening. They sat with their chairs rather farther away from her than was convenient for easy conversation. Euan wondered whose job it had been to check that Ginny was not infested and hoped they had done their job efficiently. Otherwise they were enjoying talking to Ginny and liking her American hip phraseology.

'Gee, you're a well-put-together guy,' she said to Euan. This made Sheila laugh. Equally they found Ginny's vagueness, which had infuriated the *Hopeful*'s officers, rather reassuring. It put reality properly away.

'The Crucifixion Disease — wow, man, those guys were cruel, they sure were.' But to questions about where the crucifiers had come from, who had commanded them — that sort of important factual question — Ginny had no answers.

'They were some sort of fascist cats — I never did get to read the capitalist press too much, so I guess I never did catch up with who set them up. The karma from them was bad, really bad. I sure got no waves at all from those guys. We split when we heard they were coming.'

'How did you hear?'

'Some guys told me. They heard it on the radio, I guess.'

What interested Ginny now was her Palestine trip. The *I Ching* had given her the right messages about that one and she was sure it would go well. She had quite gotten over her disappointment about her trip to Katmandu (what had the *I Ching* said about that one? Euan wondered). What Ginny planned to do was to settle down on a kibbutz for, maybe, a year or two and see how things went along. How long did Euan and Sheila really think it would be before the *Hopeful* got them there?

Euan and Sheila exchanged glances again. There had been a ship's meeting the previous night when all personnel were represented and votes were taken on major policy decisions. A vote last night had been unanimously in favour of getting out of the Mediterranean basin. What was going on there was too awful and too vast for their small group to be able to play any useful part. They were going to take their little bit of what they regarded as civilization away somewhere. They had seen the old part of Western civilization in Greece, they had looked in at the gateway to the newer civilization. If that gate — Gibraltar — was anything to go by, the Americas were not worth a visit.

And as to Palestine; there was no hope of making a landing there. The crucifixion men had been there — they knew that. They had had the usual messages from Haifa and Tel Aviv: THEY ARE CRUCIFYING US. But this morning there had come a cable from Jerusalem itself:

PONTIUS PILATE REPLACED STOP NEW GOVER-
NORS STATEMENT STOP NO THIEVES RELEASED
STOP NO BOWLS OF WATER STOP I WASH MY
HANDS IN BLOOD STOP ENDS

Some sort of sick joke no doubt, but no one on the *Hopeful* had really cared for it.

Gently Euan and Sheila tried to intimate to Ginny that the *Hopeful* would not be going to Palestine. She didn't seem inclined to accept this information.

'We'll be on our way just as soon as we get organized. You wait. There'll be no stopping us. We're really a great group when we get together — there's nothing screwed up about us. You wait till Harry's O.K. again. He'll really get things going. Harry, you know, he really knows about things. He really is the group.'

'Sure,' said Euan uncomfortably. 'If you'll excuse me I'll just go and do my night round.'

The New Governor's Statement

We start by asking: 'Why do men work?' The short, blunt answer is: 'because they have to'. But that is only the beginning of the matter. It is like saying that men swim because if they do not they sink. That is true enough, but it does not explain the difference between swimming enough to keep one's head above water and the whole range of speed strokes which gives a man mastery over water and makes swimming a thing of delight.

Management is, at bottom, the production and manipulation of power in human form. Just as the electrical engineer evokes and manipulates the power inherent in electricity, so does management evoke and manipulate the power inherent in men, and particularly in combinations of men.

It is not irrelevant to glance at the source of power, and the conditions governing its evocation where men are concerned. All power comes at source (as far as management is concerned) from the life and wills of men and women. When a man is in conflict with himself — torn, that is, in different directions by conflicting impulses or desires — his will cannot be fully engaged. It is placed in abeyance. In consequence he is powerless, ineffective. Conversely, when he is in harmony within himself, that is when his personality is well-knit and integrated, we find him powerful and effective. When a person normally rather spineless and dim, under the impulse of some situation suddenly becomes single-minded, so that his whole will is aroused and focused in that single direction, we are not seldom amazed at the transformation from weakness to an outburst of power. Those resources of power, we may note, must have been present potentially all the time; what was lacking was the condition that called the power into active expression.

The great driver is fear. It is the shark behind the swimmer. The usual forms are fear of the sack; fear of the future, and of insecurity generally; fear of reprimand or reprisal at work and of loss of prestige among the neighbours and at home. There will always be some men who will not work hard without the spur of fear to force them. So complete an absence of ability to respond to better incentives amounts to a state of disease. Such men are cases for the psychiatrist rather than for the manager, and in the absence of effective treatment by the former their best hope is to fall in with a tough and not too scrupulous employer — a Roland for an Oliver.

Euan, despite his new duties, remained formally as house physician to V. and W. under Sir Maximov. After W.'s bout of crying Euan sought out the psychiatrist and asked whether he didn't feel W. should have some antidepressants.

'No, no, no,' said Maximov. 'I feel that Maximov therapy is proceeding quite happily. Only use drugs, Euan, to make your patients accessible to human contact. If they are accessible allow them some tears, some emotion, to withstand the strains and stresses of the past and future.'

'Do you think that V. and W. have made love yet?'

'What's your opinion?'

'Well, they've been together in the same room for months now, alone lots of the time. It's hard to believe that light conversation is all they indulge in.'

'It is indeed, it is indeed,' said Sir Max. 'Well, time for my case conference. Oh by the by, Euan, I hope you keep physically examining that couple.'

'Well, no, I can't say I have really,' said Euan. 'There didn't seem much point.'

'Tch, tch, you should. Just go over them again today, could you. Let me know if you find any changes.'

Euan went down to V. and W.'s side ward puzzled. Had W. developed signs of some process, say a carcinoma, which might account for his odd behaviour all along? But no, he could find nothing. Although he was very still Euan did succeed in getting from W. a reaction to a pin-prick. His self-induced hysterical anaesthesia was disappearing. Was that what Max had wanted him to observe? He decided he would not do a rectal examination; surely nothing could have changed there.

Euan went reluctantly over to V. She looked at him, smiled faintly:

'You wish to examine me, Doctor, do you?'

'Yes, please,' said Euan coldly, pulling down her lower lid to look at her conjunctive. V. said nothing and lay quite still so Euan himself pulled down the sheet.

He found she was lying quite naked under it and he listened to her heart for a moment or two without making any further remarks. Then he began gently to palpate her stomach. There was a large lower abdominal mass.

'My God, you're pregnant. You're several months pregnant. Why, you must have ... You're ... ! No, you weren't pregnant when you came in — I know because we did all those hormone levels. You. It must be ... !'

'I'm sorry if you're shocked, Doctor. Perhaps you'd like to arrange for me to get married, Doctor.'

Euan looked at W., who was lying flat on his back looking up at the ceiling — smoking again, which Euan thought they'd managed to stop — and pretending to take no notice. Euan took the sheet and pulled it back over V.

'I don't mind you looking at my body, Doctor. I've always wanted to share its pleasures with everyone.' She smiled at him again — almost laughed — and Euan swung round and left the side ward.

'Perhaps we *should* talk about marriage again,' said W. V. as usual made no reply. W. stubbed out his cigarette and began again:

'Most of these women — the ones I was trying to love or the ones I had married — had notions of one sort or another about their role in society. These notions seemed to override or at least overpower any notions they might originally have had of loving me. Now there were those who had the notion that as part of loving me they should see that I achieved something in the world — they wanted no part in it themselves but they wanted me out there achieving. Or there were the other sort who were the "liberated women" — the women who wanted themselves to be part of the world and couldn't see why I didn't throw myself into that one with them. They had all these views about the way men had cheated them, got most of the money, had the higher status, looked on women as mere breeding factories. That was all true, maybe, but why did the men do it? Why this absurd invention of male superiority? Why this search for status, for being that sort of stupid manager, director, worker of one sort or another? To hide from themselves and from their wives their own deep feelings of futility, so they made out that their jobs as adman, dishwasher, technical assistant, transport controller, doorman at big hotel, they made out that these jobs were really something. And their women, they thought those jobs were something and they were wanting to do those jobs themselves. Who wanted to stay home, wash their own dishes, have babies, when there was all that real status, prestige or what-have-you available in the world outside?

'Only I knew, at least I began to know, I'd had all those jobs — lawyer, bank clerk, skycap, insurance salesman — I'd even been an academic, I'd taught people what it was like, and I knew that none of that meant anything. Whose respect did I want? I didn't want respect, it was a medieval love that I wanted, locked away in a castle, a hold somewhere, attempting to make it with somebody, away from all that claptrap.

'In the morning, though, I'd wake in my bed and find that that was not the case for them, I had not made it even with my singled-out person and that I was being bawled at to get up, make it to work, help with the house and get the kids to school. So finally they said I was lazy, wouldn't get up in the morning. So then I'd leave them, live alone, get up early, take long solitary silent walks. Consider suicide, think that was an easy way out but, as it rode over, not able any longer to sustain any very positive stance but hope that people were around, would realize my case and come and bail me out.

'And all that time you were in your so-called school, your nunnery, convent, what d'you you call it, getting your first-class education, learning the stations of the cross.'

V. spoke:

'It seemed to be mainly a book about a man who lived a long time ago a long way away in quite another country, not somewhere where someone like you might come from. The problems were all different. There was nothing to do. I mean there was nothing he said to do which really told you, like what a girl could do. And then there was magic — their kind of God — which helped you out. He got killed, some hours of pain. I was seven when my mother died. That was ten years ago at least. The book doesn't seem to have anything to do with the ways of the men of the West. I don't see how it could help them.'

'V.'

'Yes?'

'What are you talking about?'

'The Bible, of course — one of the only two books I ever really studied. I haven't read lots like you.'

'They don't help. Which was the other?'

'*Histoire d'O*. O. accepts, you'll recall, everything — not just the remorseless raping, but the beating, the branding and finally even the rings that are inserted in the lips of her vulva. She wants the love, admires the love that is given without pity. I don't want pity either — nor would I want to come to O.'s state, begging death as the final act of love. But O. teaches one, tells one to offer oneself like that and hope something will come of it. That I suppose is where it was like the Bible — an acceptance of death, except the crucifixion seemed so unnecessary.'

He showed her another poem (Brock 1970).

> Stand
> alone
> on a hill
>
> remember
> almost anyone
>
> cry
> and cry
> and cry
>
> as though
> hearing
> Oscar Petersen
> on almost
> any night

decide
the crucifixion
was an unnecessary
vulgarity

8   *The Syndrome Called Despair*

Desperation

The *Hopeful* had a continual problem with patients who recovered (some did). Where should they be landed? But the patients often surprised them by their willingness to go ashore. It was as if they wanted to leave the hospital. They certainly agreed to be landed in some very odd places. A group of middle-aged Americans had asked to be put ashore at Athens on that very quay where the crew of the *Hopeful* witnessed the crucifixion of most of the male inhabitants. 'We'll get to the King George,' they said, 'the ambassador will soon sort all this out for us.' They had been seen pushing their way through the Greek crowd, somehow avoiding any contact with them. They stared fixedly ahead and managed to avert their eyes from the crosses which surrounded them. They shrilled away: 'Once we are clear of this crowd we'll grab a taxi.' 'I wonder where the American Express is, I want to cash a few more travellers' cheques.'

The bunch from the caique — the Desperadoes, the crew called them — presented a particularly difficult problem. Within twenty-four hours most of them had fully recovered from their exposure and were to be found pushing their way around the ship, talking loudly and looking at the crew's smart blue uniforms with none too friendly eyes. The Captain hastily called them together and told them he was unable to land them in Israel but offered to put them ashore further along the North African coast, or he offered to allow them to stay on board until the hospital ship was out of the dangerous

Mediterranean basin. The Captain tried to be friendly, addressed the group as 'you kids' and offered to find jobs on board the ship for anyone who wanted one. This approach was somehow wrong. The man they called Harry got to his feet, started waving his arms about and talking very fast. His remarks excluded the Captain, other ship's officers and Dr Van Thofen from the conversation but sometimes he deigned to wave a hand in their direction.

'We've got a serious problem here. I reckon we've got to sit right down and think this thing right through. What we've got to do is to see where we are now and exactly where we are going — without any interference from any ... any ... What we've got to ask ourselves is: "Who are these guys anyway?" They look suspiciously like pigs to me or the very next best thing to pigs I've ever seen. What exactly is their thinking? We have to be very certain about that. What are they trying to do to us, I ask myself?'

'Harry, what about these guys sitting right here?'

'Good thinking, Sadie, good thinking. Hey, Cap'n, the group would like to throw this thing around a little. Would you have any objection if we holed up in this lounge for a little while?'

The Captain looked at them in a bewildered fashion and nodded.

'Perhaps you'll let me know what you decide.'

The members of the ship's company slid quietly out of the lounge and stood around uneasily outside for a while. No one said much and soon they departed to their respective jobs, shaking their heads as they went.

The meeting in the lounge went on for hours. Euan, who had had a vague account of what was going on from Van Thofen, passed by at about eight o'clock and heard the steady buzz of voices. Five hours, he thought to himself, worse than Grand Rounds at Johns Hopkins! Their only contact with the outside world had been regular trips to the coffee machine. They're solving someone's problems, thought Euan, listening to some shouting which included the words 'Marx' and 'Lenin'. At eleven-thirty when he and Sheila took a last stroll before going to bed they were still at it.

'They've all got to have a say,' said Sheila, 'it's good for them to have a bull session.'

In the morning the lounge, Euan noticed on his way to breakfast, was empty. He had just settled down to his scrambled eggs when he was interrupted by Sir Maximov.

'Trouble in the operating suite,' said Sir Max. 'I think we'd better go down.'

'Trouble?'

'Yes,' said Sir Max, 'they've got some sort of sit-in going on down there. They obviously need a psychiatrist.'

The anteroom to the operating suite was a milling throng. The Desperadoes were marching round shouting: 'Patient participation in Operations.' They carried banners which read: 'I Want to Chop Too', 'Health Rights for Patients', 'Democratic Prescriptions', 'We Want to Pill Push'. A worried Van Thofen was trying to argue with four or five of them at once. He was explaining the elaborate arrangements that had been made for patient representation whenever a policy decision was taken.

'You never asked us when you turned away from Palestine.'

Euan heard this remark and was able to shout back:

'You were unconscious in your bloody boat when we took that decision.'

'Doctors are all the same — hierarchical bastards — where were the porters, I'd like to know!'

Euan saw Reg, one of the theatre orderlies, and dragged him over to the girl who'd been shouting at him.

'What do you feel, Reg?' he asked.

'Fucking disgrace,' said Reg, 'look at the mess they're making of my fucking floors.' But that particular girl from the caique had turned away and didn't seem to hear the remark.

Meanwhile Blackgall, one of their senior surgeons, was getting angry and shouted:

'Get these people out of here. Go away, I've a very full list.'

On this remark the whole group of about forty promptly sat down. The one Blackgall had been pushing did this so suddenly that the surgeon himself fell over, cracking his head on a door that opened at that moment. He appeared dazed and, to Euan's relief, stopped shouting at the intruders. Sir Maximov meanwhile had battled his way through to Van Thofen's side.

'Keep 'em talking,' he muttered to Van Thofen, 'I'll fix it in a moment.'

'Here, let's sit down too,' he shouted and forced his way over to a stack of folding chairs (the anteroom was sometimes used for lectures). He dragged the chairs back through the sitters to the doctors, who were now grouped in the middle of the room. Puzzled by this move no one tried to stop him.

Shortly, then, this was the scene. Seven or eight doctors and nurses were sitting in a tight bunch on chairs in the middle of the room. Van Thofen, standing, was arguing with the people from the caique on behalf of the ship's company. Harry, their unelected representative, sitting on the ground among his 'people', was shouting back.

'Can't we go to a lounge and argue it out,' Van Thofen asked, 'then operations could start.'

'No, no, no. Pigs, pigs, pigs,' they shouted back. 'Patient Participation First.'

'We're not moving until all our demands are met,' shouted Harry.

'What are they?'

There was some confusion over this but as far as Euan could make out there were three main objectives: (1) No procedures on any patient until all other patients on his ward had approved. (2) All operations to be attended by a minimum of six other patients. (3) No medicines to be prescribed except by patients themselves.

'Come, come,' Van Thofen interrupted, 'they might be unconscious.'

The talk and shouting went on for about another five minutes and then abruptly Sir Maximov took off his cap, stood up and waved his arms and shouted very loudly:

'I want a CRAP.'

There was silence.

'No time to have one before this blew up and my bowels always work in the morning. I shall have a massive movement here if you don't let me go.'

'O.K., O.K.,' said Harry, 'see he comes back, Phil, without raising the rest of the pigs.' Phil, looking rather worried, followed Maximov out of the room.

Harry watched them go, took a deep breath and launched into a long statement about his theoretical position. Essential, he explained, if the ill-educated medical men were to understand what the arguments were about. Van Thofen's periodic pleas that surgery should be allowed to start went unheeded.

Suddenly the big double doors which let the trolleys in swung open and revealed a horde of 'walking' patients from the nearby surgical ward. Some were on crutches and there were one or two gallant souls in wheelchairs.

'We want operations. The silent majority demand medicines.' These two phrases they seemed to have been taught but after they had shouted them they looked puzzled as to what to do next. 'Why, it's a lot of student drop-outs.'

The sitters began to shout back at them and the patients shouted back:

'Disgraceful! Go away from here.'

At first the two groups simply confronted each other but more patients were arriving from other wards and, as the pressure built up, some of the patients pushed on into the room and began pulling the sitters to their feet and trying to push them towards a door. The sitting group from the caique resisted and began to chant 'Patient Participation' over and over again. The chairs the medical group were sitting on fell over. They got to their feet and stood, totally confused. What should their role now be?

Straight across from the swing doors which led into the suite was a similar pair which led into the operating theatre. When the tumult was at its height these were pulled back to reveal Sir Maximov standing in the entry.

'Heigh, heigh, heigh!' he shouted through a megaphone which he was carrying. 'Death! Death! Death!'

He had discarded his own familiar cap and was wearing the judge's sinister black cap; over his shoulder he had an immense sickle.

'Death! Death! Death!' he shouted again, and pushed on into the room. Patients, staff and the Desperadoes themselves gave way before him. Behind him was a group of children whom Euan recognized. They were a bunch of seven- or eight-year-old psychotics who skipped and twirled, shrilled out odd noises and screams as they played in their own mad world. These children Maximov ushered into the room and their shrilling could be heard in the silence that fell.

'Death! Death! Death!' Maximov shouted again and un-swung the sickle from his shoulder as if to wield it at waist height. There were screams in the room then and patients, Desperadoes, everyone bolted out through the nearest door available. Sir Maximov danced round and hurried them off.

'Grab Harry, Euan,' he ordered. Euan grabbed him. He was still standing near the centre of the room facing Van Thofen and watching bemusedly as his troops fled in all directions.

Sir Maximov grounded the sickle and pulled Van Thofen into a corner.

'Fast, Toffee. Grab each of these kids singly or in pairs and ask them what they want to do while they're aboard. Get weaving with one or two of the ship's people before they get into a group again.'

'Now then, you come along with me.' Maximov spoke kindly to Harry. 'You look a bit shaken. Euan, see those kids get back to their ward, I don't think they've come to any harm. Blackie, you can start chopping, you lucky old butcher.'

He pushed the bewildered surgeon towards the scrub room and led the unresisting Harry away, saying:

'This has all been a bit of a shock to you, old boy. Come along with me and I'll give you something to settle you down a little.'

Euan had no difficulty getting the children back to their ward. A therapist was with them.

'He just said to bring them along urgently. And he looked so mad I didn't dare refuse.'

'Where did he get all that stuff from — that black cap, I mean, and the sickle?'

'I asked him that as we were coming here and he just said, "Always carry one in my hand luggage." '

'He doesn't,' said Euan, 'I helped him to carry his bags down.'

'I expect they've got most things in the ship's stores,' said the girl. 'But that peculiar black cap?'

'Judge's black cap. They wore them to pronounce the death penalty,' said Euan, who'd seen enough television to recognize that. 'Surely ship's stores don't carry black caps.'

He hurried down to see what Sir Maximov was making of Harry. Harry was sitting in front of him drinking something. Euan looked questioningly at the glass.

'Harry has been feeling very tense, he tells me. So I suggested he should have something to make him relax. We've been having an interesting talk.'

'What is the drink?'

'100 mg of chlorpromazine as a starter. Now I've just suggested he should help one of the real working-class people we've got on the boat for a day or two so that he gets a feel of their problems, then he'll know best how to interact. Now,' Maximov went on, 'I want you to take one of these tablets twice a day for a week or so to settle your nerves. Ah, there you are, Ben,' he smiled at the neat little mortuary attendant as the latter came briskly into the room, 'I am so grateful to you for coming up.'

'A pleasure to be of assistance, Sir Maximov.'

'Good, now this is Harry who wants to help you out for a few days. Harry ... Ben. Ben will introduce you to our problems aboard this ship at rock bottom.'

'Yes, right down in the bowels we are. Come along then, young man, you'll find we're rather busy at the moment.'

'Jesus, Maxy,' said Euan when the two had left the room. 'Won't that shake him up a bit? Ben's got three thousand bodies down there in cold storage.'

'Well, the chlorpromazine will blunt his reactions for the first few days and then, when I ease him up, he'll be an old friend of Ben's and an expert on embalming, I expect. Dialecticism, that's what he's got. It's another group pathology, can be just as dangerous as the Crucifixion Disease. That mob this morning would have used bombs if they'd had any. Its origins aren't in childhood — no frozen upbringing for them — no, they have nice homes. It's something to do with education and too early an exposure to the world's ills. It's teaching them political philosophy and general theories with nothing to apply them to that does it. Now, I'd not allow people to be taught that sort of thing at all. I'd make them do anatomy. Nothing like dissecting someone's balls to make one protective of one's own and other people's. Of course I might except Aristotle — they could use a dose of him all right.'

'Did he know about the Dialectical Disease?'

'Indeed he did. Let me see — *Nichomachean Ethics*,* I think, but no, no I wasn't thinking of that. You'll recall what he reported of the camel's penis?'

'Don't they copulate back to back?'

'So it is said, though I have never witnessed the event. But I was thinking of their penises. Aristotle reports that the Egyp-

---

*'Hence a young man is not a proper hearer of lectures on political science; for he is inexperienced in the actions that occur in life but its discussions start from these and are about these; and further, since he tends to follow his passions, his study will be vain and unprofitable because the end aimed at is not knowledge but action.'

tians put them to good use. They made their bow-strings from the penises of dead camels.'

The 'womb' is a part peculiar to the female; and the 'penis' is peculiar to the male. This latter organ is external and situated at the extremity of the trunk; it is composed of two separate parts: of which the extreme part is fleshy, does not alter in size, and is called the glans; and round about it is a skin devoid of any specific title, which integument if it be cut asunder never grows together again, any more than does the jaw or the eyelid. And the connexion between the latter and the glans is called the frenum. The remaining part of the penis is composed of gristle; it is easily susceptible of enlargement; and it protrudes and recedes in the reverse directions to what is observable in the identical organ in cats. Underneath the penis are two 'testicles', and the integument of these is a skin that is termed the 'scrotum'.

Testicles are not identical with flesh, and are not altogether diverse from it. But by and by we shall treat in an exhaustive way regarding all such parts.

Of male animals the genitals of some are external, as is the case with man, the horse, and most other creatures; some are internal, as with the dolphin. With those that have the organ externally placed, the organ in some cases is situated in front, as in the cases already mentioned, and of these some have the organ detached, both penis and testicles, as man; others have penis and testicles closely attached to the belly, some more closely, some less; for this organ is not detached in the wild boar nor in the horse.

The penis of the elephant resembles that of the horse; compared with the size of the animal it is disproportionately small; the testicles are not visible, but are concealed inside in the vicinity of the kidneys; and for this reason the male speedily gives over in the act of intercourse. The genitals of the female are situated where the udder is in sheep; when she is in heat, she draws the organ back and exposes it externally, to facilitate

the act of intercourse for the male; and the organ opens out
to a considerable extent.

With most animals the genitals have the position above
assigned; but some animals discharge their urine backwards,
as the lynx, the lion, the camel and the hare. Male animals
differ from one another, as has been said, in this particular,
but all female animals are retromingent: even the female
elephant like other animals, though she has the privy part
below the thighs.

In the male organ itself there is a great diversity. For in some
cases the organ is composed of flesh and gristle, as in man; in
such cases, the fleshy part does not become inflated, but the
gristly part is subject to enlargement. In other cases, the organ
is composed of fibrous tissue, as with the camel and the deer;
in other cases it is bony, as with the fox, the wolf, the marten,
and the weasel; for this organ in the weasel has a bone.

The males of oviparous animals, whether biped or quadruped, are in all cases furnished with testicles close to the loin
underneath the midriff. With some animals the organ is whitish,
in others somewhat of a sallow hue; in all cases it is entirely
enveloped with minute and delicate veins. From each of the two
testicles extends a duct, and, as in the case of fishes, the two
ducts coalesce into one above the outlet of the residuum. This
constitutes the penis, which organ in the case of small ovipara
is inconspicuous; but in the case of the larger ovipara, as in
the goose and the like, the organ becomes quite visible just
after copulation.

The ducts in the case of fishes and in biped and quadruped
ovipara are attached to the loin under the stomach and the gut,
in betwixt them and the great vein, from which ducts or blood-
vessels extend, one to each of the two testicles. And just as with
fishes the male sperm is found in the seminal ducts, and the
ducts become plainly visible at the rutting season and in some
instances become invisible after the season is passed, so also is
it with the testicles of birds; before the breeding season the
organ is small in some birds and quite invisible in others, but

during the season the organ in all cases is greatly enlarged. This phenomenon is remarkably illustrated in the ring-dove and the partridge, so much so that some people are actually of opinion that these birds are devoid of the organ in the winter-time.

Molluscs, such as the octopus, the sepia, and the calamary, have sexual intercourse all in the same way; that is to say, they unite at the mouth, by an interlacing of their tentacles. When, then, the octopus rests its so-called head against the ground and spreads abroad its tentacles, the other sex fits into the out-spreading of these tentacles, and the two sexes then bring their suckers into mutual connexion.

Some assert that the male has a kind of penis in one of his tentacles, the one in which are the (two) largest suckers; and they further assert that the organ is tendinous in character, growing attached right up to the middle of the tentacle, and the latter enables it to enter the nostril or funnel of the female.

Now cuttle-fish and calamaries swim about closely inter-twined, with mouths and tentacles facing one another and fitting closely together, and swim thus in opposite directions; and they fit their so-called nostrils into one another, and the one sex swims backwards and the other frontwards during the operation. And the female lays its spawn by the so-called 'blow-hole'; and, by the way, some declare that it is at this organ that the coition really takes place.

OF COURSE, MIND YOU, LIFE IS A FAIR OLD BIT OF HELL ROUND THERE, BUT STILL ...

Among the flotsam floating on the Athens quayside had been some strange passengers. The *Hopeful*'s crew had tried to leave the locals behind to be looked after by their own friends and relations, whereas the foreigners, who appeared to have arrived there in some unaccountable way, they had taken aboard. Sheila, Euan found when he dropped into her clinic, was interviewing one of these. She was an English-speaking lady and she had been found bleeding from a blow on the head but still tugging two children behind her. Her own head wound had proved quite trivial and she was now consulting Sheila ostensibly about her children's sleeping problems. Sheila and her nurse were patiently trying to sort out who she was and what she had been doing in Athens.

'They're always crying at night,' Mrs Dunne was saying, always crying.'

'Do they cry when you put them to bed, or wake up and cry?'

'All night, Doctor, all night they're crying.'

'What time do you put them to bed then?'

'I try about half-past six, but they cry. They're often still awake at two in the morning.'

'And what time do you get up?'

'Well, Mr Dunne gets me a cup of tea usually around eight-thirty and I gets up round nine o'clock.'

'Are the children still in bed then?'

'They should be but they gets up.'

'It's a long time for children of two and four to be in bed, six-thirty till nine. They don't need that much sleep. What do they do when they get up?'

'They does awful things, Doctor. They spreads the jam all over the walls.'

The nurse suddenly interrupted this conversation. She had already found out Mrs Dunne's first name.

'Joycie,' she said, 'can you tell the time?' A silence.

'Not too well, I can't,' said Mrs Dunne.

Sheila looked at Euan, who was trying not to laugh, and said, 'Do you want to take over?' Euan shook his head.

Mrs Dunne started again.

'I'm worried about what they done to the two older kids. They took them away.' They? Did she mean the grey men, had her two older children been crucified?

'Who took them away?'

'The Welfare.'

'Oh, why was that?'

'Because of what Mr Dunne did.'

'What did he do?'

'Got sent to prison, you know ... Mr Dunne ... you know ... he likes having babies, he does.'

'What do you do about that?'

'I cools him off with a bucket of water.'

'What does Mr Dunne do then?'

'He went and saw Mrs Duffin. He was away, took some cigarettes, you know, he did. Mrs Duffin ... leastways *said* she'd been raped. Had three kids. You know her, she's a big strong girl. Mr Dunne, you know, he's not very strong ... '

'What happened?'

'They said he had so they gave him eighteen months.'

'I see. What about the other children?'

'Well, you see, just before Mr Dunne come out they was round about the kids, said they was going to take them away.'

'Yes.'

'They took me to court. And of course ... '

Again the nurse helped: 'Did they talk about moral danger?'

'They said Mr Dunne might do it to Rosey. But he'd never touch Rosey. He wouldn't do that. They took them away. Rosey and Jean.'

'How old?'

'Well, eleven and nine they was. They didn't want to go. Home somewhere they're in. I can't get down to see them.'

'Well,' said Sheila, 'we'd better see what we can do about these two younger ones ... '

There were two women next and a ginger-haired man. Assorted children came in with them.

'Won't you sit down,' said Sheila.

'I'd rather stand, Doctor, sir.'

The women and the man were white but two of the children who were running round the clinic were half-caste.

'Are these your children too?' asked Sheila, addressing them all vaguely.

'They're my sister's children,' said the man. The women still said nothing. Sheila smiled tentatively and said:

'These are your sister's, are they?' The man moved about uneasily and then said 'Yes' with a downcast look.

'Well, what about the baby then?' The baby was the patient Sheila was seeing, Euan realized.

'It's my baby,' said the man proudly. He took the child from the arms of one of the women who'd been nursing it and held the child up and spoke to it.

'Lovely!' he said. 'Lovely. She's coming on ever so well, Doctor.'

'How old is she?' asked Sheila.

'Two,' said the man.

Sheila took the child and laid her on the examining table. The head was totally uncontrolled and flopped back from the body. The eyes didn't focus but jerked to and fro in rhythmic nystagmoid movements. The lower limbs were stiff, in-turned and stretched out with the toes pointing down.

'Spastic Diplegia,' said Euan.

'That and a bit else,' Sheila flashed at him.

'Genetic,' said Euan, 'I bet.'

'Who is the mother?' asked Sheila, turning to the man again.

'It's my baby,' said the woman who'd been holding the child. 'It's my baby,' she shouted again.

'You're his sister?'

'Yes.'

Euan began to undress the child while Sheila, deciding to skip any more family history, enquired about the child's development since she had been born. It didn't sound too good to Euan.

'Fits?'

'Yes, she had fits sometimes. Been in the hospital with them too.' The mother was the informant about that but the brother broke in again.

'She can smile at you, Doctor. It's amazing the things she can do. I mean — I works with her. We get her to do things. Maria, Maria, smile, smile at the doctor.'

Euan had moved away from the baby which Sheila was now examining. He stood behind the women who had stayed sitting in their chairs firmly while the man was with the baby. Their hair was cut in a masculine way. It was straight and looked as if it were frequently oiled with something like Brylcreem. It was combed out so that the individual hairs were grouped in thick greasy strands through which one could see the pink/grey skin of the scalp. Euan wondered what had drawn his attention to the hair and suddenly, as he watched, he realized small objects were moving along the strands; the heads of both the ladies were alive.

Sheila had completed her examination of the child. Slowly the mother rose and came over and with clumsy motions began to put the clothes on again. All her movements seemed wooden and mechanical as if she were some sort of robot that had been programmed to dress and undress babies. As she did it she barely glanced at the child and carried out the actions as if the child were a doll.

'She's all right, isn't she, Doctor?' said the man. 'She's all right really. I mean, there's nothing really wrong?'

'Well,' said Sheila, 'she's behind. She's slow. She's really very retarded.'

'It was the priests,' burst out the mother. 'It was the priests! They made us have her.'

There are two million followers of a 25-year-old religion which claims to put together the best in the three great Eastern religions, Buddhism, Taoism and Confucianism. Probably it owes more to its graftings from Rome and from Spiritualism. It has a Pope and a College of Cardinals and — rather heavily veiled — a wonderful writing machine, the *corbeille à bec* (in fact, a planchette) which, under suitable conditions, transmits messages from great spirits of the past. Victor Hugo is a particularly communicative spirit — and now also a saint of the church.

Their Holy City is one of those things which just have to be seen to be believed. Multi-coloured dragons with darting scarlet tongues climb up and down innumerable pillars through a vast polished marble hall. Lotuses blossom in the stone grilles of the windows, and from the centre of each looks out somewhat superciliously an enormous human eye.

At one end of the hall stands the throne of the Pope entwined by seven serpents; four with downcast heads, representing the evil passions; three rearing triumphant, representing the good passions. At the far end of the hall, beyond the double rows of thrones for the Cardinals, dim and partly veiled, rises the High Altar, an immense blue globe from the centre of which, in the correct position for the Pole Star, glares out again that cold and fishy human eye: the Universal Conscience in the Universal Cosmos.

There are four masses a day — one at 6 a.m. for the peasants, one at noon for the school-children, one at 6 p.m. for the soldiers and one at midnight for the church dignitaries who number several thousands. In their long shining gowns and their conical hats, the dignitaries looked the nearest thing to wizards I ever expect to meet.

I interviewed the General before dinner and the Pope before lunch. General N.Y.T. was a tough little brown jumping bean of a man. He had no French and, sitting at his desk before the tricolour and his own personal two-star General's flag, he answered our questions in Vietnamese which he spoke with great verve and much clicking of teeth.

'Like our religion,' he said, 'the Army has incorporated the best features from all other armies. I have now fifty thousand soldiers; eight thousand first-class soldiers with rifles whom I can use in operations, twelve thousand auxiliaries trained and armed but whose command I must share, and the remaining thirty thousand who are fully trained but have no rifles.'

A silent servant in a black mandarin cap seated us in an

anteroom and in a few moments the Pope entered, and greeted us. He was wearing a long silk white gown with sleeves down to his wrists and a neat high neck, like a Victorian nightgown, and it was very soon evident that he was a man of formidable charm, a very 'bright spirit' indeed, who possessed to the full that volatility of temperament and liveliness of mind which is perhaps the most endearing Vietnamese characteristic.

'Peace,' said the Pope, 'will not come from arms. Peace is something here,' — and he raised two fingers delicately to the centre of his forehead — 'peace is a thing of the *esprit*. When all men are men of goodwill, then peace will come. C.D. recognized no races, no nations, no colours — only the great human family. We are ready for union with all other churches, particularly, I hope, the Anglican Church of England ... ' But of the other Pope, the Pope in Rome, I gathered he entertained little hope ...

The silent servant discreetly filled the porcelain teacups in their silver filigree saucers and the Pope went on:

'Man,' he said, laying a gentle hand upon my arm, 'lives on two planes – the spiritual and the physical. When the two planes come out of balance' – he gestured delicately – 'there is much trouble in the world and there is need of a prophet to restore the equilibrium. Christ was one such prophet. C.D. is another ... '

The Pope put down the porcelain teacup upon its silver saucer. He was, I knew, a married Pope, with two daughters, a former clerk in the Government Customs Service. For though C.D. prescribed celibacy for its hierarchy, it was a reasonable religion, recognizing that if you had acquired a wife before becoming a Cardinal, for instance, there was nothing much that could be done about it. Vegetarianism is prescribed six days a month for ordinary members, ten days a month for soldiers, and continuously for the priesthood.

I asked the Pope about the messages. Was he himself a medium?

'No,' he said, 'I am not a medium, but I have the faculty for discovering mediums. Sometimes they are illiterate people. But in a trance, they can write. They can even write English!' The Pope tapped my knee enthusiastically, and started back in his chair, his eyes popping with astonishment at the thought of it ...

'Ah c'est merveilleux! C'est merveilleux.'

And had they had any good messages lately? I enquired. The Pope thought a moment. Well, he said, there was one from Joan of Arc. Why, yes! and another from William Shakespeare. What had Shakespeare to say? Oh, it was on the subject of the late war.

The Pope offered me the plate of biscuits.

Love and its Disorders

'I shall start,' he pealed out in a voice like a tenor bell, 'with myself. I am a very distinguished man but I have to ask what the fuck,' glaring round, 'am I doing here. Biological scientists, gentlemen, that is what we are, not humanitarians, not do-gooders, or do-Goders, nor are we poets, painters, film-makers, cabinet-makers, cloche-makers, no sort of artists at all. Don't be led astray by the statement that doctors should be artists. Biological scientists, my boyos, science of the study of living things. As doctors we are peculiarly attached to human beings — heretofore sick ones. A mistake: well ones are much more interesting. They are our concern. How to make well people. I shall come back to well people because well people make love. Well people start being made from that act, conception — a good-looking sperm and a nice round egg.'

No, thought Sir Maximov, who was pacing up and down his cabin trying out various starts, that's wrong, something cooler, more straight, I think, i.e. what it's actually about:

'For any species, ladies and gentlemen, the most essential task is the effective reproduction of one's own ... '

For years now he had been planning to give this clinical lecture on 'Love and its Disorders'. His appointment to the *Hopeful* as clinical lecturer was forcing him to fulfil his promise but he found himself faced as ever with scraps of paper and no real plan at all of how to tackle the whole topic.

The reproductive processes lead one direct to the biology of love-making. Clearly I should review the whole subject of love in the animal kingdom. Or should I take out three animals, say, the octopus, the snail and the tortoise. The octopus because he has an arm which turns into a penis and he copulates for several hours. The snail because he shoots a dart into his lover which inflames, and the tortoise because he bangs against his lover and because of the face of the tortoise who's just had an orgasm. Bother, selecting only three leaves out that variety of lung-fish which lives on the bottom of a river in a hole and grabs members of its own species. If they are the same sex he eats them, if they are of the opposite sex he makes love to them. Is the act of 'grabbing' an act of love?

Well, so much for the animal kingdom. Now what about all the social scientists/psychiatrists and human love?

The importance of touching, doing, feeling, having contact with people. The danger of talk. The false attempts of Freud, Marx, Maynard Keynes, Marshall McLuhan, to reduce emotion to talking about. (Ought I to have read their books or can I get someone else to do it? I have read two volumes on the psychology of women — Deutsch — Hurst told me to.)

But back to Uncle Sig. F. et al. Find out whether any of them ever emptied a bed-pan. Which of them held the hands of a dying woman. Did they always insist their wives changed the babies' nappies? Why did they send their sons away to be educated? Did they dislike their 15-year-old daughter's boy-friend? When did they last wash their women's bodies?

Moving to literary sources actually about love (Ortega y Gasset and all that) and then real accounts of love.

A TIME OF HOPE

Nadezhda Mandelstam wrote a biography (1972). In Russian she gave it no title but in English she suggested it should be called *Hope Against Hope*. Nadezhda means 'Hope' in Russian. Nadezhda was married to a great poet. They loved deeply. He was taken to a prison camp. He never returned. The exact date of his death is uncertain. Hand-copied by Nadezhda, poems survive. Others she learnt by heart. Was their survival what allowed her to use that title?

We know each other. We love each other deeply. I hope that in old age we might do some loving and spend some time together. Will all our passion be spent? Existing personal commitments appear to intervene in our love. However, these are not the real dangers, they are outside our persons. There may be a collapse (Yeats 1921) Jack surprised me the other day: 'It's good having you here, you're always optimistic.' I will end this book going up. In the context/content that is logical. I am Hopeful.

MORE NOTES FOR SIR MAXIMOV'S LECTURE

So far I have been drawing your attention to the importance of adult love because of the very serious effects breakdown of that relationship may have on the growth and development of the human child. As I have indicated, breakdowns in this relationship lead to adults stunted emotionally and intellectually. Elsewhere I've recorded my feeling that urban society itself may lead to an increase in such breakdowns (Bax & Whitmore 1974). These however leave us with maimed individuals and societies of all sorts have accepted the principle that there shall be maimed individuals. I want, however, to draw your attention to something else about adult lovers. Lovers are usually nicer people in all senses of the word than non-lovers. It is true they may be self-absorbed but if one can distract them, their interests are simple, their aims idealistic. They are not usually interested in luxury, or even in owning a lot of worldly possessions. Bread, cheese, a bed and a bottle of cheap wine and they are in luxury. They work hard and cheerfully and prefer tasks which they can sustain, in front of each other, as useful. They are the least neurotic of people. Provided they are together they can live anywhere. Conventions bore them.

At some point during this lecture, during this saga, your mind will wander off. Not, of course, that you won't concentrate because you always do that, but you will begin to wonder and say, 'Well, where is the explanation which you promised me in the first-floor restaurant?'

'It's about an open love,' I said, and floundered to explain. You leant against me.

'I don't quite understand.'

'It's all in the book,' I said.

'Is it? When you come to the end will you be able to offer me a more open love? Will you be able to stand in the corner beyond the big brass bed and say, not in a whisper but aloud, "I love you". And will you, notwithstanding all the other loads/loves, hold to that?'

'The hardware is all right, nothing wrong with nuclear physics; in fact better for finding out about the gods than any form of religion. Religions, even lacking an effective technology, were dangerous enough. Hardware technology works; its very effectiveness makes it dangerous. It matters who uses it. Look at medicine. O.K., a technology beginning to work some time around 1900. Working O.K. and knowing a lot about how to do some things. But look at your doctors – bastards all of them, narrow-minded bigoted bastards. Showing them how something works doesn't make people nice Something else does that. That's what I'm trying to lecture about.'

Maximov paused again, took another cramped turn up his cabin. There was the point that the hardware might intrude right into the software. Get right inside the love. Paolozzi (1967) and Ballard (1973) had both been working on those lines. It was another whole area he could explore. Then he would have to look at the biological intrusions, there was all that stuff about A.I. Should he get into that? The lecture would last for ever. There was the danger of its being about nothing, like the man who came and talked of his research into love.

Suddenly it's Spring

We want you to know that in Federal Funding, we care ... It — the idea — translates ... These goals — the hope and promise goals ... I have been finding out these past two weeks ... programme planning ... media information ... innovative concepts ... process thrives. Evaluation, that's what we are talking about. Hopefully we offer you options ... permit the use of action systems early. We must learn to give them the opportunity to show us. Decisions can be made.

Additionally evaluate its effectiveness. Evaluation Design. Difficulties of evaluating this kind of intricate processing. Individualized constructional objectives. We are getting involved in a long-term milieu ... closely related dilemma of instrumentation ... options differed ... input from T.A.D.S. To date the overall evaluation plan consists of five thrusts ... ah ... ah ... ah ... ah ... ah. Other project ... hopefully the analysis of all data collected.

Some time next spring ... attempts will be made ... their pressure to bear ... to gather together what you have seen ... hopefully provide ... and reach a peak at the end.

9 *The Sexual Childbirth*

Slipping at the last moment into the lecture room, Euan was glad to find Max had attracted a big audience. His fame would account in part for this and his title 'Love and its Disorders' would have special appeal to the staff of the *Hopeful*. Euan recalled the ship's application form:

GENERAL APPLICATION FORM: HOSPITAL SHIP 'HOPEFUL'

(Note: this form to be filled in by all grades of staff before specialized application forms are issued.)

1. Are you in love?   (a) Yes
                       (b) No

If (a), apply jointly on form X2/OF/US.

2. If (b), do you want to be in love?   (a) No
                                         (b) Yes

If (b), state whether you wish to love
                          (a) Same sexed humans
                          (b) Opposite sexed humans
                          (c) Beasts*

*Opportunities for bestiality aboard the *Hopeful* are limited. Applicants who have no inclination for aquatic species are advised to withdraw.

3.   How long will you love for?   (a) Ever
                                     (b) 50 years +
                                     (c) 35 years +
                                     (d) 18 years +
                                     (e) 13–18 years
                                     (f) 5–13 years
                                     (g) 1–5 years
                                     (h) Into the new year

4. How many people can you love? State a number
between nought and infinity.

When I came in you were sitting on the sofa reading, you
glanced up at me negligently and gave me a chaste kiss and then
turned your head down to your book again. We were expecting
a late caller. I didn't know whether to try to do some work or
not. You said, 'Yes, M.'s late,' and went on reading. So in the
end I got out the papers and settled down in a chair.

   Your thighs are very long and you had bought some new
stocking tights with just the suggestion of a pinkish tinge to
them. After a bit I came over again and touched then kissed
you again. I suggested I should take the tights off. 'No,' you
said, 'I'm reading.' I ran my hand up to your crotch. 'Wouldn't
you like me to suck you there?' I said. 'No,' you said, 'I'm
reading.' 'Could I do it later?' 'Maybe.'

   Then M. was there, a lot of talk and walking upstairs and
down to look at bedrooms. You'd gone to bed to avoid all that
but when I eventually came up you were still awake, lying on
your side curled up and facing away as you always do from
my half of the bed. I didn't know whether to ask or act so I
said something, I think, and you made that maybe sort of reply
so I lay down beside you pulling the sheets down past your
thighs and began to kiss slowly from your arse forward. I
placed my tongue firmly against you just in front of your hole
and sucked hard. Finally I knew I was there, you moved a
little and shut the book. Then you suddenly rolled over

pulling your body away from me but placing a hand at the same time on my thigh. 'Do you want me to suck you?' you asked. I nodded. 'Let's do it together,' I said. 'No,' you replied, 'I want to concentrate on you,' and you took my cock in your mouth; later you bit the shaft of my cock and buried my balls in your mouth.

These are all false beginnings, thought Sir Max. It must be precise — the nature of adult love — and its disorders:

Walking into the sea in her knickers to drown. Ann. Why the knickers?

She was a simple girl to start with, a secretary or something. Quite beautiful. Long black hair, gay, a good smile though teeth showing early signs of decay. Not good. A sign of not caring. But early on writing things down, achieving something, not a lot but trying to come out of a very simple life. Moving about Europe — America. When with a man almost domineering.

But then Robert after one year: 'I couldn't live with a girl with a glass jaw.' What did he mean? Glass — a very hard substance for a jaw, very tough to touch. Perhaps, but glass brittle, cracks easily. Fractures into myriad pieces.

So, Ann. Without saying any more about her, we all know girls called Ann. We know the age at which they — the girls — kill themselves. Any rate here is Ann late at night taking off her clothes, all of them except her knickers, and walking into the sea. Not quite alone, for a fisherman — one imagines a gnarled man mulling over nets — sees her walking into the sea. In the morning a pile of clothes (no knickers) and a week later a bloated shape on a deserted shore.

Vague rumours, stories in unreliable papers. Searching for a proper account. But walking out into the sea, perhaps just a late-night swim, trying to make it an accident but knowing Ann, knowing that it was not an accident. Cast up on a deserted shore in the same year as other people who died more naturally or more unnaturally. Herb. His son howled like a dog when he heard (Jack expected more restraint). G. eaten into by cancer. Another one (her name began with V.) who rang the bell at seven in the morning saying, 'I'm high' and wanting to come in and talk but me pushing her out and saying, 'Later.' And later her husband, whom we never met, on the phone to say, did I know she killed herself? 'No, I hadn't heard.'

Is that to do with human love? Why cover herself at all before that last moment? Keeping a scrap of civilization around her loins, not for any prudish decency but so that when she was cast up on that deserted shore people who found her could say, this was something recognizably human. And wonder what had happened to the human bonds which might have kept her afloat, swimming in towards the shore.

All this is about the nature of adult love. A quick irrational act like somebody suddenly unstable on a high building but not the slow walk into the sea and swimming out to the point of no return. Nothing pulling one back.

WHAT THE CAPTAIN THOUGHT

While they were all working, listening to the lectures, doing things to their patients or being patients lying in their beds, I could, as we passed through the gateway of the Mediterranean, the gateway to the New World, passed Gibraltar ... I could push the ship very hard, very fast and then open all cocks and sea valves and keep her going fast, block off the warning sirens and she would dive on towards the new world, depressing her bows down under the waves, and all the busy people aboard would barely notice the ship flooding. They would be working, busy, alive at one moment and then the water cutting them off and silence. No mark left at all. An unruffled sea. No sign of the millennia of civilizations when boats went out west from Europe (killing what they found there). Went west and thought they were going to achieve a new world, something beyond and better than anything they saw in Greece. Something more than a rock discerned from afar on a morning when two great lines of ships were moving slowly together to demonstrate to each other what they stood for and to make heroes for men to admire because their bloody deeds were discernibly human and seemed better than simply walking straight out into and under the sea.

This is a lecture, thought the Captain, about adult love. Why should I think of death and the sea?

Reaching and keeping that physical state where a mere glance calls to mind the ecstasy of orgasm. Where fucking can be continuous or where there can be long days simply of eye glances, simply of mood exchange. Feeling that telepathy has been achieved. That study by Beloff is wrong because what lover would want to communicate about shapes on cards? It is maintaining and communicating the ecstasy.

THE ONSET OF LABOUR

At a time the woman will say to her man, 'It's starting.' For her it will be a very precise moment when she is sure that now her labour is upon her. Her man might be doing anything. Taking a truck to New Mexico, hanging by a strap to clean the windows on a skyscraper, playing a crap game with friends in a bar, being an essential link in a conveyor belt on a factory line. Be what it may, the first duty of the attendants is to summon the man to his lover.

Sometimes the onset is signalled by a show. A show of blood and mucus. A plug which blocks the doorway to the uterus is expelled, the door is unbarred and labour can begin. No, not can begin but will begin; the start once signalled, no power on earth can prevent a continuation of the process. Unlike a theatrical event that indeed can be called off by an indisposition of one of the players, by damage to the building, by a failure in the electricity supply, there is nothing that can stop labour. It is a show that must go on.

The attendants will take the couple to airy rooms, clean

naturally, but luxurious in their appointments. Firm wide beds, deep drowsy chairs, ornate tables and soft deep carpets on the floor. On the walls pictures chosen for their vigour, softly lit with concealed lights; disguised cabinets will conceal wealthy wines and tasty fruits, stereophonic tapes in profusion to meet all tastes will be relayed on the most expensive equipment. The colours of the room should be in pastel shades, huge drapes should hang sweeping over the windows but they should be easily pulled aside to reveal long views across the city. On the balcony plants at their prime thrust their virile shoots against the panes and leaves of vine and ivy burst into the room.

The attendants of course must know their job, be intimate with the inner anatomy of the body, be able to handle the array of scientific instruments carefully concealed behind the panelled walls, be thoroughly knowing of all the stages of a labour, but their minds also should be alert not only to the mechanics of labour but to what comes after, the essential nature of life itself. They should of course be familiar with the habits of newborn babies, be skilled at summoning forth their first breaths, but more they should be adept at knowing what happens to babies, what possibilities there are for infants and should be able to expound on every possible future for the human child.

They should be lovers themselves. The girls with wombs conceived or ready and willing to conceive, aching to receive the seed of their lovers and absorb themselves in their own creative processes. The elders will have borne themselves, proven their fertility through successful conception. The men should be strong lovers whose seed is eagerly poured into the vaginas of loving women, whose eyes, encountering female eyes, look at them saying: You are a human female — all such I love and desire. I will not take you from your chosen man but remember my desire for you, remember my constant need to be a lover.

Their dress should be varied. Some may themselves choose

to be naked, to display the glories of their own flesh, there own limbs. Others will appear in full evening dress, Astaires in top hat, white tie and tails, or others may wear multicoloured jeans or dresses designed for dancing. Their clothes should be special for each occasion, freshly laundered and pressed, put on with care. They should wear what trappings they like — rings, amethyst pendants, diamond tiaras. The men if they shave should be freshly shaven, the women's flesh should be scented, the eyes of both should be bedewed with smouldering fires of passion.

Considerable forethought must be exercised in regard to the preparation for a confinement if the delivery is to be properly and safely conducted.

Labour is the process by which the products of conception (foetus, placenta, membranes and liquor amnii) are expelled from the uterine cavity through the lower uterine segment, cervix and vagina. Normal labour is difficult to define, but in general it may be stated that labour is normal.

THE FIRST STAGE: In most cases the first symptom of the onset of labour is the occurrence of intermittent pains referred to the abdomen or to the back or sometimes to both places. At first these pains are not severe, of short (half-minute) duration and they recur at irregular intervals (from ten to thirty minutes).

DILATATION OF THE INTERNAL OS: The length, dilation and texture of the cervix before the onset of labour is extremely variable. It may be long and undilated, very short (effaced) and patulous; and it may be firm or soft. A 'ripe' cervix is the ideal at term — soft, effaced, slightly patulous and closely applied to the head. The alterations induced by the onset of labour are shown in Fig. 136, where it will be seen that the cervix is shortened and the canal open at both ends, the internal os being rather wider than the external. These figures represent the actual conditions found in frozen sections of women who died, the former before labour, the latter soon after its onset;

they have therefore the value of precise anatomical observations. This is known as the 'taking up' of the cervix. It is also referred to as the shortening, effacement or obliteration of the cervix. If a rectal or vaginal examination is made at this stage, the external os will be found sufficiently dilated to admit only one finger and the cervix will feel like a thick membrane stretched tightly over the advancing head. The external os then gradually dilates and is drawn upwards. Full dilatation has taken place when the greatest diameter of the head has passed through the external os. The cervix will then be out of reach of the examining finger.

FIRST STAGE

The attendants take the couple and thrusting aside the great double doors of the palatial room they admit them to the marbled bathroom. They strip them, wash and bathe them, paying great attention to the most intimate parts of their bodies. With clean horn combs they lightly comb out the magnificent bushy pubic hair where it branches over the mound of love and gently separating the woman's legs they comb it back from the vagina so that the hair rests to the sides of the legs along the labia. While they do this, while they admire this fount of love and praise, they congratulate the man whose choice lies there on his discriminatory wisdom in picking such beauty.

Dried, powdered and scented the couple are led back to their room where everything is done and arranged for their entertainment. First they should embrace firmly and strongly, then their every wish should be granted. Some would like to entertain friends, drink with them, chat and laugh while yet attending to those moments when the pangs in the girl's body testify to the excitement in her womb as it prepares to thrust forth its genesial offering. Others I have known liked a musical group in one corner playing while they clapped and rhythmically expressed their pleasure. Others again will like the time to be spent more quietly with perhaps the occasional dancer to move softly round the room while music and coloured lights gently saturate the walls.

Always the man and the girl attend to the girl's body. The attendants are skilled in helping him to comfort and alleviate pains with his hands gently running over her back or pressing her to him so that the contractions seem to involve not only her body but his as well.

Both the man and the girl will have been prepared for this moment and the girl will have been given special training to help her manage those moments when pangs of pain flow through her. She may have chosen to study those ways whereby rhythmical breathing and control allow the diaphragm to relax while the huge muscle her uterus has become continues its task. Others will eschew the actual practice of mechanical exercises to control their bodies but by exertion of the will push into the subconscious obtrusive messages from their bodies. Others will depend more on the aroused feelings of sexuality, the admixture of pain and eroticism, the realization that this is the culmination of those many moments when they have opened their bodies to allow the penetration of their lovers – to welcome into them those powerful thrusts which seem almost to tear them apart and yet at the same time cause such sweet pleasures that, half wishing to pull back, they yet spur their lovers on.

The attendants will attend. It is their task to see that every moment of this occasion, like the coronation of a prince, sticks in the mind of the father, of the mother, as a truly sublime moment in their lives. The attendants may take what steps they choose to help this occasion; they may wish to administer soothing draughts but nothing must be done to confuse the mind of the mother. To do this, to cloud her mind with sleep, is wrong for she will wish to know and comprehend what she has to endure.

At some time during this stage it is likely that the waters will burst. Wrapped round the baby are these bags – the membranes enclosing the baby in a watery grave from which he must arise. They rupture and gush forth. They have a particular smell to them which you should notice. It is not entirely pleasant but faintly reminiscent of a rich sea of plankton. The attendants will wash it away.

Over the mother now, as labour proceeds, wave after wave breaks incessantly so that she seems to have no time to relax before another immense contraction seizes her body. 'It's coming again,' she cries out. Her lover should throw himself beside her, grasp her body to him if she desires, strain with her in her labour, groan when she groans, relax back when she relaxes. Enjoy the coolness as the attendants mop their brows and urge them on with their task.

CLEANSING THE VULVA: Wherever possible the patient should have a complete bath at the very commencement of labour, and the nurse should see to it that the rectum and bladder are emptied. It is usually well to give an enema in every case, irrespective of whether the bowels have acted naturally or not, unless the patient is in strong labour when the nurse arrives. The nurse should then pay special attention to the genitals. The hair should be shaved. The vulva is swabbed, the labia minora must be separated and wiped with pledgets of wool.

The part of the vagina above the levator ani is rapidly dilated. It is soft, capacious and unsupported by muscle. The enlargement of the pelvic aperture and the dilatation of the lower half of the vagina is usually accomplished by a series of advances and recessions of the head.

In normal labour the uterine contraction begins before the patient appreciates the pain of it and continues for some time after the pain has left her.

The expulsion of the child is accomplished by the uterus strongly reinforced by the voluntary muscles which are vigorously used by the patient. The participation of the voluntary muscles is the chief factor causing the characteristic feature of the pains of the second stage. The onset of each pain is accompanied by a deep inspiration, followed by straining or 'bearing down' in which the patient holds her breath and employs her diaphragm, abdominal and back muscles, and sometimes apparently all the muscles in her body. The face becomes congested, the pulse quickens; she perspires a little and groans deeply during the pains.

The resistance of the pelvic floor and perineum is now almost completely overcome, the greatest diameter of the head passes between the levator ani muscles and is held by them, the head does not now recede. This is called 'crowning'.

The head escapes completely with the next contraction, forehead, face and chin passing in succession over the perineum. The movement of restitution corrects the slight twist on the neck, and with the next contraction the face turns towards one of the mother's thighs — the right thigh is a first vertex. The next contraction carries the anterior shoulder beyond the symphyis and forces the posterior shoulder over the anterior edge of the perineum. The body follows immediately.

With the infant still in a partially inverted position the cord is now tied and the infant separated from its mother. The cord should be divided as soon as is conveniently possible after delivery.

SECOND STAGE

A feeling of excitement builds up, a tension almost, as the climax approaches. The attendants cry out with elation, turn the mother to the position they feel appropriate to delivery, position the man so he supports his girl's head against his bare breast while at the same time an attendant gently handles his genitals so that he is reminded that their ferocious activity has led to this climax. Thrusting down now through the vagina is coming a great head out through that cavity through which his head rammed. His head he pressed as hard into that cavity as it would go. He really dived into it and exploded all over the inside of the cavity, covering with a thick cream that interior surface. That coming has led to this coming.

There is no denying too — although some would deny — that this coming out is often accompanied by pain. The heroines of nature's childbirth say there is no pain, there need be no pain at all. Pain may seem unbearable but it is borne and afterwards it is a pain that did not matter. It is part of one's commitment. The girl when she accepts the man, when she conceives, accepts from him a whole process that will dominate her life and if it — loving — brings pain with it, that, as a part of love, must be borne.

The baby twists and turns in the mouth, the crown of his head is seen at first only a little and then more and more is viewed through the vaginal opening. For the man it is a moment of extreme eroticism; he is watching this great expansion of his woman's vagina, forced apart in a way which he could never achieve but which in fact he has achieved. He kisses his wife between the surges of her uterus, he may stroke her clitoris.

She seems to be going away from him. She is absorbed in her task. She listens and tries to do what the attendants tell her to do. The man must know what the attendants want so that the girl remembers him as one of those who helped her.

Slowly the whole of the top of the baby's head is in view and suddenly the face pops out and peers startled, looking backwards away from the mother. The baby seems to wait for a moment and then the head turns slowly round to the left or the right and so it faces the mother's thigh. So now the rest of the baby suddenly shoots forward out of the mother into the world. The father can clench her tightly and cry out. The baby is placed in the mother's arms between the mother and father on the bed.

The placenta should be received in a clean basin, and later floated out in water to see that it and the membranes are quite complete. Hold the placenta in both hands, maternal side up.

The placenta may appear at the vulva inverted, drawing the membranes after it and followed by a quantity of blood or blood clot. This is known as *Schultze*'s method. Less frequently the placenta may come sideways, like a button through a button-hole; *Duncan's* method. Labour is now ended, the parturient has become a puerpera and the puerperium has begun.

(He) emphasized how much less suffering parturition appears to cause in animals and among the primitive races of mankind, attributing largely the more acute suffering so frequently encountered to the emotion of fear. This fear is engendered and perpetuated by various influences. Public opinion, attributing great suffering to labour, has been formed as a result of historical teaching, including that of the Bible, and of written or verbal accounts of labour often distorted or exaggerated.

THIRD STAGE

There is a pause. Everyone is still. The baby may cry quietly and gently. The midwife takes the cord, clamps it with the clean instruments, cuts it and ties the ends. Then suddenly the placenta separates and slides away from the mother. It lies in a bowl with its membranes. It is a meaty, bloody object and most mothers do not wish to see it. It has a firmish texture not unlike liver but not quite as solid as that, so that you can push your fingers into it and feel it break up beneath your fingers. The attendants inspect it carefully to see that none has been left inside.

Gently now the father and mother lying on their beds are bathed. Cooling water runs across the mother's open vagina. It is inspected; sometimes it has been torn during that last moment and then it must be stitched firmly together again. The baby has gently suckled at the breast. The baby is taken from the mother and weighed, then placed in the cot beside them. The man and the woman hold each other firmly in each other's arms. The attendants cover them gently and together they sleep.

The man thinks of the fantasy: from that belly pressed

against his has come this small but well-shaped human and now the space from whence it came seems to have shrunk. He wonders if he could take hold of the baby and in some way force it back inside her, would it fit again? How did it ever fit? While the woman wonders about the child, how it will change, but also immediately the thought of how she will manage with the baby. Will her breasts give milk? And then the man. She feels his penis, how soon will she be able to welcome him back thrusting again into her vagina? Sleep.

The Far East presents itself to the attentive traveller under two aspects. It is the last Wonderland of the World; and it is also the seed-bed of a multitude of new political issues. I have endeavoured to reflect in these pages this two-fold quality of my subject. Therefore the record of mere travel is interwoven with that of investigation: the incidents and the adventures of the hour are mingled with the factors and the statistics of the permanent problems. By this means I have hoped to reproduce upon the reader's mind something of the effect of the Far East upon my own. It is a picture which is destined, either in bright colours or in sombre, to become increasingly familiar to him in the future.

Of the native inhabitants, of whom Hanoi has seventy thousand, there is much that might be said. After China, with its hundreds of thousands of great brown coolies, and its slim ones who will walk all day uphill under burdens that would break down a European athlete on the level, the Annamites strike the visitor as a nation of pigmies. Their average height must be under five feet; they are narrow-chested and thin-legged, their mouths are always stained a slobbering filthy red with the areca-nut and lime they chew unceasingly, and they are stupid beyond the power of words to tell. Whether it is in any degree due to the fault of their conquerors or not, I cannot say, but they appear to be a people destitute of the sense of self-respect. At any rate, the French treat them as if they had none. The first time I went into déjeuner at the hotel at

Haiphong one of the 'boys' had left a dirty plate on the little table to which the host showed me.

'*Qu'est-ce que tu fais, toi?*' demanded the latter, pointing to the plate, and smack, a box on the ears followed that you could have heard fifty yards off. And this in the middle of a crowded dining-room. You would no more think of striking a Chinese servant like that than of pulling a policeman's nose in Piccadilly. Before a Frenchman, an Annamite too often appears to have no rights.

Lest it be thought that there is exaggeration or prejudice in these suggestions of impropriety in the administration of French Indo-China, I will reproduce a passage from the verbatim official report of the discussion of the national Budget of 1891 in the Chamber of Deputies. M. Etienne, Under-secretary of State for the Colonies, was making a long and important speech in explanation and defence of the portion of the Budget relating to the Colonies. He was interrupted at one moment by M. Clemenceau, and the following conversation occurred:

M. CLEMENCEAU. While you are still upon the question of Tongking will you be good enough to say a word to us about the exemptions from the customs duties? That is one of the important points of the Report of M. le Myre de Vilers. You have forgotten to speak of it.

M. ETIENNE. M. Clemenceau points out to me that the Governor-General has taken it upon himself to exempt from import duties certain classes of goods intended for young industries in Tongking and Annam. He declares that the Governor-General had not the right to deprive the Budget of the Protectorate of these receipts. I reply that the Governor-General acted by virtue of the powers which he holds from the State; he has done what is done — I am obliged to say it — in the other colonies. The Councils-General, when a customs tariff has been voted and has received the sanction of the Council of State, have the right to reduce duties without incurring remarks from any one.

M. LEYDET. In favour of private persons?

M. ETIENNE. Precisely.

M. CLEMENCEAU. Then there is no law any more.

M. ETIENNE. It is the Constitution.

A MEMBER OF THE LEFT. It is the absence of a Constitution!

M. ETIENNE. It is thus.

M. LE COMTE DE MONTFORT. Then everything is explained!

In conclusion I will say simply this. I believe, as everyone who has looked into the matter believes, that Tongking might have a prosperous future under the control of a colonizing nation. But I know, as everybody who has looked into the matter knows, that she will never reach it along the present road. A certain permanency of appointment for the Governor-General; a relaxing of restrictions upon the colonists all round; a hundred times more respect paid by officials to colonial wishes and requests; far greater consideration for native rights and sentiments; the encouragement of the Chinese; a glad welcome to capital and enterprise from any source; an immediate and equable reduction of the tariff; the decentralization of authority — these are some of the primal conditions of progress. If they do not come, then France may prepare for the humiliation which the very name of 'Indo-China' will ultimately carry with it.

What Happened to the Colonial Powers

Nobly, nobly Cape St Vincent to the north-west died away. Sunset ran one glorious blood-red reeking into Cadiz Bay. Here the *Hopeful*, the hospital ship, was hove to. In the dimmest north-east distance stood Gibraltar grim and grey. The sea around held the ghosts of dead seamen, men who took the decision to fight. Coming out to fight against a vastly better fleet, they stood impudently out to sea and were annihilated. The *Hopeful* was more cautious; they were seamen with vast experience but they were doubtful whether they should approach the distant embattled fleets whose presence they could sense, almost smell, through the faint mist.

In the main mess the debate had been going on for hours. Where should the *Hopeful* go next? For some time Timothy Anders, a psychologist from Michigan, had been arguing in favour of crossing the Atlantic to the U.S.A. He had been quoting figures of internal domestic production. Even if the rest of the world had been overwhelmed, the United States had the resources to keep going. Other members of staff were cautious; there had been no news from North America for a long time, pointed out Arbace, whereas they knew that in parts of Africa life was near normal.

'It won't be for long, it won't be for long; they don't have the natural resources that North America has. Look at these data.' He shot up a slide: 'Look at coal, look at oil, look at steel. We can hardly afford to ignore that sort of data.'

'No, no, no,' said a clear voice, 'I can't bear it, Timothy. You are interpreting the data all wrong.'

Euan, who was standing up leaning against the wall, had been trying to spot Sheila for some time. It amazed him when she spoke in public, which she did too rarely — that quiet but clear voice, that cool authority and knowledge.

'You are looking at the data wrong. We are not concerned with technical resources. We have the hardware, we know the technology. It's who's to handle it. It's the human resources that we need. Look at the human resources in America. You know them, I know them. That is why we are both here. If Europe is like this, the Americans will be doing all that's being done here only more. It will be worse. I cannot bear to go to America.'

There was a pause for a moment. Anders didn't reply. Sheila spoke again quietly:

'Remember the suicide who was waiting to jump? The crowd — the American crowd — shouted, "come on, come on! Jump, jump!" They jeered at her when she didn't. What will that crowd do for the crucifixion men? They will hand up the hammer and nails.'

Euan hammered with his open hand hard against the steel side of the ship against which he was leaning. Other men took it up. The noise resonated along through the ship. Others in the hall began to stamp hard. Sir Maximov, who was sitting on a camp stool on the edge of the platform, took off his cap and began pounding one great fist into the other. Soon the whole room took up that too. Boom, boom, boom, the whole ship seemed to shake with the pounding. As suddenly as it had started it faded and within half a minute had stopped. The Captain, who was in the chair, said quietly:

'O.K. Not America.'

A long discussion then developed about Europe. Leblanc, the French geneticist, had plotted on a map the places that Tafteria had recorded messages from. He demonstrated that western France, the United Kingdom, Belgium and Holland had been spared. It may be chance, several people pointed out, and tried tactfully to question the efficiency of Tafteria's communications section. It might be a wireless effect? Messages had come from Narvik and Oulu in Scandinavia. Leblanc said maybe western Europe had been spared. The Celtic Fringe is still alive. Max stood up and said:

'Here and here did England help me; how can I help England? — say? Sail north.' So they did.

November in the Channel. Season of mists and mellow fruitfulness. Fogs and bitter cold but calm flat seas. They cannot decide whether to sound their foghorn or not. They don't; the radar scanners are watched anxiously. They cut speed and creep along. They have seen nothing, there is not a sign of shipping. They have cut across from just south of the Isle of Wight over to the French coast and up towards Boulogne and Calais. No coastal shipping. Back towards England and gently down the south coast from Dover. There is a tiny object in the sea, a small brown rowing-boat. Wrapped up in a rug and lying asleep in it is a woman with her six-month-old child. The sea is so calm that a cargo port low down is opened and when the rowing-boat gently bumps the side it is quickly secured.

The woman awoke and looked up at Van Thofen who had elected to go down into the boat to her. She looked up at him standing over her in his white coat with his label: Dr Van Thofen. She stared at him; he said quietly, 'Don't worry, we're a hospital ship,' and then she screamed and shouted aloud ——

'It's the doctors — AAAoh! — It's the doctors!' She shook off her rug, clasped hold of her child and was about to jump overboard. Van Thofen held her and two sailors jumped down and grabbed her. The child, frightened, began to cry. She was detached from her mother and handed up into the cargo hold. Then the mother, still screaming, was manhandled into the ship. Once on board she paused and said, 'Give me my child.' This was done and then she allowed herself to be led along the gangway, moaning out, 'My Gawd, the doctors, they've got me'!

'Max's, I'd say,' said Van Thofen, rather ruffled. 'Stay with her, Euan, we'll send for him.'

Euan sat in the corner of one of the emergency rooms trying to look inconspicuous and wishing Max would come. The woman sank into a chair, nursing her baby, hugging it to her and quietly moaning, 'The doctors. My Gawd, the doctors ... '

What was holding Max up was his need to change; he had borrowed a pair of sailor's heavy serge trousers and a dark blue T-shirt and he came in accompanied by Ben.

'Hello, love,' he said, 'what's to do?'

'You're not doctors, then?' she said.

'Naow,' said Ben, hastily joining in, 'naow.'

'Take it easy, love,' said Sir Max. The woman looked over at Euan and Sir Max said, 'He's only a student really. Here, fetch us some teas, lad.'

When Euan had got back Mrs Miller had relaxed somewhat. The baby had been put on an examining couch wrapped up in a blanket and was sound asleep again. Mrs Miller was talking fast and disjointedly while Sir Maximov was trying to throw in a few questions to direct her answers.

'Crucifixion. Them people, they're everywhere. I think it's

the doctors behind them. That's how it started. It all started with the doctors.'

Mrs Miller was a woman who got worried about her babies. She thought they had things wrong with them and this one, she had thought, was going blind. It was here that her troubles had begun.

'You see, it's not like it used to be, I mean, there used to be this place on the corner and you just nipped in and there was always someone there you knew. Well, they done away with all that. They ripped down that nice little row of houses. You remember them, Mister Ben?'

Ben, in some strange way, did.

'Anyway, those houses. You remember old Mrs Howes. Funny ole thing she was. Couldn't read nor write. "I bain't no scholard," she would say. Anyway she lived in one of those little houses.'

'When she died,' said Ben, 'I had to cut orf her skirts. Tied on with string, they were. Fleas and all.'

'Poor old thing. Her two sons was coalmen ... Anyhow that row of houses they pulled down and they shut the bits of the hospital we knew and they built this tower. Twenty-six storeys, they say. Anyway I was in there with the kid.'

'Which kid?' interrupted Max.

'Why, this one, of course. About her eyes. Well, yes, they'd say, her eyes are odd. I mean, she didn't follow like the other one did.

'Anyway they didn't really seem interested in the eyes when I got in. They asked me about the kid. How did I feel about her. Well, I said, a bit awkward, you know. Bit funny to hold. Then they started talking, talking about the kid. I mean I was holding ... well, hugging, her, you know. But they had this idea about her. Thought that I didn't like her somehow. What I'd said, they said, showed I wanted her to ... Well, I'd come about the eyes, hadn't I? Well, then there was this psychiatrist and he was saying I really wanted this baby to be handicapped in some way, that's why I said she couldn't see.

'Then they started asking me about my husband. What did I want with him. Well I explained, yeah, he drove me mad sometimes. So they said didn't I feel we both needed help? Well yes, I said, of course we do. So they took us into the hospital, I mean, and there we were. The baby, you know, by then she was looking round the place lovely. But the things they did to us. They took my husband away, said he shouldn't have babies. I think they crucified him. Then me, well, they wouldn't really let me have my baby. She was in this glass cubicle, see, but I could go and look at her.

'Then last Wednesday it was foggy, see. There was all these young doctors too running round taking blood from us. Said they was surprised at us — the way we behaved — something about England. And the rot having to stop somewhere. Then there was this banging and hammering so I just went to look at the baby to see if she was safe and they'd left the door unlocked so I took her. I mean, it was the young doctors saying it was up to them to clean the place up. They started it off, that's my belief. So I just walked out down to the river, I went, and found that little boat. I mean, I only went to ask about the eyes. Crosses, there was. All up the Mall, they told me. It was the doctors!'

'Yesterday,' said Sir Maximov, 'all of the past. Yesterday the classic lecture on the origin of mankind. But today the struggle. I shall tell the Captain to attempt no landing in Europe, there is no hope for this civilization. We must head back to the Pacific and try to ride out a few storms before checking in there.'

The New Declaration of Independence

Nature is not interested in happy endings.

At the beginning of time she laid down her own laws of comedy and tragedy, then abruptly left for parts unknown and bade us write our little phantasies as we saw fit.

The result so far has not been entirely satisfactory.

That, however, was our own fault.

A buzz-saw is a very useful instrument — provided it is used the right way. But when it gets hold of our fingers, it is a terrible instrument of destruction.

But another group refuses to accept this philosophy of defeat.

'Too bad,' they will agree, 'too bad about Rome and Greece and Jerusalem and all those other states and nations. But it was their own fault. They perished through their own folly. And anyway, they are dead and gone. We, on the contrary, are very much alive. We know infinitely more than they did. It is up to us to escape their fate. And we can do it. Only it will take a terrible lot of dreadfully hard work. There is only one question. Have we got the courage to do it?'

Personally, I think that we have.

Not because I am an inordinate admirer of that state of mind commonly known as optimism. Newspapermen and doctors are rarely addicted to that dangerous social drug. Their daily dose of Stark Reality prevents them from getting this one particular bad habit. But they also know that there is a force in this world, much stronger than themselves, something within them and yet without, something that will carry on when they themselves are ready to drop by the roadside and devote the rest of their days to the collecting of butterflies or stamps.

And just when it seemed that all was lost, that the western world had committed suicide, that the days of the white race were counted, there came a first ray of faint hope and the name thereof was the Younger Generation.

America has always been devoid of pageantry. The gorgeous and elaborate symbolism of Crown and Church which for so many centuries delighted the heart of the European peasants and burghers was banished from our shores.

It is of course very difficult to write about these things. We are in the midst of a revolution, the greatest revolution the world has seen since the invention of the written word. But we are so utterly in the midst of it that we cannot possibly know what is happening or what the outcome will be.

This is only the tenth year of a war that will last at least another half-century.

That means that we have forty more years to go and that I shall not see the end.

But speaking strictly for the twelfth of February of the year of grace   this is the way I see the present development of the conflict from the point of view of America.

Not only did we stop and look and listen but the most intelligent leaders of a nation that was never yet accused of a lack of brains or courage carefully inspected the surrounding landscape and asked whether perchance we were not on the wrong road? And for the first time in more than half a century the American people applied the yardstick of sober common sense to the achievements of the last two generations, and said, 'Let us see what we have really done that is worth while.'

Such a nationwide inventory is not finished in a week or a month. In truth we ourselves, who are responsible for the dreadful failure of the immediate past, shall not live to read the final report.

The younger generation will have to finish the job. And then, in truth, the world shall stand at the crossroads of destiny.

For our nation, our country, the fortunate strip of land which we call our own, by a strange turn of fate has been called upon to be the guardian of mankind's future.

Characteristic and species-specific maternal behaviour, such as nesting, retrieving, grooming and exploring have been observed in non-human mammalian mothers immediately after delivery. During studies designed to assess the effects of immediate, prolonged separation of the human mother from her premature infant following delivery, we observed an unusual routine. When mothers first touched their young, they began by poking and picking at the infants' extremities with the tips of their fingers. To explore this behaviour in the human mother we made detailed observations of women during their first postnatal contacts with their premature or full-term infants.

The two groups of mothers were photographed in different surroundings and both groups were told they were being photographed. Women and their full-term infants were filmed 0.5 to 13.5 hours after delivery (average 5.3 hours) with a camera eight to ten feet from their beds, either in a recovery room on the delivery floor or in a room on the maternity division. The mother's bed was flat, the infant was undressed and the top of the infant's head was placed at the level of the shoulder, approximately six to eight inches from its mother. Only the first contact was recorded for the mothers of full-term infants. Mothers of premature infants were first filmed one to three days after delivery (average 1.2 days) with the camera placed inconspicuously outside the glass wall of the nursery.

The following activities were recorded from the film: the movement of the infant, position of the mother's finger-tips and palms on the trunk or extremities of the infant, the amount of time she was smiling, and the amount of time either physically supporting or encompassing the infant; and, for mothers of premature infants only, the proximity of their heads to the incubator and the amount of time spent with their hands inside the portholes. Behaviour was considered 'encompassing' if the mother enclosed either the trunk or head of her infant with her entire hand. We also measured the amount of 'en face' (a position defined by Robson, in which the mother's face is rotated so that her eyes and those of the infant meet fully in the same vertical plane of rotation).

An orderly and predictable pattern of behaviour was observed when each mother of the full-term infants first saw her infant. Commencing hesitantly with finger-tip contact on the extremities, within four to five minutes she began caressing the trunk with her palm, simultaneously showing progressively heightened excitement, which continued for several minutes. Her activity then often diminished, sometimes to such a degree that she fell asleep with the infant at her side. Fig. 2 summarizes changes during three time periods in finger-tip and palm contact on either the extremities or trunk with the mothers of full-term infants. When behaviour in the first and third periods — only three minutes apart — is compared, the decrease in finger-tip contact from 52 to 26 per cent, the increase in palm contact from 28 to 62 per cent, the decrease in touching the infant's extremities from 38 to 22 per cent, and the increase in touching the infant's trunk from 24 to 49 per cent are all significant (p < .02) using the sign test. Comparing the same periods, encompassing significantly increased from 12 to 30 per cent (p < .05), while smiling decreased from 45 to 34 per cent (p < .01).

Interest in the eyes of the infants in both groups was measured from the amount of verbalization on the audiotapes and from the amount of time the mothers spent in the 'en face' position. An intense interest in waking the infants in an attempt to see their eyes open was verbalized by 73 per cent of the mothers. Some mothers even voiced a relationship between the condition of the babies and their eyes. For example, 'Open your eyes. Oh,

come on now, open up your eyes.' 'If you open your eyes, I will
know you are alive.' Several mentioned that once the infants
looked at them they felt much closer to them. The mothers of
full-term infants showed a remarkable increase in the time
spent in the 'en face' position in only four to five minutes. Fig. 4
shows the percentages of 'en face' in the two groups.

No significant differences in behaviour were observed when
multiparous and primiparous or married and unmarried
mothers were compared.

Our results reveal strong evidence for species-specific behaviour in human mothers at the time of the first contact with
their full-term infants. Although each full-term mother's
experiences, plans, and expectations differed and the period
of time between delivery and filming varied, the observed
sequences and patterns of behaviour were strikingly similar. The
rapid progression from finger-tip to palm and encompassing
contact within a period of ten minutes does not agree with the
observations of Rubin, who noted palm and close contact to
develop only after several days. In our study, the nude state
of the infant during the contact period might have stimulated a
more rapid progression. Differences in maternal anaesthesia
might also have altered the affective state of either the mother
or infant — a limp, sleepy, unresponsive infant whose eyes were
closed would not provide the same stimulus as an active, wide-
awake baby.

Clear-cut patterns and orders of behaviour (cradling, grooming, nursing, restraining and retrieving) have been described
in primates (Rhesus monkey) as components in establishing
early affectional ties between mothers and their newborn
infants. This report has disclosed that a common pattern
appears to occur in the human mother at the first contact after
birth, although, as Bowlby has stated, 'What a mother brings
to the situation ... derives not only from her native endowment
but from a long history of interpersonal relations within her
family of origin (and perhaps also within other families) and
also from long absorption of the values and practices of her

culture.' What other common behavioural sequences are present in women as they establish affectional ties with their infants? Have these been obscured by child- and mother-care practices?

A comparison of immediate postnatal behaviour with that observed in many non-human species suggests that this period may be especially sensitive for the development of close affectional ties in the human mother as well as the goat and sheep. Does separation during this period in the human result in distinctly aberrant behaviour when the mother and infant are reunited?

Euan was trying to apologize to V. but she was laughing, turning from side to side, picking up the babies and saying, 'Two of them, two of them!' Bob, who had assisted at the delivery, was stripping off gown and clothes and shouting, 'Twins, undiagnosed twins,' and, quite unnaturally for him, roaring with laughter. He pushed open a cupboard and suddenly emerged with two bottles of champagne.

'Come on, Bill, get this open. Hey, we'll drink a health to these young Mois. Where are some glasses, Sister? A health to the Mois.'

V. had at last turned from her children and understood that Euan had some concern about something. She gave him a great smile.

'Euan,' she said, 'Euan, what is it?'

'I'm sorry I didn't know about it being twins,' he said. 'I ought to have ... '

'Euan,' laughed V. and she caught his arm and pulled him down and put an arm up round his neck and kissed him.

'Thank you for calling me Euan at last,' he whispered.

'Euan, Euan,' she said mockingly, imitating the voice she had used when she had called him Doctor in the past.

Bill was squatting on the pillow by V.'s head looking pale, indeed more tired than V., who since the babies had been born seemed to have acquired a great burst of energy. He had wrestled successfully with the champagne bottle and Bob had his open as well. Sister handed round glasses and they all shouted, 'The Mois twins,' and drank.

'Give them a drink too,' said Sheila. 'Here, I'll show you,' and she eased each twin and arranged them so that V.'s nipples were in their mouths. They all stood and watched while the babies sucked for a moment or two at the breasts and then Sister wheeled up two bassinets and the babies were gently removed. They refilled their glasses and toasted them again.

At that moment Sir Maximov burst into the room. He was wearing a white coat but had no trousers on and his long legs stretched down into a pair of very old-fashioned carpet-slippers. He rushed over to Bill who was still perched at the top of the bed holding V.'s hand. Sir Maximov gave Bill a hug and bent down and kissed V. Then he hurried over to the cot and lifted out the larger baby, a five-pounder, still crying lustily.

'Beautiful, beautiful baby, V.' he cried. 'Can I show him the stars outside?' he asked. 'It's better than an incubator.'

'Well, if you really want to you can,' said V., considerably puzzled.

'I'll show the baby the world,' shouted Sir Maximov, and he suddenly pushed his way backwards through the doors and into the night outside.

'Will he be all right?' said V., alarmed.

'Of course he will,' said Euan, 'you know Max wouldn't harm a flea, but I'll go and get him back.'

'Please do that for me, Euan, Euan.' Euan looked down at her and smiled. The loss of the title Doctor was like shedding a load — a title he had sweated for, been proud to have but which had suddenly, between him and V. at least and at last, become obsolete. He patted her head, smiled at Bill and hurried after Sir Maximov.

Maximov had unbuttoned his coat, revealing his fat hairy body, kicked his shoes overboard and was tramping the decks almost naked. He was holding the baby up in front and striding along shouting, 'Twins — a case of undiagnosed twins!

Ha-ha! Undiagnosed twins. Ha-ha.' A few startled crewmen stood to one side to let him pass while a junior nurse pursued him bleating, 'Give me the baby back, Sir Maximov.' As Euan arrived on the deck, Matron appeared, doing her turn of night duty:

'Behave, Sir Maximov!'

Euan suddenly noticed Sheila had come quietly out after him into the moonlight and was leaning against a mast. Sir Maximov turned to her, held out the baby and said:

'My darling girl, a case of undiagnosed twins.' There was silence and Sheila, looking vaguely puzzled, turned towards Euan. Euan suddenly shouted:

'You can fuck Sheila if you like, Max.'

Sir Maximov roared with laughter, turned and handed the baby to the frightened junior nurse.

'No, no, Euan, wrong again. It's Matron I want. Matron,' he shouted, 'I intend to rape you.'

'Sir Maximov!' cried Matron, dodging back from him as he lunged at her and slipping hastily away behind the mast Sheila was leaning against. She could be heard running back down the deck. Sir Maximov bounded after her and could be heard shouting:

'A rapist, Matron, a rapist is after you.'

Matron, running hard, doubled back in front of Sheila and Euan and Sir Max came stumbling back after her. He was shouting too much to be able to make very much pace and Euan realized that Matron did not wish to escape.

'You and I, Matron,' shouted Max, 'we could do incredible things together. What if you and I combined, Matron? What would happen to mankind, Matron? What great events in medicine and biology will happen once we two, Matron, are among the world's leaders? Matron, you are my fantasy. Make me yours, Matron, Matron, Matron ... '

Will medicine and biology discover a way of restoring deep-frozen men to life?

Will men from earth colonize new planets?

Will they mate with the inhabitants they find there?

Will men create a second, third and fourth earth?

Will special robots replace surgeons one day?

Will hospitals in the year 2100 be spare-part stores for defective men?

Will it become possible in the distant future to prolong man's life indefinitely with artificial hearts, lungs, kidneys, etc.?

Will Huxley's *Brave New World* come true one day in all its improbability and chilling inhumanity?

A compendium of such questions could easily get as big as the London telephone directory. Not a day passes without something brand-new being invented somewhere in the world — every day another question can be struck from the list of impossibilities as answered.

Think tanks are springing up all over the world; what they amount to are monasteries of scientists of today, who are thinking for tomorrow. One hundred and sixty-four of these think tanks are at work in America alone. They accept commissions from the government and heavy industry. The most celebrated think tank is the Rand Corporation at Santa Monica in California. The U.S. Air Force were responsible for its foundation in 1945. The reason? High-ranking officers wanted a research programme of their own on intercontinental warfare. Eight hundred and forty-three selected scientific authorities now work in the two-storeyed magnificently laid-out research centre. The first ideas and plans for the foundations of mankind's most improbable adventures are born here.

There is no end in sight to this research work, and there is unlikely to be one.

Governments and big business simply cannot manage without these thinkers for the future. Governments have to decide on their military plans far in advance; big businesses have to calculate their investments for decades ahead. Futurology will have to plan the development of capital cities for a hundred or more years ahead.

Equipped with present-day knowledge, it would not be difficult to estimate, say, the development of Mexico for the next fifty years. In making such a forecast every conceivable fact would be taken into account, such as the existing technology, means of communication and transport, political currents and Mexico's potential opponents.

Mankind has a compulsive urge to think out in advance and investigate the future with all the potentialities at its command.

It is not our fault that there are millions of other planets in the universe.

It is not our fault that Admiral Piri Reis did not burn his ancient maps.

It is not our fault that the old books and traditions of human history exhibit so many absurdities.

But it is our fault if we know all this, but disregard it and refuse to take it seriously.

The previous afternoon Euan had awakened from sleep and had looked up to see Sheila staring down at him.

'I don't think,' she'd said, 'that I can give you all you want from me.'

'But,' Euan said, 'you'll do anything for me.'

'Yes,' said Sheila, 'I can give you all you ask from me, but there will be other things you'll need. There'll be other touches you'll want which you cannot express to me. There will be other lovers whose thighs you want to kiss. I want you to have them. Loving me will be loving them.' She had dropped down beside him and pillowed her head on his shoulder with a sigh of relief and fallen asleep almost at once.

Now Euan felt he understood what she had meant. The relationship between them was not to close other relationships but to open them. Their love would make it easy for them to contact/touch others. With Sheila he could even cope with the crucifixion men if need be. He had felt tired after the hours in the delivery room but now the smile in Sheila's eyes made him burst with drive. He could make love to her, and would soon, but he had energy to do more than that.

'I think,' he said, 'it is time to go. I think we should have a baby. We should have something formal between us like a marriage. I think we should, I think we could go ashore. I think that we shall survive. But if not ... well ... we should go.'

'The suicide pact,' Sheila replied. 'The romantic death? Very well, I accept, for I am your choice, your decision, yes, I am ... '

'Come on,' said Euan, 'it's time to be going.' He grabbed her hand, lifted it, made a bow towards her and then still holding her hand in his he led her forward like a bride along the deck towards the bow.

The origin of the Moi is uncertain. Malay-Polynesian is the conjecture most generally accepted. Their history seems to have been a matter of retreat after retreat from stronger tribes: Siamese, Chinese, Thai, Annamite, Cambodian. Small wonder, too, that they fear the European newcomers.

The Moi peoples are not, and never were, a nation. The term is applied comprehensively to many clans, independent of each other; each governed and protected by a chief who is usually a sorcerer. Sadet of the Fire, Sadet of the Water, Jarai, Rade and Bahnar are only a few of the apparently numberless clan names that one hears when travelling about the district. Each sub-tribe has its own vernacular, differing so widely from the others that a Moi-Annamite-French dictionary given to me by a missionary in Djiring was useful, he warned me, only among the Koho and Sore clans.

In the matter of dress the clans vary but little; the men wear only loin-cloths or g-string; the women wear waists and long skirts. But in physique, in temperament and in customs there are notable differences. In some of the clans matriarchy obtains in one or another of its forms: transmission of name, or property, or both, through the mother; polyandry; or dominance of woman in some other way. Wherever this social system exists it is proclaimed by the proud bearing of the women.

In the presence of the chief and one other witness, bride and groom clench their teeth against the blade of a home-made hatchet. 'My vow is stronger than the iron against which I bite' is thus symbolized. I regret that I had no chance to see this rite.

Beyond the village and deeper in the forest is the cemetery. Under trees which are sacred both rich and poor are buried but in different manner. The rich are laid in coffins made of the bark of trees. The poor are wrapped in mats and put under-ground as soon as possible after death. A bamboo hut, small as a doll's-house, provides habitation for the souls of the dead whenever such shelter is desired. Under the thatched huts, between the poles, were rough board coffins all ready and waiting — small coffins for the children, large ones for the adults. It seemed to me then that death was the event the natives had most in mind.

THE WALK ALONG THE DECK

They paraded forward and as they continued across the open deck of the carrier they became aware that the other couples had formed up behind them. Sir Maximov Flint had caught up with Matron and she had yielded to him at last. He had cast off his white coat and proceeded quite naked but Matron retained her sober grey tunic and gave to the couple a curious air of propriety.

Ginny and Harry were there, Ginny carrying the cage with the white doves which she released when Euan glanced back at her, and they flew up above the ship but then swooped back low over Euan's and Sheila's heads as they swept on, over the bows and away forward into the distance. They were not the only animals: a curious squeaking made them look down, and a little to their left they saw Ben's white mice proceeding along with a family of five tiny babies trying to keep up with the adult mice, all squeaking as they went.

But there were hundreds too of older friends. There were tall J. and Ann. There was big bearded Larry with Elaine, a couple who'd set out to India to learn about the East. There were Paul and Margaret. There was the paediatrician Ronnie with his sailor wife Elizabeth whom they had first heard of in Copenhagen dancing a sword-dance with the dinner-knives on the tables in the Tivoli Gardens.

There were Coma and Kline. The long and usually gloomy face of the analyst was alight and he was shouting out: 'The Million-year Girl! The Million-year Girl! Is here! With me!' Like Euan and Sheila they held their hands high in the air and marched along in a stately poised way, but with his free hand Kline waved towards people who were off the ship, shouting: 'Look at me, I have been here for a million years.'

The deck was gradually filling up as couples took up their positions, formed lines neatly spaced and marched onwards in unison. There were Henry, the big bearded redhead from Liverpool with Liz from Richmond. There were Edwin and Liz. There were O.T. and Euphoria — the ten-foot-tall girl from Trinidad with the body she loved to show. There were Hugh and Rachel. There was big fat rumbustious Jeff with the skinny Prissy, the astronauts, the first couple to copulate in free fall. There were Chris and Jenny.

Dressed neatly in a blazer with his slacks freshly pressed came Ben, the mortuary man, with Mrs Miller still carrying her baby, marching soberly enough, she was, but shouting out: 'The doctors are gone, the doctors, the doctors are gone.' Big John was with Night Sister, his cap in his hand, waving and singing, 'Farewell, Trenton my lovely.' Bob had — good! good! — made it with Sally. She was leaning against him, only just out of an orgasm, panting still but walking beside him, and Bob laughing and relaxed again. There were Mike and Freire together — good! good!

There were hundreds and hundreds of people. There were Jack and Barbara. There were people after all alive. Kingsley and Pam. It was a day to wake up and dream you were alive again. V. had come out on deck, her body bare, and W. too, and they moved over towards some central place in the procession. W. with his arm wrapped round V. but V. looking well, strong, V. alive and moving again. W. silent, not talking but walking forward with V., turning to look from time to time, touching his head on to her head. There were Pierre and Natasha.

Henry had got the group on deck again. Trevor had arrived last but he was there and the drum-beat began. Art was without his shoes but had all his instruments with him. They rendered the Wedding March and then Phil started again, the guitar notes building up and slowly first Dave on the bass and then Trevor with brushes and the wind instruments. They were playing the Vietnam Symphony. Norma was there echoing the texts, her extraordinary voice giving a new dimension to the words: 'He-he-he Moi,' and all the ship echoed it 'He-he-he Moi.'

As Sheila and Euan reached the bows they turned and looked behind them and the whole vast deck of the carrier was a crowd of couples. Each pair turned and they bowed formally to each other and then waited a moment. Cymbals clanged and the band for a moment was silent. In the silence from somewhere way back down the ship there came a cry. The cry of a baby. The birth cry, as Lind (1967) has remarked, the birth cry is a unique cry.

References

ALEXANDER, F., 'The Dynamics of Psychotherapy in the Light of Learning Theory', *Amer. J. Psychiat.*, **120**, 440, 1963.

ALLPORT, G. W., *Personality: A Psychological Interpretation* (London: Constable, 1960).

BALLARD, J. G., 'The Sound Sweep', *Science Fantasy*, 1960.

——, 'Terminal Beach', *New Worlds*, 4, 1964.

——, *Crash* (London: Jonathan Cape, 1973).

BAX, M., 'You, Me and the Lovelight in Your Eyes' *Palantir*, **3**, 1976.

BAX, M. and WHITMORE, K., 'Health and Welfare of London School Children', paper presented to the Brit. Paediatric Assoc. An. Meet. at Harrogate, 1974.

BELOFF, J., 'The Sweethearts' experiment', *J. Soc. Phys. Res.*, **45**, 1, 1969.

BERRY, M. F. and EISENSON, J., *Speech Disorders* (New York: Appleton-Century-Crofts, 1956).

BOWLBY, J., *Attachment and Loss*, Vol. 1 (New York: Basic Books, 1969).

BROCK, E., 'Instruction', *A Cold Day at the Zoo* (London: Rapp and Whiting, 1970).

BÜHLER, C., *The First Year of Life* (New York: Day, 1930).

CLANCY, H., DUGDALE, A and RENDLE-SHORT, J., 'The Diagnosis of Infantile Autism', *Develop. Med. and Child Neurol.* **11**, 432, 1969.

DARWIN, C. R., 'The Life of an Infant', *Mind*, 1877.

FREUD, S., 'The Dynamics of the Transference' (1912), *Collected Papers*, Vol. 2 (London: Hogarth Press, 1924).

GESELL, A., *The First Five Years of Life* (New York: Harper, 1940).

HOLLO, A., 'The Seventh Lady', *Ambit*, **17**, 27, 1963.

HURLOCK, E. B., *Child Development* (New York: McGraw-Hill, 1950).

ISLER, W., *Acute Hemiplegias and Hemisyndromes in Childhood* (London: Spastics Internat. Med. Pub./Heinemann, 1971).

KARPMAN, B., *The Alcoholic Woman* (Washington: Linacre Press, 1948).

KUNZ, P. R., 'Romantic Love and Reciprocity', *Family Co-ordinator*, **18**, 111, 1969.

LIBBY, W. L., 'Eye Contact and Direction of Looking as Stable Individual Differences', *J. of Exper. Res. in Personality*, **4**, 303, 1970.

LIND, J., Speaking in 'New Worlds', B.B.C. Radio 4, 1967.

MACBETH, G., 'Fin du Globe', *Ambit*, **17**, 21, 1963.

MACARTNEY, J. L., *Understanding Human Behavior* (New York: Vantage Press, 1956).

MANDELSTAM, N., *Hope Against Hope* (London: Collins/Harvill, 1972).

MEYERS, T. J., 'The Psychodynamics of the Female Pelvis', *Dis. Nerv. Syst.*, **24**, 682, 1963.

MILLER, G. A., *Language and Communication* (New York: McGraw-Hill, 1951).

ORTEGA Y GASSET, J., *On Love ... Aspects of a Single Theme* (London: Jonathan Cape, 1967).

OSGOOD, C. E., *Method and Theory in Experimental Psychology* (New York: Oxford University Press, 1953).

PAOLOZZI, E., *Moonstrips Empire News* (London: Editions Electo, 1967).

PRECHTL, H. and BEINTEMA, D., *The Neurological Examination of the Full-Term Newborn Infant* (London: Spastics Soc. Med. Educ. Inf. Unit/Heinemann, 1964).

REICH, W., *Character Analysis* (New York: Orgone Press, 1949).

ROBSON, K., 'The Role of Eye-to-eye Contact', *J. Child Psychol. Psychiat.*, **8**, 13, 1967.

RUBIN, R., 'Maternity Care in our Society', *Nursing Outlook*, **11**, 519, 1963.

SHERIF, M. and SHERIF, C. W., *Groups in Harmony and Tension* (New York: Harper, 1953).

SHERMAN, M., 'The Differentiation of Emotional Response in Infants', *J. Comp. Psychol.*, **7**, 335, 1927.

SPITZ, R. A. and COBLINER, W. G., *The First Year of Life* (New York: International Universities Press, 1965).

TROJAN, F., 'General Semantics', In L. Kaiser (ed.), *Manual of Phonetics* (Amsterdam: North Holland, 1957).

VAN RIPER, C., *Speech Correction: Principles and Methods* (Englewood Cliffs, N.J.: Prentice-Hall, 1954).

YATES, D., *She Fell Among Thieves* (London: Ward, Lock, 1935).

YEATS, W. B., *Michael Robartes and The Dancer* (London: Macmillan, 1921).